VERGANN

BOOK ONE OF
THE DELPINE DIARIES

L.C. WATKINS

This book is dedicated to my wonderful husband and three awesome daughters. Their love and encouragement has helped me through every step of this long journey. My heartfelt thanks to my daughter, Skyler, for lending her talent and imagination to the project. This book could not have been completed without your help. I also would like to thank my friend, Jan. Your support and interest throughout the process has been invaluable.

PROLOGUE

King Hulbert of Draven pulled back on the reigns of his mighty steed and stopped.

He narrowed his eyes, anger building as he struggled to keep the bony old man ahead of him in sight. This chase was proving to be more troublesome than planned, thanks to the dense greenery and uneven terrain hindering his progress. Perhaps travelling by horseback had been unwise.

A strange silence in the air kept Hulbert alert. It was an almost expectant sort of silence—as though his every move was being watched.

For all he knew, that might be the case. The EliSann Forest was not a place one ventured unless completely necessary. It was easy to understand why. The forest was alive—beautiful, yet not at all welcoming. Nature's finest work mixed with man's basic fears. Misty rays from the bright morning sun shone with a hazy brilliance into the darkest reaches of the rich forest as an eerie tranquility filled the air. An unfelt wind whistled through the trees as though a thousand shrill voices screamed from the shadows, demanding to be noticed.

A lesser man would flee. But Hulbert was not that man, and he would *not* be deterred.

Turning his attention back to the pitiful old man attempting to navigate through a thick hedge without success, Hulbert grinned to himself. The chase would soon come to an end.

He had first encountered the man two days prior. At the time, though, his attention had been on the woman and boy rumored to have the object he sought—not some weak old man holding a baby, cowering in the corner of the room.

Images of the events of that day flooded Hulbert's mind. A tiny village burning, women clasping their infants to them as they ran for their lives, the lifeless bodies of the men foolish enough to fight back littering the road. Chaos, utter chaos... And there had always been something Hulbert loved about chaos.

He felt no remorse for his actions. Why should he? The woman and her son had sealed their own demise by not giving him what he sought. Both were now dead.

The cowering old man with the baby, however...

How had he managed to get past Hulbert's men? The entire village had been devastated, every soul snuffed out. To find that one had escaped was infuriating.

There was some relief to be had, though. Hulbert had been convinced he had failed in his quest. Now, there was some hope, however small. Perhaps the man stumbling through the brush ahead *had* the most prized object of objects. Perhaps the woman and boy had given it to him for safekeeping. It was worth the painstakingly slow pursuit through the forest to find out.

The man gave up trying to push his way through the impenetrable wall of brush, his frail body heaving with the effort it seemed to take to remain on his feet.

"You there!" Hulbert shouted, signaling his men with a wave of his arm. The thirteen guards dismounted, surrounding the man.

Clutching the screaming infant to his chest, the old man's pale eyes darted from one guard to the next, recoiling into the hedge the best he could. He looked up at Hulbert slowly, trembling.

He knew who sat atop the palace horse, of course. Everyone from the surrounding countryside knew. Hulbert was aware of his reputation and embraced it. He was hated, yes—but also feared, as he should be.

The king gave a swift tug to the reigns of his horse. The beast strode forward until he towered over the old man.

"Please, Sire. Spare the child, spare me." The old man's voice was barely more than a whisper. He struggled to stand while cradling the baby.

"Give it to me!" Hulbert demanded, dismounting his horse. His boot crushed a twig beneath it as he approached the old man.

Eyes wide, the fearful man pulled the baby to him protectively. "Please, this is my granddaughter. I'm all she has. I…"

"The GraVinn!" King Hulbert drew his sword and angled it toward the man's heart. His already-low patience was dwindling, and there was nothing the old man could do to placate him.

Nothing mattered except the Stone of GraVinn.

"I don't know what you speak of, sire, please," the bony old man pleaded.

King Hulbert laughed. The man must be a fool, to expect him to believe that.

"I don't have—"

Before he could finish his sentence, the old man's many years had come to an end. His strangled scream echoed through the forest as King Hulbert's razor-edged sword pierced his chest in one sure blow, the baby slipping to the ground at his side.

Ignoring the ragged, faint sound of the old man's dying breaths, Hulbert turned away, sheathing his sword as two guards searched the body. When he looked back, the guards were shaking their heads up at their king.

The GraVinn was nowhere to be found.

Hulbert scowled. That entire chase—all for nothing. And now, he had a screaming infant on his hands.

"Shut that thing up!" he roared over the baby's cries, and stomped back toward his horse.

A guard stepped forward and raised his sword, ready to do as commanded.

"You will not harm the child."

The female voice was unexpected. The surprised guard, weapon still hovering over the infant, looked up at the king, perplexed.

Hulbert felt his blood run cold as he slowly turned around to see an intense auburn glow emerging from the shadows of the forest behind the child.

This was not some ray of morning sun finding its way through the dense foliage, that much was clear. The light grew brighter and brighter until in one sudden flash of warm color, it took the form of a woman.

She stared directly at Hulbert. Her eyes, deep as the bluest sea, made it clear that she feared no one—in fact, she seemed to be looking down on him with something like disdain.

Two guards dropped their weapons and retreated, their petrified screams ringing through the forest, leaving no question as to how they felt.

Undaunted, King Hulbert squared his shoulders. Although appearing to be a human female, clearly this woman was something more, something much more. Her soft, flowing, red velvet gown rippled in waves, although there was no wind. Her long, golden hair hung in perfect ringlets that framed her emotionless face. The woman exuded otherworldliness.

With those piercing eyes, she stared back at Hulbert as if she could see deep to the core of his very being. Perhaps she could.

"You will not harm the child," she repeated, in the same cold tone as before.

Hulbert's fingers brushed over his goatee, his scowl deepening. He, the king, had been given an order, and by a woman at that! He did not take orders, he gave them. And as certain as the sky was blue, he did not answer to a female.

He shoved one terrified guard to the side, coming to stand over the baby. He did not know who or what this woman was, but she would soon see how serious he was. Nobody was going to stand between him and the GraVinn, be it a bony old man and a baby, or some otherworldly *being* from the EliSann Forest.

"Watch me," he snapped, raising his sword over the child, bringing it down with expert precision...

Hulbert stumbled forward as the weapon vanished from his grip—along with the baby. He just managed to catch himself before hitting the ground.

He looked from his empty hand back up at the woman, gritting his teeth angrily as he noted that the infant was now on the ground at her feet.

"The GraVinn is mine! Give it to me and I might forget about this," he roared.

Marlott, Seratine of EliSann, stepped forward over the baby, glancing down at the old man's limp, lifeless body.

"This man had nothing to do with what you seek... and yet you killed him."

"He was in my way," Hulbert snarled, and then worked to hide his unease as eight young men—boys, really—appeared at the woman's side, out of thin air. They each stared at him with the same blank expression the woman wore.

He turned his attention back to the crying infant, catching a glimpse of lime-colored light from behind the seratine, and found himself at a loss for words—the pocket of the tattered blue shirt the baby was swaddled in had lit up. In a brilliant flash, the light disappeared, leaving a faceted aquamarine stone attached to a simple leather cord necklace lying across the infant's neck.

"The power of the Stone of GraVinn is not for one such as you to possess," the seratine said matter-of-factly.

Pure hatred seeped from every pore of Hulbert's body. He surveyed the eight boys. They said nothing, but like their seratine, they exuded power. It was clear from their icy stares that they would not permit any movement toward the baby or the woman, either.

Hulbert took stock of his remaining eleven men—all in various stages of shock and disbelief. They were by no means outnumbered by those in EliSann, but their disadvantage was understood.

With a voice as void of emotion as her expression, Marlott spoke one last time.

"You shall never know the power of the Stone of GraVinn, King Hulbert of Draven."

In the next moment she, and the eight young men, disappeared with the baby, right before his eyes.

King Hulbert studied the immediate area again with renewed caution. He knew their immediate retreat was expected. Remembering the cold gaze of that strange woman, he shivered. Suddenly, he wasn't sure he wanted to discover what the penalty would be if he lingered in the forest much longer.

Snarling, Hulbert forced his way through his guards.

"Out of my way!" he growled, mounting his horse. His quest had come to a screeching halt for the time being, but it was far from over. This he swore.

Only those chosen specifically by the seratine could sit on the EliSann Council. Nardin, nymph, delpin, and sprite—all beings that called the forest home had at least one representative, and Marlott watched these chosen few with the pride of a mother as they entered the underground meeting room.

First to enter were the nardins and nymphs. Male and female respectively, they possessed very little supernatural power to speak of. Tending to shy away from adventure and new experiences, the nardins and nymphs did not venture far from their woodland home. They lived simple lives, firm on tradition and customs of old, and represented the largest population in the forest. The two nymphs and six nardins now finding their seats at the wooden-planked table were among the most respected of their kind.

Marlott eyed the three quiet young men occupying the remaining chairs at the table. The delpins were undisputedly the most powerful of the EliSann Forest's inhabitants, aside from herself. Their abilities were vast and difficult to understand, the very embodiment of what those on the outside feared. It was for this reason above all others that the safety of her secluded people was entrusted to the delpins.

Despite being the oldest of those in EliSann, they appeared to be young men, sixteen at most in human years. Youthful, intelligent, powerful; the delpins were a force not to be taken lightly.

Finally, there were the sprites, winged human-like beings standing no more than five inches high, also a loved, integral part of the EliSann community. Known for their mischievousness, they were prone to journey from the forest from time to time. Tucked away in their beloved ErinDarr Hollow deep in the forest, the sprites lived separate yet as one with the rest of EliSann. They held no seat on Council themselves, as much of their time was spent managing affairs in their own tiny community, but the delpins had always been especially trusted by the sprites, and served as representatives for them.

With all eleven Council members accounted for, Marlott stood at the head of the table. She stepped to the side.

There was a resounding gasp throughout the room.

Slumbering in a makeshift cradle lay a baby—a human baby.

"The child from this morning," a nymph said, appearing uncomfortable as murmurs spread throughout the room.

"Yes." Marlott looked the baby over—sleeping so peacefully, in stark contrast with the day's events. "We'll care for her now."

No one dared speak—all were shocked as they processed the seratine's words.

"She wears the Stone of GraVinn," a nardin observed, noting the teardrop shaped aquamarine stone so plainly in view around the baby's neck.

"Also entrusted to our care." Marlott walked to stand behind the crib, eyeing the stone warily. "As you know, the GraVinn has been sought by many over the years. The promise of unimaginable power is an irresistible lure. The stone already has a long and bloody history." The child stirred slightly in her sleep, and Marlott continued. "I'm not strong enough to destroy it outright, but without safeguards in place, it could bring an end to our way of life."

Before that statement started weighing too heavily on the Council, she took a deep breath. "I can, though, contain the stone's power. It is finally, after all this time, in our possession—our *control*. It would be a mistake to risk losing it without first limiting it."

"And what of the child, my lady?" The nardin sounded anxious.

"It's because of the Stone of GraVinn that this child has been left with no family. It's only right that we now care for her."

An elder nymph spoke up. "But—a human baby in EliSann? Are you sure that we should take her in as one of our own, my lady? It *would* be a first."

"While a human child's needs are no different than any child from the EliSann Forest, it would be best to have her raised by her own kind," Marlott said. "We must turn to Draven to tend to her. But as the child is in possession of the Stone of GraVinn, we must also keep watch over her. I've selected one among you to be her guardian."

The tension in the room was almost tangible as she made eye contact with the blond delpin at the center of the table.

"VerGann."

The delpin stood and approached the seratine slowly. Although appearing to be a fourteen year old human boy, his years numbered far more—and his power far surpassed even that of his fellow delpins.

"The GraVinn must be guarded at all costs," Marlott warned. "Close proximity to the girl is necessary. You will befriend her. It will be easier for her to relate to you if you appear to be her own age, so at the appropriate time—"

His brilliant blue eyes flicked from the baby in the cradle up to the seratine.

"I'm going to grow?" He sounded perplexed, for a delpin.

The question was expected. A delpin appeared as a teenage human boy, never a full grown man.

"In appearance, my son," the seratine clarified. "The GraVinn is under EliSann's protection, but it is you, VerGann, who bears the most responsibility for its keep. There will be those who seek to take it, but know this; once removed from the girl by force, the stone's power will cease. But should she willingly give it away…"

She locked eyes with VerGann. There was no need to finish her statement. The unspoken seriousness of such an action was understood. The girl was never to relinquish the GraVinn. This was his charge.

VerGann turned back to the baby. "She's the key to its power."

"Now she is. What I ask of you is a great task," Marlott agreed gravely. Her final warning must be heeded. "The GraVinn isn't meant for our kind, my son. Do you understand?"

After staring at the baby a few moments more in deep concentration, VerGann straightened.

"I do."

CHAPTER 1

(17 years later)

Natty peered cautiously out of the old, hollowed log which she had sought refuge in moments before.

It was by sheer instinct that she had darted into the fallen timber in the first place. King Hulbert's voice, echoing over the castle grounds and into the reaches of the forest, had startled her.

The sprite knew it was silly to suddenly let the sound alarm her, after listening to the commotion for the better part of the morning. But the king's last angry, bellowing outburst far exceeded anything she had heard yet.

Looking up at KaiDinn, Natty smiled. Her dear friend's disinterest was etched across his face– not surprising. Very little unnerved the delpins, a trait she knew she would never in a million years possess.

"Nat?"

Natty stifled a giggle—she'd always found KaiDinn's bug-like nickname for her funny. Exiting the security of her hiding place, she returned to his shoulder.

"I know, I know," she said. "But you have to admit that King Hulbert's just a little bit scary."

"I don't think that *scary* is the word I'd choose to describe him," KaiDinn corrected. "He's just angry... All of the time."

"And resonant," she suggested, studying the rather short distance between where she and KaiDinn sat and the castle's outer wall. The edge of the forest was but a field away from the city of Draven.

"Hm..." The corner of KaiDinn's mouth downturned a bit. "Yes, resonant is also a good word."

Natty tugged at the ends of her short golden hair as she turned her attention to the north. Just the uppermost peaks of the sparkling white towers of the Draven castle could be seen over the enormous fortified outer wall. "I wonder what the problem is today? He seems particularly agitated this morning, don't you think?"

Hearing no answer, she tapped her foot on KaiDinn's shoulder. He huffed dismissively, and she let out a deep breath. As far as KaiDinn was concerned, any amount of time spent thinking about King Hulbert was too much. He was not at all interested in anything to do with the egregious king.

KaiDinn settled back against the tree behind him. "There doesn't have to be something wrong. Breakfast served late, cold bath water, a nephew that refuses to jump at every order he's given; take your pick, the possibilities are endless."

"Still not knowing the location of the Stone of GraVinn."

That got KaiDinn's attention. He turned to her.

"That was seventeen years ago." He was only twelve, and had not been around during Hulbert's famed search for the Stone, but it was impossible to live in EliSann and *not* hear about that day.

"He blames EliSann. Or more to the point, Marlott and the delpins." Natty pivoted on her toes to face him. "A man like that doesn't forgive or forget. I'd be careful, if I were you."

Hearing no immediate response, she smoothed her skirt with her hand and cleared her throat. "I'm joking, you know. You're probably safe. He has no idea where the GraVinn is now, at least."

KaiDinn nodded, his gaze turning distant. "And we're going to make sure it stays that way. The GraVinn is better left lost."

"Natty!"

She gasped at the sudden screeching sound of her name from behind. Arms out at her side like a bird in flight, the sprite fought to regain her balance before falling off KaiDinn's shoulder.

"Sorry," a sheepish male sprite apologized as KaiDinn put his hand up to catch her. "Anyway, a group of us are going to the castle to see what the ruckus is all about. Want to come?"

"Well, I..." Natty had to admit that she *was*, in fact, very curious. Given how rare it was for her to leave the EliSann Forest without KaiDinn, though, it was hard to convince herself that a trip to Draven was in her best interest.

"Go ahead," KaiDinn said. "You know that you want to."

"But..."

"*Go.* You'll be fine. No one's going to see you peeking through a window four stories up, anyway."

"I guess it would be harmless," she agreed. "But what about you? I told you that I would help with—"

"It's fine," KaiDinn cut her off. "Fill me in on all of the delicious details when you get back." He smirked. "I know you'll look forward to that."

He had a point. She did enjoy a bit of gossip from time to time.

In the next instance, KaiDinn had disappeared—leaving Natty with no footing. She shrieked and fell a short distance before managing to spread her wings and get her bearings. Spying four sprites ahead, she darted off to join them.

"I can't wait to hear what the problem is this time," one shouted. "He's been at it all morning."

"I am going to guess someone is in trouble," another chimed in. "And I think we all know who that *someone* is."

Natty nodded in agreement. It was a well known fact that Hulbert spent most of his time frustrated with his nephew, Prince Breydon.

It had been eighteen years since Breydon's father, King Lundane, had left for battle and never returned—presumed dead, of course. His brother Hulbert ascended the throne and stepped into the role of father to Breydon, almost two years old at the time. Preparing his nephew for the throne had been at the forefront of his mind for several years now.

Prince Breydon, however, did not share his uncle's priorities. The young prince's relationship with the king grew more strained by the day—which was saying something, since strained relationships were all there were to begin with when it came to King Hulbert.

They flew past the pines lining the northern edge of the forest and darted across the field, finally coming to the castle grounds. Natty focused on the towers rising in front of her and sped ahead of her companions, excitement building.

"Princess Gwenevieve will be here in three days, and you'll accompany her during her stay as though you are already married." The booming sound of Hulbert's deep voice reverberated off of every stone wall in the castle. "Is this understood?"

As usual, Breydon's morning had started with another of his uncle's tirades. His gaze shifted from his uncle to the six servants on the king's left and the eight guards to the right. All of them very carefully avoided his gaze. Even the nosy servants peeking around the doors to watch the showdown in the Great Hall appeared to feel bad for him.

Over it all sat King Hulbert on his throne, a permanent scowl on his face.

Is this understood? Breydon clenched his jaw, fighting the urge to answer. Nothing good could come from his response.

He *understood* a lot when it came to his uncle. His uncle was a hard, cold, calculating man, not at all like his father. As sole heir to the throne, Breydon was expected not only to tolerate, but to embrace the same unfavorable behavior.

King Hulbert and King Lundane were like day and night. Hulbert was well known for his cruelty; Lundane had been loved by his people, strong but compassionate.

At least that was what Breydon was told. He could not say for certain—he had but a few disjointed memories of his father.

Breydon squared his shoulders. No matter how bad the disagreement—and the one at present was worse than any other he could remember in recent history—he knew his uncle would tire at some point. If he could just hold out for a little while longer, the whole humiliating scene would be over, and he would be free to go back and sulk in his room, alone.

The problem was that *he* was the one beginning to tire. The subject of the morning's tirade was love. Or perhaps that wasn't accurate. Not love, *marriage.* Of all subjects, this one had garnered the most attention recently. His uncle's continued attempts to have him married were at the top of Breydon's mental list of things he detested about his life. How could they not be? He was not going to entertain, much less marry, whoever Princess Gwenevieve was.

Of course, he had been hearing about the beautiful princess from Santerine for some time, as an arrangement had been made when he was young in regard to their marriage, but he did not care. Hulbert had hand-picked the girl as his bride. That was more than enough reason to resist pursuing her.

"Uncle, you seem so enamored with the girl, why don't you show her around? Or better yet, why don't you just marry her yourself?"

Breydon swallowed hard as his uncle's glare narrowed. He had crossed a line.

"This isn't up for discussion," Hulbert snarled, despite the fact that they had been discussing it all morning. "You will marry this girl. Once you get that fact through your thick skull, things will perhaps be less tense around here!"

"I don't love her, Uncle," Breydon snapped, wishing there was a way to make his point without sounding so juvenile. "I don't even know her! I have no interest in *Princess Gwenevieve*. I don't want to get married."

"Your marriage to Gwenevieve isn't about love," his uncle continued, ignoring Breydon's attempt to bring the conversation to a close. "Your happiness is not a priority here. This marriage brings with it an alliance of two kingdoms, two kingdoms so long intertwined in battle that—"

"So I am a peace offering in your time of war?" Breydon interrupted, his anger boiling over. "Of course, you're already on the verge of war with Tatrus—anything to avoid two war fronts…" He trailed off at his uncle's furious expression.

Breydon took another deep breath to calm himself. He had pushed the argument to a point where it had never been. The king had been paranoid about Tatrus' increasing military strength for years now, but he preferred not to put that paranoia on display. Especially not in front of an entire palace full of servants.

"This is not a sudden decision. Princess Gwenevieve was promised to you at birth." His uncle's fingernails dug into the carved oak arms of his stately chair.

"When I was two," Breydon corrected. It was hard to believe that so much time had been spent on what he viewed as a ridiculous subject. He was just shy of twenty. Although he knew this was an appropriate age to be married, he did not believe it to be such a pressing matter. "This is absurd. What if I do not want her?"

"It doesn't matter!" Hulbert's voice boomed, his face reddening. "I don't care!"

"I guess I just hoped that I would be allowed to marry a girl I choose, at a *time* I choose."

"That will never happen, Breydon."

"I will *not* marry her!" Breydon protested. His uncle stood to loom over him, his eyes flashing angrily.

"Enough!" Hulbert roared, his face turning an even deeper shade of red—an impressive feat. "This matter is closed."

Closed. Breydon cursed under his breath. There was nothing else to be gained from his presence here. Exasperated, he turned to take his leave. He would just have to find another way of dealing with the situation.

"Halt!"

Breydon stopped, taking yet another deep breath to manage his response. He knew what was coming next. His uncle demanded respect from everyone—his nephew included.

To his uncle's chagrin, *he* only tended to give respect to those who deserved it.

"Turn and face me."

Slowly, Breydon turned as commanded. He had to force his body to move.

"You may be my nephew, not to mention my sole heir, but first and foremost I am King, *your king*, and no one leaves my presence until dismissed."

Breydon seethed to himself as Hulbert scoured the room to make sure he had everyone's attention, a satisfied smile crossing his face. His uncle viewed him as defiant, and for the time being he was also going to be embarrassed. In his eyes, this was a small price to pay for the inexcusable exchange they had just had.

After being forced to stand there for a few moments longer, Hulbert's pleasure at his torment obvious, Breydon was relieved to see the king wave his hand dismissively toward him.

"Go!" his uncle barked, taking his seat back at the head of the room. "Drink!"

Not giving Hulbert any more time to think of something else to say, Breydon made his way to the door. His personal servant Samuel, stood in the corridor, smirking.

Ignoring the servant's amused expression, Breydon made his way through the long, narrow, stone corridor outside the Great Hall with deliberate steps. He did not even have to look up to know that every face he passed was fixated on him. Understandably so—after such a heated argument, it stood to reason that he would be either furious or humiliated. But the door to the eastern tower was just ahead, and he was not about to let either emotion show.

Feeling Samuel right on his heels, the prince pushed open the large wooden door to the eastern tower and started his ascent up the spiraling staircase. Rounding the corner to the large landing midway up, Breydon finally felt the tension leave his shoulders.

The eastern tower was the one place where he did not have to worry about being under the constant eye of every servant. These were his private chambers, and only a select few were allowed into the tower. This was an absolute necessity if he ever hoped to maintain even an ounce of sanity about him.

Leaping up to stand in the oversized arched window and leaning against its cold stone side, Breydon's gaze drifted to his servant. Samuel knew of his ongoing battle with the king. After the morning's entertainment, he hoped his friend had some words of wisdom to offer.

"You bring it on yourself, you know," Samuel began. "You do. I mean, look at it this way. You're going to be king of this magnificent kingdom. All of this will be yours." With a dramatic wave, he motioned to the vast city stretched out below them. "You have the power, the castle, the land, the subjects, and now you have the girl."

They were not the consoling words of comfort Breydon had hoped to hear. Exasperated, he sat on the ledge of the window. As his closest friend and confidant for the better part of five years, Breydon found himself baffled at the blunt statement, but he would indulge Samuel for a while.

"True," he agreed. "And as I understand it, this marriage will bring peace to Draven and Santerine. That's more important than my happiness any day, isn't it?" He sighed. "If I really believed this marriage would bring peace, I would do it."

"You would?"

He swallowed hard. "I didn't say I'd like it. But, in my position, I know that there are some things I'll have to do that I won't like."

"Well, all right," Samuel agreed, laughing, scratching the stubble at his chin. "I guess the worst that could happen would be for Princess Gwenevieve to turn out to be the ugliest woman in the world. Even so, once you have a son, there's no need to interact with her at all."

It was difficult to say what bothered Breydon more, the simplicity of Samuel's statement, given its reprehensible nature, or the fact that Samuel had even been able to think such thoughts in the first place.

"What?" Samuel asked as Breydon shot a disgusted look his way.

There was no good answer he could offer. "Right..." he mumbled, annoyed. "Well, it won't work. Peace won't come to Draven from my marriage. Look at Tatrus. We haven't heard a peep from them in years, yet my uncle speaks of King Sandis as if his armies are just outside our city gates. If there's no fight, my uncle will create one." He shook his head. "Well, I'm not going to play into his trap. I'm not going to marry Princess Gwenevieve. If I marry—and that is a big *if* at this point—I am going to marry someone of my choosing." Jumping down from the window and brushing past Samuel, he hesitated. "Gwenevieve. Why does that name sound so familiar?"

"Maybe because she's all you've heard about for the past seventeen years."

"No, I never knew the girl's name, only that I had a bride-to-be waiting for me when I came of age. *Santerine's beautiful princess.*"

"Breydon, I still think you're being ridiculous," Samuel complained, following him up the stairs. "It's your duty to marry an appropriate princess. Your uncle secured that girl for you—"

"When I was two!"

"When you were two or when you are twenty, it doesn't matter. Now, the only thing left to do is marry her." The servant shrugged. "You're lucky."

"Please," Breydon retorted, pushing open the door at the top of the stairs. "You're beginning to sound like my uncle."

"Not quite." Samuel smirked. "I am not screaming."

Breydon stared, dumbfounded.

"Right," he muttered. Patting Samuel on the shoulder, Breydon closed the door on him before he could utter another word.

The early morning sounds of shoppers flooding into the streets echoed throughout the city, mingling with the creaking of wagons and whinnying of horses. Tiaponine, walking amongst the merchants setting up shop along the road, sighed in resignation.

These were the lower streets of Draven. These were the streets she had grown up on, and these were the streets she feared she may never escape.

Having awakened at the first morning rays of the sun, she had been wandering around for several hours. After taking on a few random errands here and there, she had managed to secure her breakfast as payment. Not a bad start to her morning.

Tiaponine glanced behind her and grimaced. It appeared that breakfast was not all she had managed to secure.

Drake, the tall, dark-haired bane of her existence and his three equally dislikeable friends, had been following her ever since she finished her last errand a couple hours earlier. As the *only* son of the *only* baker on the lower streets of Draven, Drake was under the delusion he held a position of some importance.

For reasons unknown, he seemed to enjoy pestering Tiaponine every chance he got.

"I heard the man who runs the fruit stand in the north alley complaining that a pair of his trousers came up missing the other day."

"Really?" Drake said, far too loudly. "Well, I think we know what happened to them, don't we?"

Tiaponine risked a quick glance at her clothing, picking up her pace. Dirty, loose white men's shirt, baggy dark brown pants gathered at the waist with a large brown leather belt, the extra length hanging at her side. Her fingers glided over the back of the floppy black hat atop her head that secured her long auburn hair.

She bit her lip. It was not like she had a dozen dresses to choose from. Hardly anyone noticed her, and her unconventional choice of clothing for a woman guaranteed that few ever *would* take notice. It was unfortunate that this did not apply to Drake.

"You wouldn't know the first thing about acting like a girl," Drake chided. "Look at you. You don't even dress like one."

Tiaponine felt her jaw tighten. The temptation to launch a verbal attack on Drake was difficult to ignore. Perhaps, if she had the means to do so, she would have dressed up from time to time. But she didn't. There was no call for it, anyway.

"Well, you're quiet today." Drake bumped shoulders with her as he fell in step beside her. "You really take the fun out of harassing you."

"Apologies," she said, not even bothering to look up at him. She smiled to herself with a sense of accomplishment as he sighed, already bored, and fell back to rejoin his friends.

When she stopped walking a few paces later, she looked back in his direction, her smile turning into a smirk as she fingered his ivory-handled knife between two fingers.

It was his prized possession. He never left home without it. She could not believe she had managed to slip it out of his side pocket without him even noticing.

She waited. The anticipation was killing her. She had to see Drake's reaction when he found it missing.

It was but a moment later when she saw all four men stop in their tracks. Drake's face paled. She could not keep herself from grinning.

But then all four turned toward her, and she swallowed hard, her previous sense of accomplishment vanishing.

"Get her!" Drake yelled.

He'd barely finished speaking before they were racing for her. Tiaponine bolted into a side street, clutching the knife in her pocket. Through a tangle of wooden carts overstuffed with flowers, past the sweet scent of fresh pastries, behind the candle maker's shop, around the corner, and...

Tiaponine stopped. Drake was nowhere to be seen, but still—it was wise to put as much distance between herself and him as possible.

She darted to the right, narrowly missing a merchant with a tray of bread in his hands. Around the fountain, past a large tub of fish, the pungent smell causing her nose to wrinkle...

She staggered to another stop, searching the crowds of people around her. Her breath halted as she glimpsed Drake and his trusty companions emerging from the crowd. They appeared amused—which could not be good for her.

She took inventory of her surroundings again, a knot forming in the pit of her stomach. She was standing at the end of a dock, her only exit, now blocked by Drake and his friends. How could she be so careless?

"Great," she grumbled.

Drake edged closer. "I ought to..."

"You ought to what?"

At the unexpected male voice, Drake turned around, coming face to face with a tall blond man about his own age. Tiaponine allowed herself a snicker as Drake scowled.

"This is between me and her, VerGann. Get lost!" he snapped, turning his back on the delpin to focus again on Tiaponine.

She was still cornered. She had only two choices available—jump into the chilly morning water of the merchants' canal, or take a chance at getting past Drake and his friends. Neither option sounded favorable.

The time had come to end the game she had started. Someone was going to get hurt, and if she was not careful, it might end up being her. With newfound determination, Tiaponine pulled Drake's knife from her pocket.

"Give it back!" He lunged at her, which would have sent her into the canal, but she stepped to the side at the last moment. He teetered for a second at the edge of the dock before regaining his balance and whirling on her again.

She threw the knife.

"Heads up!" she screamed, pleased to see the weapon whiz past Drake's head. The knife missed him by a few fingers' length as it traveled on to embed itself in the side of a passing wooden boat with a resounding thud.

She'd never had much skill in handling knives, but it appeared that her limited amount of practice had paid off nicely.

Drake, caught off guard, lost his balance and fell backwards into the water. One of his three friends dove into the canal after him. The two remaining hapless thugs looked at each other, mouths agape.

"You're crazy!" one of them shouted, pushing Tiaponine to the side and diving into the water. Without a word, the third boy followed.

Tiaponine laughed as all four young men tried without success to catch up to the merchant's boat making its way down the canal. Feeling very self-satisfied, she turned away from the retreating boat, only to find herself face to face with VerGann.

"Nice throw," he offered, his tone dry.

"Thank you," she mused, very proud of herself. Registering the delpin's continued deadpan stare, Tiaponine felt a twinge of guilt dampen her sense of accomplishment. "Trust me, they deserved it."

VerGann finally looked away, a slight smile creeping into his features.

"I know. And the look on his face was priceless." He laughed. "Of course, the look on his face if you *hadn't* had any throwing practice would've been something entirely different."

At the sound of a watery slap against the wooden slat beneath her foot, Tiaponine glanced down to find that one of Drake's friends had somehow managed to find his way back to the dock. Soaked through and fatigued, the embarrassed young man tried clumsily to pull himself onto the dock. She almost felt bad for him.

Almost.

With the slightest push from VerGann's foot to the top of his head, the man fell back into the muddy water of the canal. Not bothering to even look back at him, the delpin walked past her.

After amusing herself watching the man flail around in the water a moment longer, Tiaponine laughed and ran ahead to join VerGann.

CHAPTER 2

Breydon's day could not possibly get any worse at this point.

He'd thought he had heard the last about Santerine's princess for at least the next three days—until Gwenevieve was scheduled to arrive. But life seemed determined not to afford him a break.

She had shown up early. Three full days early. He had almost fallen off his bed when Samuel had told him.

The oversized double-door to the Great Hall was just ahead, Breydon straightened, taking a deep breath. He would greet Princess Gwenevieve and then make his exit as soon as possible.

As he entered the hall, Breydon wondered if he should have risked ignoring his uncle's summons altogether. Judging by the forced smiles around him, patience appeared to be in short supply.

It was understandable. He *had* been summoned over an hour earlier.

"Ah," Hulbert began, with a very unconvincing attempt at a cordial tone. "And here's Prince Breydon now."

Breydon's whole body tensed. The grand introduction was an obvious—and ineffective—attempt to overshadow his blatant rudeness.

"Breydon, may I present Princess Gwenevieve from Santerine."

With heavy steps, Breydon made his way to the front of the Great Hall. Rude or not, he could not bring himself to look at the woman ahead. He could imagine what the Santerine princess had been told about him. No doubt his immense displeasure at this forced marriage had not been revealed. For all he knew, Gwenevieve was under the impression that he was looking forward to their future together.

Catching a glimpse of Samuel's pained expression beside him, Breydon slowed. "What is it?" he grumbled.

"Why's she looking at you like that?" Samuel asked, gesturing with his eyes toward the blonde ahead of them.

Against his better judgment, Breydon glanced at Princess Gwenevieve. His brief glance turned into a stunned stare.

He swallowed hard.

"Look," Hulbert deadpanned, his tone dripping with sarcasm. "Love blossoms already."

Breydon strode to the front of the room, head down as he passed the princess. He went straight for his uncle.

"Her?" he whispered, trying to be discreet. "Uncle, I *cannot* marry her." He cringed as his words echoed in the massive room. A deafening hush fell over the hall. So much for not drawing attention.

Gwenevieve took a step forward, her eyes wild as she inspected him. A measure of respect was demanded in the presence of a lady, and his reaction did not even come close. The princess squared her shoulders, her chin held high. His obvious displeasure clearly did not faze Princess Gwenevieve in the least, but rather spurred an indignant determination.

"Well, I had no idea," she chimed with feigned innocence. "I never expected to see *you* again."

Breydon made no effort to hide his irritation as he glared at her.

She sauntered toward him, her gaze almost hungry. Breydon fought the urge to recoil—while she certainly was beautiful, her whole demeanor approached something much closer to *intimidating* than attractive. A predator in a dress. It appeared that here, *he* was the damsel in distress.

Not surprisingly, his uncle was smiling with firm approval, pleased with his matchmaking skills. Princess Gwenevieve moved closer, her eyes brightening. She was *also* very pleased.

He forced a smile and prepared to make his exit. Feeling Gwenevieve lean in, her hand resting on his right arm, he froze.

"I think we make a great couple," Gwenevieve whispered.

It was impossible to put into words what Breydon felt at that exact moment. She knew he was in a difficult position—it was incredibly obvious—and no amount of protest would change the king's mind about their marriage. She had him.

He felt sick to his stomach. He couldn't even begin to come to terms with the fact that once again, the whole castle was audience to his mortification.

"Not going to happen," he said flatly. He turned and stormed out of the hall, praying his uncle did not stop him.

"My apologies, princess. Prince Breydon is a bit out of sorts today."

At his uncle's less than believable apology, Breydon laughed to himself. He was more than a bit out of sorts. He stepped into the long marble hallway leading to the eastern tower. As expected, curious onlookers crowded close to the doors, clearly having heard everything. He wondered how many more times today he would endure this cruel journey. He picked up his pace.

"Do you know her?" Samuel asked, pushing through the crowd to walk at Breydon's side.

"Do I *know* her?" He laughed mirthlessly. "Remember the girl at King Bartholomew's spring gathering three years ago, his only daughter? The one who followed me around all night?"

"The girl that never let you get a word in," Samuel said, thinking out loud. "No regard for personal space—or, at least, *your* personal space? The girl who—"

"Yes," Breydon interrupted. "The same insufferable girl who invited herself to Draven for a week. Thank goodness I got out of that one."

"But that girl was King Bartholomew's daughter. Gwenevieve is from Santerine," Samuel reasoned. "You must be confused."

Breydon shook his head. "She never said she was King Bartholomew's daughter. I just assumed. Turns out she was not from DenWinn." He looked at Samuel. "She was my Santerine princess."

Samuel stared at him for a long moment. Then he started laughing.

Breydon gritted his teeth as the door to the east tower came into view. *He* certainly did not find this funny.

"Oh, come, Breydon. That was three years ago. People change." Samuel's snigger made it clear that he did not believe that in the slightest.

Breydon glared at him. "Give me a break," he said shortly. "I just cannot believe that *this* is the woman I've been hearing about all this time. I could have started my protests three years ago."

"But—"

"Please, no," Breydon interrupted. Stopping at the familiar wooden door to the eastern tower, he took a deep breath. "I need space to think."

"Come," Samuel said, tugging on his left arm. "Don't hole yourself up in your tower again. Let's find something better to do."

Breydon studied the servant for a moment, his curiosity piqued. Maybe he had a point—dwelling on the mess he was in would not make him feel any better, would it?

With only a moment's hesitation, he followed Samuel.

"Oh, decisions, decisions," the stout shopkeeper sang, fingering the stacks of cloth piled in Tiaponine's arms. "I know she'll take almost anything, but of course you understand that I want to send her the best."

VerGann surveyed the array of floral weaves and striped cottons with utter disinterest. Such a task should never require as much concentration as the shopkeeper was investing in it.

Tiaponine adjusted the cloth in her arms, eyes glazed over with boredom as well. What they had hoped would be a quick errand for a little extra change had turned into a lengthy one-sided discussion on modern fashion.

VerGann stifled a yawn. Another chase through the lower streets with the likes of Drake sounded better than this.

"What do you think, Tiaponine, dear?"

VerGann laughed to himself as Tiaponine's attention jolted back to the shopkeeper, her whole body jumping in surprise. He had to admit, it was curious that the shopkeeper sought Tiaponine's advice in this matter. Given her attire, she did not seem an obvious choice for fashion opinions.

"Which one do you like, dear?" the shopkeeper repeated.

"Oh," she offered, clearly embarrassed. "I suppose the blue one, and the green."

The shopkeeper squealed with delight. "I *do* believe you're right, my dear. These two are the prettiest of the bunch, aren't they? The blue and the green it is, then." Adding the two pieces of cloth to the pile in Tiaponine's arms, she giggled, very pleased with herself. "I know my daughters would agree—"

As the sound of footsteps echoed down the stairs, her smile brightened.

"Oh, Lerra, Eva, there you are," she beamed, her attention moving to the two young women skipping into the room.

VerGann stiffened, unable to bring himself to turn around. The addition of the shopkeeper's daughters was something that he did *not* have the patience to deal with at the moment. A quick glance at Tiaponine made it clear that she shared his irritation.

It was not that either woman was particularly dislikeable. They were just clueless in all things appropriate and prone to overly candid comments which tended to make people uncomfortable. *Very* uncomfortable.

"I'll be out for the next few hours. The shop's yours for that time," the shopkeeper continued, oblivious to her guests' sudden discomfort. With a quick peck to each girl's cheek, she left.

Lerra and Eva's attention turned from their mother's retreating form to Tiaponine... And then to VerGann, the only male in the room.

With a respectful nod of acknowledgment their way, he glanced again at Tiaponine, who was already backing toward the door. "We should be going. We still have a few more stops to—"

"So, Tiaponine, I'm sure you've heard that Prince Breydon is looking for a wife."

Shoving Lerra in the shoulder, Eva rolled her eyes.

"No, she's already here. Some princess from another kingdom arrived this morning for him."

"There've been rumors of the prince taking a wife for years, and it hasn't happened yet. Why should this time be any different?" Lerra shot back. "Men his age don't want to be tied to one woman. Who can blame him? What fun is that?"

Eva's face crinkled. "*What fun is that?*" she repeated, her tone almost accusatory. "And what does that mean, may I ask?"

Please don't elaborate, VerGann thought helplessly.

"The prince is young. *We're* young," Lerra answered, poking Tiaponine in the ribs with her elbow. Tiaponine recoiled from the clear invasion of her personal space. "People our age should have fun. That's all I'm saying. Once you're married, the rules change." She tugged firmly at her ill-fitting bodice to reveal even more of her already protruding chest.

Hearing Tiaponine's muffled groan at his side, VerGann tried to manage his reaction. The shopkeeper's daughters each had a style that, for lack of better words, demanded to be noticed.

Tiaponine backed toward the door some more. "We really should be—"

"Prince Breydon is almost twenty years old," Eva complained. "The king's right. He should be married by now. What do you think, Tiaponine?"

With that, any hope of an immediate retreat was lost. VerGann and Tiaponine exchanged fatigued looks. The discussion was a ridiculous one. They had a lot to deal with on a daily basis, and the prince's love life was quite inconsequential in comparison.

Tiaponine's lips tightened the way they always did when she was irritated. Ignoring VerGann's amused snicker beside her, she turned to the sisters.

"Actually, I don't."

"Don't?" Eva asked dryly. "You don't what, dear?"

"Think about it, about him. I don't keep up on Prince Breydon's romantic troubles," she said flatly. "I've never met him, and I cannot pretend to understand his struggles. Nor do I care to."

Direct and to the point. Tiaponine had summed up VerGann's thoughts on the matter quite well. Perhaps now they could be on their way.

He smiled respectfully at the two sisters, ready to take his leave, but upon seeing Lerra and Eva both staring uncomprehendingly at Tiaponine, he had to stifle a groan. They weren't finished yet.

"You like the prince." Although the statement was directed at her sister, Eva seemed to be announcing it for all to hear.

"How can I like the prince? I don't even know him, Eva," Lerra countered. Turning back to Tiaponine, she shook her head in mock annoyance.

VerGann resisted the urge to roll his eyes. It was clearly a rehearsed conversation between the sisters, as if each knew what the other would say, a mere exhibition for their new audience.

"And this *fun* you spoke of," Eva persisted, "Perhaps you would like to elaborate for Mother?"

Lerra took one more approving glance at her tight fitting dress. "Despite what Mother says, there's nothing wrong with a little innocent time alone with a man. You both know what I mean."

Both. VerGann risked a glance at Tiaponine, whose face was already beginning to flush in embarrassment. He had known her almost all of her life, and although the streets had exposed her to many things, such relations with a man were not among them. Regardless, it was not Lerra's place to put her on the spot. His irritation was reaching its peak.

Not hearing an immediate answer, Lerra's brow furrowed. "You know what I mean, right?"

Tiaponine stared at Lerra, her eyes wide.

"Well, I understand," Eva said after an uncomfortable silence, focusing on the tall, attractive, tousled blond-haired man in front of her.

VerGann swallowed, very certain he did not want the young woman to continue speaking.

"A man that many a girl eyes. To be able to say that you know what it's like to be close to him, while everyone else wishes they could be so lucky. I can see the appeal." With her delicate thumb and forefinger, Eva fluffed the lacy ruffle along the neckline of her emerald green dress, her mouth curving into a grin.

He swallowed again, turning to look at a still-mortified Tiaponine. As long as he didn't have to keep staring back at Eva.

"Well, I guess you *do* understand," Lerra said. "Anyone special in mind, Eva?"

"Perhaps," Eva mused, continuing to stare at VerGann. He risked another glance her way and instantly regretted it.

Tiaponine nudged him, turning again toward the door, and he breathed a sigh of relief.

"Ladies," he offered, forcing a smile. Not giving either sister a chance to say anything further, they left.

Almost as soon as they had stepped into the street, Tiaponine smirked at him.

"What?" he demanded.

She tried unsuccessfully to stifle a laugh. "Well, that was..."

"Please don't," VerGann muttered, running his hand through his hair, still embarrassed.

"I don't think they could've been more—"

"*Tee.*" He could not look at her. Taking in a deep, much needed breath, he shook his head. It was time to change the subject.

"Sorry." Tiaponine giggled again.

"I know I promised I'd help you this afternoon, but..." VerGann smiled, hoping he could smooth over any disappointment that was to come. "I need to go back to EliSann for a Council meeting. Marlott requested that I be there, so I'll have to meet up with you later."

Tiaponine blinked, studying him with a slight frown on her face.

"No, it's all right," she said, just a hint of displeasure in her tone. "If she requested you, it must be important."

VerGann agreed. Something had to have come up for him to be called to Council on such short notice. His curiosity was piqued. He was running late already, and any further delay would not be met with approval.

"You know that I wouldn't go unless I had to," he added. "Given certain personalities on the Council, I'm very happy to avoid it when possible." He hesitated for a moment—he really *did* hate to leave Tiaponine alone like this.

"Tell you what," he offered. "When I return this evening, we'll take a walk by the ElinDann River. If that sounds at all appealing, that is."

It was not often that they made the trip to the crystal blue river flowing through the middle of the EliSann Forest, but when they did, he knew Tiaponine found the peaceful river's edge much to her liking. VerGann doubted she had to put much thought into his proposition.

Smiling, she shifted the pile of fabric in her arms. "I guess I'll see you later, then," she said. "Gives me a good reason to finish my errands early."

VerGann breathed a sigh of relief. Crisis averted. He would attend the Council meeting, deal with any unpleasantness waiting for him there and leave. At least he had something to look forward to this evening.

"And I hope *certain personalities* are in a better mood this time," Tiaponine teased.

"One can hope," VerGann agreed with a playful wink. "Until later."

* * *

VerGann leaned against the cold earthen wall outside the Council chambers with resigned obedience. He had returned to EliSann as requested.

Now that he was here, though, he had a bad feeling about this meeting. It was rare for him to be called back home, especially on short notice, and it did not sit well with him. So he had not yet entered the Council chambers. Unbeknownst to those inside, though, he could hear every discussion taking place.

"I think I can guess who's responsible for calling us here."

VerGann's attention was caught by the voice speaking inside his head. It was Vrenler, the eldest of the delpins.

"And here he comes now," KaiDinn added, joining the silent conversation.

The delpins were the only beings in the EliSann Forest with the ability to communicate telepathically. Although not part of the conversation, VerGann could hear everything being said. He knew who his friends were talking about without even looking.

"Dreesdin looks pleased," Vrenler noted dryly.

"Why shouldn't he be?" KaiDinn complained. *"He's getting everything he wanted."*

"Not quite," Vrenler started. *"Where is..."*

Inside the room, someone pushed their chair away from the table, its heavy wooden legs scratching loudly on the ground. "Where's VerGann?"

VerGann stifled a laugh.

"*VerGann?*" Vrenler's voice sounded much clearer as he addressed VerGann directly.

He closed his eyes and sighed. He'd known it would only be a matter of time before KaiDinn and Vrenler would feel his presence—another ability the delpins possessed.

"*You're not planning on leaving us with this nardin much longer, are you?*" KaiDinn already sounded sour.

VerGann peeked into the Council chambers. "*Planning it, no. Considering it...*"

"It was made very clear to VerGann that he was expected at this meeting." Dreesdin's tone was probably meant to be aggressive, but he just sounded whiny as usual. "There's no point to this if he isn't here."

"There's no point to this even if he *is* here," Vrenler countered. "The delpins won't support you."

VerGann leaned back against the wall. "*Support him in what?*"

"I hope he doesn't intend to..." Dreesdin continued, unaware of the delpins' private conversation.

"*I'm going to kick him,*" Vrenler grumbled.

"*Please do,*" KaiDinn said.

"*Fine, I'm coming.*" Gathering what patience he could muster, VerGann stepped into the room.

"VerGann," Dreesdin greeted with a half nod and furrowed brow, dropping whatever accusation he had been about to make.

Taking his seat beside Vrenler, VerGann offered the slightest of nods to the impertinent nardin across the table.

In general, the nardins and nymphs of EliSann were gentle beings, but there were exceptions. Dreesdin was one of them. To say that he possessed a difficult personality was a gross understatement. Nosy, abrasive, with a permanent chip on his shoulder...

And he had a great dislike for VerGann. The feeling was mutual.

Noticing Marlott appear at the head of the long wooden table, VerGann smiled mockingly at the nardin, a cocky gesture he knew would infuriate him. Satisfied as Dreesdin's eyes narrowed in frustration, he turned his attention to the seratine.

Taking a moment to view the Council members each in turn, Marlott raised her hand, calling the Council to order.

"As most of you are aware, recent unexpected developments have made it necessary to call this meeting. There are questions that must be addressed. VerGann, your presence here is appreciated." She turned to him. "I wish to hear a status on the Stone of GraVinn."

"The GraVinn is secure, my lady," he assured her. "May I ask why I was called from Draven about this now? You must know that I'd relay any concerns back to the Council immediately."

Marlott nodded. "Yes, I trust that you would. This meeting wasn't called at my request, though. A member of the Council has some questions regarding the GraVinn." The seratine's attention shifted to the nardin sitting across from VerGann. "Dreesdin will address his concerns with you."

VerGann knew his sudden change in posture as Dreesdin's name was mentioned was difficult to miss.

Hearing a snicker, he glanced at KaiDinn, who lowered his head so as to avoid making direct eye contact with him.

VerGann straightened, preparing himself for what was sure to be another tirade of admonishments and grievances. It was far from the first time he had been the focus of such an attack by the nardin.

After acknowledging the seratine, Dreesdin surveyed the room. Satisfied he had everyone's full attention, he spoke, casting an accusing stare VerGann's way. "A nymph had a vision involving problems surrounding the GraVinn."

Although not exactly sure what to expect, VerGann had not at all been prepared for Dreesdin's sudden disclosure. For a moment, he found himself staring, not sure what to think.

"*Is he serious?*" VerGann asked.

"*Just wait,*" Vrenler answered. "*It gets better.*"

"*I was called from Draven because a nymph had a bad dream?*"

KaiDinn still seemed to be trying to hide a grin. "*You're going to wish it was a bad dream, trust me.*"

The brief yet unmistakable exchange of bemused glances between the three delpins did not go unnoticed. Dreesdin cleared his throat. "Perhaps the delpins would like to share their thoughts with the rest of us."

"A nymph had a vision," VerGann said with an exaggerated deadpan tone. "A vision, as in…"

"She has a gift," Dreesdin blurted. "She can see into the future." He motioned above his head in a grand arc, as if to emphasize the spiritual nature of such a wondrous gift.

VerGann pushed against the inside of his left cheek with his tongue. What a waste of time. He could already feel an intense foul mood starting to overtake him. It would be best to at least *appear* to consider the matter, though.

"And what nymph are we talking about?"

"Nelliah," Dreesdin answered, apparently surprised to find VerGann asking for more information. "She's lived with us for the past month. Of course, had you been back home in that time, you'd already know this."

VerGann managed his reaction.

"Having been exiled by the BarLonn, Nelliah has been on her own for many years. She came to our people because she thought her gift might be of use."

At that, VerGann clenched his jaw. The nymphs and nardins that now resided in the BarLonn Mountains had once been, a very long time ago, a part of EliSann. After an ill-conceived revolt against the seratine, they had all been exiled from the forest, never to return. They had taken to rewriting history for their descendants in the years since, preventing time from healing the rifts between the two communities.

Marlott did not tolerate any contact with them—such an action would be viewed as traitorous. For obvious reasons, the very mention of BarLonn in connection with this nymph, Nelliah, was enough for VerGann not to trust her, gift or no gift.

"Nelliah saw the Stone of GraVinn in a vision," Dreesdin continued. "The stone's location will be discovered. A great battle will ensue. The delpins will be defeated as they fight to keep the GraVinn from the forces of evil."

The story was curious… and unsettling. No one knew that Tiaponine carried the Stone of GraVinn. No one was *supposed* to know, except members of the Council. Particularly a nymph from the BarLonn Mountains. Unless…

VerGann locked eyes with Dreesdin, pleased to see the nardin acknowledge his unspoken accusation.

"No, Nelliah doesn't know where the stone is, VerGann," he spat. "It would be inappropriate for me to tell her."

VerGann was not ready to believe him, but he did not challenge the nardin. "So did her vision reveal when the stone's exact location would be discovered?" he pressed with feigned concern.

"No," Dreesdin answered, his annoyance evident in his tone. "Nelliah cannot control what visions come to her. She can only take the reading and wait for one to come."

This tale was getting better with every passing moment. VerGann tried to suppress a grin without success. Visions, readings, the delpins' defeat; the conversation had moved from implausible to just plain laughable.

"Reading?" he repeated, the word rolling off his tongue as though he was speaking to a young child. Dreesdin's eyes flared in irritation.

"*Careful,*" KaiDinn interjected, shifting uncomfortably. *"I'm the one sitting closest to him."*

"*Oh, I'm not done yet,*" VerGann said. He was aware Dreesdin did not appreciate his cutting wit. The nardin had to be second guessing his decision to call him to Council.

"Nelliah's visions come only after she's read the stones," Dreesdin continued, forcing himself to sit up straight in his armless, wooden-planked chair.

The stones. As in… rocks.

VerGann laughed out loud. He was aware of the awkward silence in the room. Although no one else on Council would be so bold as to express doubt about the nardin's concern, VerGann harbored no such reluctance. He did not want to be bothered with such a ridiculous subject.

"*I was called back from Draven for this?*" he asked silently.

"*We already thought it was a waste of time,*" KaiDinn said apologetically.

"*None of us want to be bothered with this,*" Vrenler added.

"I guess it should come as no surprise that you're not taking this very seriously, VerGann," Dreesdin said curtly. "Almost all on Council have witnessed one of Nelliah's visions. All except for the delpins."

"And you say the nymph saw the delpins' defeat?" VerGann inquired, grinning. Dreesdin gritted his teeth.

"*You should've heard the in-depth description of what happens,*" Vrenler mused.

"Was this part of the vision or just a secret fantasy he has?" VerGann asked. Dreesdin's relationship with the delpins had always been strained, and everyone knew it.

"Nelliah was quite certain of it," Dreesdin answered. "So, VerGann, will you at least listen to what she has to say? You'll come away quite amazed."

"I'm sure I would," he agreed, sarcasm dripping from every word as a deep flush overtook Dreesdin's face.

"I'm sure you've developed a friendship with that human girl in Draven. I'd think her safety would be a concern for you." Dreesdin leaned forward. "Will you meet with Nelliah?"

He should have left the topic of Tiaponine's safety alone. VerGann managed a long breath, forcing himself to calm down as he took in the many concerned faces around him. Everyone in the room appeared anxious enough with what little confrontation had taken place. There was no need to drag this out longer.

"No," he said flatly.

With a sound of disgust, Dreesdin turned to Marlott. "I know the delpins have a deep rooted dislike of this type of thing because of their *religious* beliefs, but I don't see why they won't listen."

"At no point have I said that Nelliah's visions are to be accepted as fact," Marlott reminded. "The nymph believes what she claims to see. I leave it to the rest of the Council to decide whether or not to believe her as well. Your concerns have been addressed as promised. The delpins have made it clear that they want nothing to do with Nelliah's foresight, be it for religious reasons or not. All will respect their decision. My children, I take my leave." With that, she disappeared.

The seratine was a woman of few words. Never one to linger for lengthy discussions, she had stated her decision on the matter and left. There was an uncomfortable moment of silence.

Then, all at once, the room was a bustle of activity as all started for the door.

"The nymph has a gift, VerGann," Dreesdin persisted, approaching the three delpins now in the doorway.

"It's possible that she does," VerGann agreed, turning back to the bothersome nardin. "My question, though, is where this gift comes from."

"Comes from?" Dreesdin repeated, perplexed.

"In what darkness is Nelliah meddling to receive these visions?"

"There's nothing dark about what she's doing," Dreesdin protested.

Glancing at Vrenler and KaiDinn, VerGann laughed. "I cannot say that I've ever taken the time to sit and study a pile of rocks. I can say with great certainty, however, that if I did, they wouldn't say anything to me."

Dreesdin's face contorted in uncontrollable anger.

"Go ahead and mock me, *delpin*," he warned. "When Nelliah's vision comes to pass, we'll see just how cocky you are."

VerGann inched closer. "Well, since we're no longer on a first name basis, be advised, *nardin*. Not only do we not care what the nymph sees in her visions—the more you try to push them on us, the more strained our relationship will become. You find me frustrating now. You have no idea how much worse it can get."

KaiDinn and Vrenler did not speak, but stared at Dreesdin with the same intensity as VerGann.

"I refuse to stand here and—"

It was unbelievable that Dreesdin was still talking. Seeing KaiDinn and Vrenler vanish—with KaiDinn rolling his eyes not-so-subtly—VerGann focused back on the nardin—whose irritation still seemed to be rising rapidly.

"You'll regret dismissing Nelliah so—"

VerGann

Dreesdin didn't get to finish his sentence, though. VerGann vanished, leaving him to stew in his anger.

CHAPTER 3

Restlessly fingering a scrap of stale bread between her fingers, Tiaponine leaned against the window ledge, watching the silhouettes of the castle towers in the distance as the sun began to set behind them.

Drake, Lerra, Eva—it had been an exhausting day. With VerGann's departure, the hours dragged even more, and she could not ignore the foreboding feeling in her stomach. Something felt off, but she couldn't explain what.

She stood and tossed the bread into her mouth, the uncomfortable crunchy texture causing her nose to wrinkle. She looked from the makeshift bed on the floor in the adjoining room to the pile of blankets at her feet.

The tiny two room attic was not much to brag about, but to her and VerGann, it was home. The fact that she shared a living space with a man was frowned upon by most, but Tiaponine did not care. It was what they could afford. They had a roof over their heads every night. Many had no such luxury.

Forcing down the last piece of bread in her hand, Tiaponine exited the dwelling and began her slow descent down the ladder outside the door to the bustling streets below. The old wooden staircase had fallen away many years before.

At last feeling the ground beneath her feet, Tiaponine turned, surveying the street as she left the building. An ominous cloud still seemed to hang over her, as if something was about to go wrong in a very big way.

But nothing looked amiss. A wrinkled old woman selling daisies from her rickety wooden cart, a fisherman returning from a successful day, his catch slung over his left shoulder, children laughing as they darted through the crowd in a game of chase; everything looked ordinary. Tiaponine smiled in spite of herself at the familiarity of the scene.

Venturing down the busy street a bit farther, her gaze leveled on a rather peculiar sight ahead—two men trying to make their way through one very crowded intersection, their fine clothing an advertisement that they did not belong there. It was rare to see Draven's elite gracing the lower streets.

Much to their apparent chagrin, their presence was attracting attention. The man in front pushed through the crowd with an arrogance she would expect from someone in his position. The man behind him, however...

Tiaponine studied the second man. His eyes were downcast in a deliberate attempt to avoid contact with the masses, but it was impossible to hide his obvious unease or foul mood. He seemed, if possible, even more out of place than his companion.

Following a bit closer, Tiaponine was relieved to see the crowd thin out—better to get a good look at him. Tall, dark brown hair, wide shoulders; the man was handsome. As he stopped walking, a grimace forming as he inspected a fresh scuff of dirt across the toe of his left shoe, Tiaponine snickered to herself.

She narrowed her eyes, spying a hunched-over old beggar man approaching the pair. She recognized him, and knew what was coming next.

Tiaponine moved closer as the beggar grabbed the second man's arm tightly. The two men exchanged words, and she shoved her way through the crowd, straining to hear what was being said.

"—The last thing I want is to be swarmed by a mass of hopeful daughters. I have enough trouble as it is—"

It was all Tiaponine could do not to laugh. The second man thought quite a bit of himself, that much was clear.

The front man attempted to push the beggar to the side, which was a mistake. The beggar began to flop around, hanging off the second man's arm for support as though he had not a single sturdy bone in his body. What had started as an irritating beggar hoping for a quick hand-out had now blossomed into a half-naked old man flopping around the street.

Failing at his first attempt to rid his companion of the old man, the front man leaned in close to the beggar. Tiaponine could not believe what she was seeing, torn between amusement and pity for the men. Were they trying to reason with him? This approach was ridiculous at best.

Approaching the beggar from behind, she took hold of his shoulders and turned him so that he was facing her.

The beggar stared at her for a moment in stunned disbelief.

Gripping the tattered tunic and pulling it over the beggar's exposed shoulder, Tiaponine grimaced. Her aerial view of the man's pale, white-haired chest as his clothing buckled in front of him was something she would not soon forget.

"Don't you have somewhere to be?" she asked, her tone direct. She was not surprised to see the beggar snarl. His game was up. He would have to find someone else to bother.

With a quick half nod the two men, each appearing confused yet grateful, Tiaponine turned and pushed the beggar ahead of her.

The beggar offered no resistance as he left his prey in the street. Stopping, he turned to Tiaponine. "Here," he said, handing her a small brown leather pouch.

"What is it?" Tiaponine asked, taking specific note of the fine, gold-threaded detail on the side.

The beggar offered a snaggle-toothed grin and ran off, now void of his previous crippled stature.

"Wait!" she began, but he had already vanished in the crowd.

Tiaponine studied the pouch in her hand. Although simple, the object possessed an undeniable beauty. No merchant in the lower streets was capable of such fine workmanship, to her knowledge.

"Oh, no!"

Hearing the desperate cry pierce the normal chatter of the streets, Tiaponine searched the crowd around her. Nothing out of place, except...

The handsome man, the same man she had just saved from the beggar, was staring at her. Her blood ran cold.

"My coin pouch!" The man's strangled voice echoed through the streets.

Coin pouch.

Tiaponine glanced back down at the pouch in her hand.

"You!" He was pointing at her.

"Get him!" the other man yelled.

Him.

Tiaponine was sure she would have been hurt by the mix-up, if not for the fact that she *did* have on men's clothing. Regardless, there was no time to dwell on it. The two men were rushing toward her, and she doubted they would be willing to let her explain how she came to be in possession of the pouch. She was holding it. As far as they were concerned—as far as *anyone* from the upper class would be concerned—she was the thief.

Tiaponine darted into a side street. With any luck, she could lose her pursuers in the crowd and just leave the pouch somewhere conspicuous for them to find. Behind the butcher's shop, past the baker; she ran as fast as she could. This was not

Drake—the men were part of Draven's elite. Should she be caught, they would exact the full measure of the law upon her.

Tiaponine spied the two men closing in on her. As expected, it did not appear that either man was eager to give up any time soon.

As she sprinted even faster, the pounding of the men's feet behind her continued getting louder. It was curious that they were able to gain ground on her. Her nerves mounting, she barreled around a corner.

At the sight of the stone wall ahead, she skidded to a stop.

A dead end. *Great.*

"Seize him!"

She had two choices—give up and face the consequences or try to escape two grown men. Neither sounded good.

Tiaponine looked from one man to the other, irritation welling up inside her. She had just been cornered for the second time that day. How could she be so stupid?

"Hold him, Samuel!"

Tiaponine audibly gulped as the handsome man as his companion—perhaps a servant of some sort—took three long strides to reach her. The handsome man gave orders like he was someone important.

She felt Samuel grip her upper arms from behind. She wriggled left and right, determined to fight back.

Pushing back with as much strength as she could muster after such a chase, Tiaponine struggled against the man's strength. Not prepared for her last desperate effort, Samuel tried unsuccessfully to regain control, but Tiaponine wriggled free. She inhaled sharply and turned again to run.

Right into the other man.

She did not have time to react—in the next instance she was thrown to the ground, her arms pinned at either side of her head as the handsome man straddled her fallen form. Tiaponine gasped, her breath coming in short, uneven spurts.

She glared at him, her anger building. Never had she been in such a physical confrontation.

"Careful, Breydon!" Samuel warned from nearby. "This one's got a lot of fight in him."

"He's not going anywhere," Breydon said. He looked down at his captive. "Now what? There's no way you're going to out-muscle me."

Although she knew she wasn't particularly strong, Tiaponine was not about to make her capture so easy. She thrashed about wildly, grimacing when Breydon pushed down on her arms with all of his weight.

Her floppy black hat fell to the side, her auburn hair spilling out onto the ground.

Immediately, she felt him recoil slightly in surprise. Some part of her was relieved—surely his life of privilege frowned upon manhandling a woman. He lightened his hold and moved to crouch at her side, although he continued to restrain her, seeming at a loss for words.

Tiaponine had to agree. The situation was awkward.

"He's a girl!" Samuel exclaimed.

This one seems a bit slow, Tiaponine thought.

She turned her icy stare toward Samuel. "Very observant. Now let me go!" she spat.

"If I let you go, will you return my coin pouch?" Breydon seemed to have regained his ability to speak.

"I didn't know it was yours," she countered, venom in her voice. "The old man gave it to me. I didn't know where he got it from."

Judging from Breydon's deep, exaggerated breath, he did not believe her.

"Yes." She rolled her eyes. "I promise."

Finally, he released her arms. She stood and readjusted her ill-fitting clothing, glaring daggers at the man. Inspecting the pouch once more, Tiaponine threw the object at Breydon and was pleased to see it hit his left shoulder, hard. He winced.

"I didn't take it, you know," she spat.

"Thank you," Breydon shot back flatly, checking the contents before turning to walk away.

Tiaponine allowed Breydon to get a head start before she followed him out of the alley. It was best to keep her distance.

She became aware of Samuel studying her as they approached the street, and her anxiety returned. It did not appear that the servant was done with her yet.

"What is it?" Breydon asked irritably, noting Samuel's shrewd look.

Tiaponine frowned as Samuel stepped in front of her to block her way.

"I was just thinking," he said. "What if you told your uncle you wanted to marry someone else? The point is to have you married, right? How far would he press the issue? His own name in history means much more to him than any promise made to Gwenevieve's parents way back when."

His own name in history. Tiaponine scoffed, crossing her arms. These wealthy elite really thought a lot of themselves. She side-stepped Samuel, but again the servant blocked her from leaving.

"Do you *mind*—" she began.

"What if you were to marry a girl you knew your uncle wouldn't approve of? No one would know she wasn't nobility until it was too late," Samuel said, grinning. "Say, someone like this girl," he mused, motioning vaguely to Tiaponine.

Her breath caught in her throat. "*Excuse* me?"

"That would really anger your uncle, wouldn't it?" Samuel continued, glancing at Breydon. "There's no way he would allow you to marry the likes of her. And a woman like Gwenevieve won't stay if she thinks she has competition. It would be beneath her breeding. Once Gwenevieve leaves, you can send this urchin on her way. I'm sure some arrangement can be worked out so that everyone involved is happy."

Breydon's features creased thoughtfully.

"A nice way to escape an unwanted marriage, if you ask me," Samuel continued. "You'd be by yourself again, as you like it."

"You're not serious," Breydon said.

"Look at her," Samuel pressed, looking down his nose at Tiaponine. "If there's a reward in the end, she'll agree to anything." Tiaponine took an instinctive step back as Samuel inspected her head to toe. "She has nothing to lose."

"She could never pass as a princess." Breydon laughed and turned to walk away.

Tiaponine's jaw dropped. This man was arrogant enough to think he should marry a princess? He really thought he was a prize. She had to say, *she* was not impressed.

"Not a princess," Samuel corrected. "We'll make her a daughter of a lord or something. An appropriate match that won't attract scrutiny."

Tiaponine sighed, tapping her fingers against her arm impatiently. Breydon and Samuel's discussion—or, rather, scheming—had long passed the point of being interesting. They could sort out whatever romantic problems they had on their own time.

Catching sight of VerGann approaching from the street ahead, Tiaponine breathed a sigh of relief. Angling herself between Breydon and Samuel, she pushed them both to the side. "I have to be going."

"Actually, there's just one more thing." Samuel stepped again in front of her. At the sound of someone clearing his throat behind him, he stiffened and slowly turned around. At the sight of VerGann, his jaw tightened in irritation.

"Tell me," Samuel began, turning back to Tiaponine and opting to ignore VerGann altogether. "Do you have any idea who this is that you just stole from?"

Her patience long gone, Tiaponine was immediately on the defense. "I didn't steal anything from him. I already told you that."

"Save it," Samuel snapped. "This is Prince Breydon, this kingdom's only heir."

A cold fear began to consume Tiaponine. Whether she took the coin pouch or not, it was of no importance. Prince Breydon was the king's nephew. King Hulbert would view her as guilty.

Even VerGann appeared uncomfortable with the sudden direction the conversation had taken as well.

"You see," Samuel continued, "King Hulbert has decided that it's time for your esteemed prince to marry. He's even gone so far as to hand-pick a bride. Problem is that..."

Samuel seemed at a temporary loss for words. Tiaponine let a frustrated sigh escape.

"He..."

"I'm not ready for marriage, plain and simple," Breydon interjected.

Tiaponine audibly groaned. This was the second discussion involving Prince Breydon's romantic issues that she and VerGann had been involved in that day, and she was no more interested now than she had been earlier. There were far more important things to think about.

"Well, that's just *horrible*. Not to mention, very sad," VerGann said, the thick sarcasm in his voice undeniable. "How does this translate into being her problem?"

Samuel glared at VerGann, as though he'd been trying to forget he was there.

"Anyway," Samuel continued. "You heard the plan. Pose as Breydon's love interest and convince the king. Once Santerine's princess is out of the way, you drop out of sight and everyone can go their separate ways."

Tiaponine studied Prince Breydon with a critical eye. The fact was, she did not feel obliged to help him out of the kindness of her heart. Perhaps when the bruises on her back healed from where he had thrown her to the ground, she might feel differently. Perhaps.

"I don't see a benefit," she said bluntly.

"I could give you everything you need," Breydon said. "Everything."

Tiaponine pursed her lips. *Everything you need* seemed a very general promise, and she wasn't sure the prince had the same understanding of the phrase as she did. "Such as…"

"Always assured a roof over your head—"

"I already have—"

"A *good* roof over your head," he corrected. "Plenty of food, more money than you'd know what to do with, more… fitting clothing."

Tiaponine might have been mildly insulted by the clothing comment, but something in her was imagining the life the prince was describing. A life she could not see as real, although he spoke of it as though it was perfectly ordinary. A life of prosperity, where she and VerGann could flourish.

"You could… do that?" she asked, aware that she sounded quite the simpleton, but not particularly upset by that fact.

"I could," Breydon assured. "And I would."

She glanced at VerGann. "I couldn't leave…"

"Your brother?" Breydon guessed.

"Friend," Tiaponine corrected.

"My offer is for you and your friend, then."

She could not believe that she was considering the prince's offer. It couldn't be true. There had to be a catch.

"I could never pass for a princess," she said, defeated. The task would be next to impossible.

"Daughter of a lord," Samuel muttered.

"Whatever," Tiaponine snapped, now very sure that she did not like Samuel one bit. The prince's arm circled her shoulders in what seemed to be an attempt at comforting her.

"You're making the right decision," he cooed.

Tiaponine laughed out loud, clearly startling him. He recoiled slightly. Of course—Breydon had likely never known a girl not to be undone by his advances. A little attention her way would nudge her into agreement. After all, he was the Prince of Draven. Who could deny him?

She could.

She turned to VerGann as Breydon attempted to regain his composure after being so blatantly rejected, not surprised to see him amused as well.

"Excuse me, I must've missed something," VerGann said. "Did you agree to this?"

Tiaponine pushed the prince's arm from her shoulders and took her place beside VerGann, smirking back at Breydon. "As a matter of fact, no. I did not."

"Listen up, you little…" Samuel started, stepping closer to Tiaponine, his face just inches from hers. She stood tall, setting her jaw.

"Look," Breydon said, pushing Samuel to the side. "There's no downside for you."

No charm, no deep-voiced, sultry words; it seemed Prince Breydon had realized she was immune to such tactics. At least he was a quick learner.

"It seems like a lot of trouble, just to get out of a marriage," Tiaponine complained, placing her black floppy hat atop her head. "Why not just tell this Princess Gwenevieve that you don't want to marry her?"

Breydon's shoulders fell. "If only. This marriage was arranged a long time ago, and with the recent strained relations with Santerine, my marriage to their princess should theoretically keep us from war with them."

"Wonderful." VerGann said. "Our peace depends on the marriage of two people who don't like, let alone love, each other."

"That's how it goes," Breydon said, defeated. "I'm not in a position to be choosy. I do think, however, that my uncle would rather drop the idea of marrying Gwenevieve altogether than run the risk of alienating his only heir. War with Santerine is just an excuse, anyway." Pausing, he blew out a deep, controlled breath. "If you're worried that I'll fall back on my promise, you shouldn't be. You'll get everything I said."

Tiaponine bit her bottom lip a moment in thought. She and VerGann had never lived in a way anywhere close to what the prince was describing. From stale bread to an abundance of food—an abundance of *everything*—was quite the leap.

Her eyes drifted to VerGann. He said nothing. The decision was hers.

"You'd better deliver," Tiaponine snapped, offering the prince her hand. "I'll do it."

"Great," Breydon exclaimed, clasping her hand in his in an awkward handshake. "You won't be disappointed. I guess I should ask your name."

"Tiaponine."

"Well, Tiaponine, I know we got off to a rough start, so," Breydon started, his charm returning as he bowed formally to her. "Here's to a fresh one."

"Since your friend here will be accompanying you," Samuel said, his attention on VerGann—although he was speaking as though VerGann weren't even there. "Might we know his name as well?"

"VerGann," Tiaponine said, trying not to give the servant more attention than he deserved.

"VerGann. Interesting name," Samuel cleared his throat, unimpressed. He stepped forward so that he was face to face with VerGann. "I'm sure this turn of events gives meaning to your otherwise, I assume, *dull* life."

Tiaponine tried to remain calm.

"I just don't know how to thank you," the delpin said, clasping his hands in over-exaggerated emotion. "For a simpleton like me—I mean, it's all just so overwhelming, and—" He cut off suddenly, barely stifling his laughter as he brushed past Samuel and cast a skeptical look toward the prince.

"So tell me, *Your Majesty*, will the obnoxious one here be playing a part in all this?"

CHAPTER 4

Draven's grand castle was breathtaking.

Tiaponine followed Madame Farault through the hallway with quick steps. In the few brief minutes since their introduction, she had already shown herself to be a kind woman. With thick, grayed hair pulled back into a tight bun, her simple emerald green gown swishing against her legs as she walked, Tiaponine had no doubt that the servant had been quite the beauty in her earlier years.

At last coming to an ornately carved oversized door, Tiaponine's eyes widened. The door opened as if it had a mind of its own. Following Madame Farault's lead, she stepped inside.

Tiaponine stopped short in the doorway, her jaw dropping as she took in one beautiful sight after another. She was in a dressing room of sorts. Inlaid wood wardrobes framed the door opposite her. Yards of silk and damask were piled high on two gold-leafed tables. She had never been close to this many fine things at once.

Hearing amused snickers from three maidservants nearby, Tiaponine's daydream ended. Even the castle help could tell that she was not where she belonged.

As Madame Farault cast a stern look their way, all three rude maidservants fell silent.

Tiaponine continued past the wardrobes through the tall, Gothic-arched wooden door, at a loss for words. It was not the sparkling white marble walls or the four grand Corinthian columns that caught her attention, though.

It was the enormous, rounded bath in the center of the room, bubbles spilling over the sides. Resting between the four columns, lush green vines draped around the edges, the bath had the appeal of a secluded lagoon. It was enchanting and inviting. The freezing cold dips she normally took at midnight in the most secluded part of the merchants' canal suddenly looked even less appealing than they already were.

The three maidservants followed her in and surrounded her.

"Hat, please," one maid, the tallest of the three, said, casting a critical eye over her clothing.

Tiaponine hesitantly handed over her hat, as the other two maidservants began to strip away her worn clothing. She wanted to protest—she *did* know how to undress herself—but somehow she knew that her arguments would fall on deaf ears.

"My dear girl, where did that come from?" Madame Farault exclaimed, studying the greenish-purple bruise on Tiaponine's bare shoulder.

Tiaponine felt the cool air of the room hit her now exposed left shoulder.

"Oh," she began, her voice sheepish, "I was chased by a couple street boys the other day. I ran into a merchant's cart."

Despite Madame Farault's silent warning, the maidservants could not hide their snickering.

"Why would they chase you?

"I may or may not have hid their shoes while they were dipping their feet in the canal." Tiaponine smiled sweetly. "They deserved it."

The snickering turned into barely-contained giggling. Madame Farault again cast a quick look of admonishment toward the three maidservants. "Come, Tiaponine dear, we have much work to do."

The maidservants made fast work of disrobing her, tossing each article of clothing to the side as though just the touch of the material to their skin would somehow scar them for life. Tiaponine endured the attention with forced patience.

"Into the water before you catch a cold," Madame Farault ordered, stepping to the side to reveal the steamy bath water. "Fetch some fresh linen for the dear from the other room," she added, waving the maidservants away.

The welcoming warmth of the water enveloped her as she lowered herself into the large bath basin. Tiaponine sighed. There were no words to describe how nice the water felt. It was incredible, and—for a few moments, anyway—she could let go of any misgivings or worries she had in life. Even the intrusive, unwanted, small crowd of people accompanying her while she bathed could be forgotten.

Blowing a couple bubbles from her hand, Tiaponine laid back against the side of the bath. All that was left to do was to close her eyes and...

Noticing a second door in the room start to open, a door which she had somehow failed to notice earlier, she felt a building sense of unease. It was awkward enough taking a bath in the company of four people, let alone however many more were about to step through that door.

A new sense of dread enveloped her as VerGann backed through the door, his full attention on the hallway. As though relieved to have escaped the corridor, the delpin ran his right hand through his hair, as he often did when he was nervous.

And then he turned around.

His shock, discomfort, and a hefty amount of embarrassment could not have been more obvious. VerGann's eyes darted from the marble columns to the tub, to the collection of frothy bubbles covering her submerged shoulders.

Tiaponine swallowed hard as VerGann made eye contact with her, very briefly, before averting his eyes to focus on an imaginary object of interest on the wall to her right. It was difficult to tell which of them was more mortified.

Alarmed, Tiaponine glanced back toward Madame Farault. Lucky for her, the servant was not aware of the extra person in the room, and the three maidservants were bustling around the wardrobes near the entrance to the room, not paying attention to Tiaponine.

"Oh, the prince has a full day planned for you tomorrow, dear. It'll be an early morning for sure, and you'll need plenty of rest…" Madame Farault continued speaking, oblivious to the painfully awkward scene going on behind her.

"What're you doing?" Tiaponine mouthed. If the question had been accompanied by sound, she knew it would sound like a high-pitched squeak. For the first time in as long as she could remember, she saw a shade of light pink creep into the delpin's cheeks. No doubt finding her at the center of the bubbly concoction, her clothes nowhere in sight, was not at all what he had expected to find when he entered the room.

"—Known him since he was just a boy, you know. His father, King Lundane, was a giant among men. Wonderful king, it's such a shame he…" Madame Farault turned back to Tiaponine, then hesitated, her eyes narrowing. "Hello?" She leaned forward, trying to see between the two columns flanking either side of the door, where VerGann was standing.

A look of horror crossed VerGann's face. He vanished in the blink of an eye.

"How odd…" the old servant muttered to herself, squinting at the doorway.

Tiaponine could not breathe. The fleeting glimpse of a man in the room now had Madame Farault's full attention. The servant may be old, but Tiaponine was sure she could take care of any male visitor if need be.

Taking one more look behind the right column, Madame Farault turned back to Tiaponine, clearly perplexed. "I could've sworn that I saw someone. Did you see anything, dear?"

She was clearly waiting for an answer, but there was no answer Tiaponine wanted to give. The best thing to do was feign ignorance.

She smiled mildly and returned her focus to the multitude of bubbles collecting on the surface of the water.

⁂

"Breydon, you cannot expect your uncle not to find out about that girl. I mean, before you want him to."

"That girl," Breydon grumbled.

That girl was the answer to his problems. It had not even been a whole day, and Samuel was second guessing the plan. He didn't even seem capable of using her name.

Breydon's eyes settled on the scores of shapes crowding his uncle's statuary garden ahead. He ducked under a low hanging arch of vines.

"Yes, *that girl*," Samuel repeated, mimicking his exaggerated tone. "We really scraped the bottom for this one, Breydon. Have you seen her? Madame Farault spent three hours with the urchin, and she still looks as though she should be getting into brawls with the local boys."

Breydon sighed loudly. With his upcoming engagement imminent, he did not have time to deal with Samuel's misgivings.

"Now, this doesn't make me nervous or anything," Samuel complained, his focus drifting upward.

Breydon's eyes narrowed. "What?"

"Of all the places to stop, you had to pick here? I mean, look at him."

Still confused, Breydon followed Samuel's gaze. The edges of his mouth curled in annoyance. They were standing in front of one of his uncle's favorite marble statues. It was no accident that the face of the brave warrior, chest puffed out to accentuate his masculinity, sword planted in the breast of the terrifying beast at his feet, bore a striking resemblance to Draven's magnanimous King Hulbert.

It was tacky.

Breydon gave the ridiculous statue one last wary, sidelong glance before moving on. "Samuel, what's going on here? This was your idea, and now you want to give up? No, you don't. This might just work. You are *not* backing out now."

"Yes, it was my idea. But it was a bad idea. I realize that now."

"And why is that?" Breydon's patience was dwindling.

"Do you really want something so important to be contingent on how this no-account street urchin performs? We can do better," Samuel said.

"You're determined not to like her no matter what," Breydon accused.

"You're right," he agreed. "I don't like her."

"If you make her feel as though she'll always belong on the streets, then she won't try to fit in here."

Samuel frowned. "The creature's been in the castle mere hours, and already Draven's most eligible man is sticking up for her. I must say, I much prefer your usual dismissive nature toward women."

Breydon did not quite agree with that evaluation, but that was beside the point.

"For lack of better words, this is a business agreement. Anything beyond that's just too complicated." Waving Samuel off, Breydon made his way through the flowered arches along the far wall. "I haven't figured out what's-his-name, though."

"VerGann," Samuel remarked, shaking his head in agreement. Of course, he remembered *his* name. "Cocky, self-assured, in the way. And there's something strange about him."

"To say the least," Breydon said. Something about the man's manner, how he carried himself, was peculiar. But he wasn't bothered enough to dwell on it. "Where is Tiaponine now?"

"Last time I saw her, she was being escorted to her room," Samuel answered, not even attempting to disguise his displeasure. "We do have time to find another girl, Breydon."

Breydon charged ahead, hoping to communicate his desire for the conversation to end. The plan was going to work. Whether Samuel liked the girl or not was inconsequential. "She will do fine."

"Different world," VerGann noted, taking in the posh guest room around him. Tiaponine's silhouette against the night sky in the room's sole window caught his attention. She was clearly in the lap of luxury, running her fingers over the intricate carvings in the windowsill as though in a daze.

Perhaps he should be miffed at the prince's lack of offering in the way of similar accommodations for himself. He had not even been offered a room in the castle for the duration of Tiaponine's stay. Breydon's promise of shelter and food for both of them must only start after the prince got what he wanted.

VerGann smiled to himself. He doubted the lapse in hospitality was accidental. If one did not feel welcome, one would not stick around. He was at the castle only because he followed Tiaponine there, and the prince would not dare anger her by throwing him out. And besides, Hulbert was not to know they were there. The use of one guest room could go unnoticed; the use of two might start to draw attention.

Jumping down from her perch in the large, open window, Tiaponine sighed. "I could get used to this," she said, rushing to dig her fingers into the plush, woolen blankets on the large four-post bed in front of her. "Not that I like all of the pomp and circumstance, of course, but there's something to be said about the perks of castle life."

VerGann surveyed the elaborate bedroom once again. "The accommodations, great. The prince, I'm not sure. Samuel…" He slipped the worn, leather bag from his shoulder and threw it onto a chaise nearby. "Absolutely not." They had not even known the disagreeable servant for a whole day, and he disliked everything about Samuel.

"The prince will be alright. Once he starts thinking for himself, that is. But Samuel…" Lying back on the bed, Tiaponine laughed. "No. No way."

"Face it, Tee," VerGann said, turning his attention to the contents of his leather bag. "This idea didn't come from Samuel wanting to save the prince from marrying a stranger. He's doing this for one reason and one reason only—his own personal gain. He's using the prince just as the prince is using you."

"And the same way that I'm using the prince?" Tiaponine whispered.

Refastening the sole buckle on the leather bag, VerGann sighed.

"No," he corrected. "You had nothing to do with all of this. You didn't ask for it and you didn't go looking for it. There's nothing wrong with accepting what the prince offered. It's not greedy. It's just smart."

"I suppose you're right," Tiaponine agreed, albeit reluctantly. "I guess we'll just have to wait and see how this all ends up." Sitting up, she glanced at the pile of folded clothes left for her on the bedside table. "I should be heading to bed. Prince Breydon told me that my training would begin first thing in the morning, and something makes me think he was not joking. He does seem rather focused."

Yes, the prince was focused. What an understatement that was. Noticing Tiaponine's less than discreet nervous glance around the room, VerGann took a quick cautious look himself. The accommodations *were* intimidating, but…

"Is everything all right?"

"Oh," Tiaponine said, sounding embarrassed. "I just keep expecting to see a small crowd of servants barge in to dress me for bed. I guess privacy isn't something that a royal views as very important." She cringed. "You should've seen them earlier…" She stopped, her eyes drifting to VerGann.

There was a moment of awkward silence as a few mental images came to mind from earlier in the day. He was quite sure he had seen a bit too much of what she was talking about.

"I'll see you tomorrow, right?" Tiaponine asked, quickly changing the topic.

"No, I'm staying here," VerGann answered. He stood and walked toward the door.

"You aren't going back to EliSann?"

While leaving Tiaponine with the Stone of GraVinn unattended in such close proximity to King Hulbert would be unacceptable in itself, that was not the source of his concern. He could not put a finger on it.

"No, I'm staying here tonight."

"What is it?"

Smiling, VerGann turned to her. "Nothing. Don't worry about it." Nothing would be served by delving into his vague concerns.

"Are you sure?"

"It's nothing, Tee," he reassured. "I'd just feel better knowing that you were safe your first night in the castle."

"The castle's the safest place in Draven, VerGann," Tiaponine laughed. "You saw or heard something that concerned you. Didn't you?"

"No, I didn't."

It was not a lie. He did not see or hear anything. He sensed something.

Tiaponine raised an eyebrow. They knew each other too well to not know when one of them was being less than truthful.

"You worry too much," he teased, hoping to let the topic be. Seeing a more content smile cross Tiaponine's face, VerGann breathed a sigh of relief.

"If you'll excuse me," he said with a playful wink, his eyes traveling from the night dress in her hands back to her. "One awkward moment a day is all I can handle, and I'm already at two," he mused. With a slight nod at Tiaponine, he opened the door to the hall.

Careful not to let the soft glow from the hallway penetrate the darkness more than necessary, the lone assassin slipped into the guest bedroom.

His orders were clear. Kill the auburn haired girl. No payment would come until his mission was complete.

Letting the heavy wooden door close behind him, the assassin surveyed his surroundings. His target was asleep on the large bed in front of him. He stepped toward the bed, knife drawn, and then stopped, his focus now on the slumbering form of a man on a chaise nearby.

He had been told the girl was alone.

Studying the sleeping man a moment, the assassin smiled. He could accomplish his mission without disturbing the man, if he was quiet about it.

"May I help you?"

At the unexpected question from the male voice behind him, the assassin jumped. His head jerked to the right, his throat tightening. Standing not an arm's length from him was the man he had just seen slumbering on the chaise. The man's eyes carried a curious, bewildered intensity about them that made the assassin's blood run cold.

Confused, the assassin glanced at the chaise. The man was still there, asleep. The assassin turned back to the man at his side, anxiety building as he confirmed again that it was the same man.

He looked back again. The chaise was now empty, a single crumpled, woolen blanket dangling off the side.

"What's going on here?" he grumbled.

"You haven't answered my question," the man at his side stated, his tone matter-of-fact.

The assassin's breath caught in his throat. Gone was the curious, baffled gaze from before. The man's features now displayed nothing but a calm seriousness and a strong sense of other-worldliness.

The assassin backed through the doorway behind him. He did not want any part of this. No amount of coinage would be enough for him to mess with this man.

When he glanced back into the room, the man had vanished again.

The assassin turned and ran.

CHAPTER 5

Although she understood why the secluded swine pits were Prince Breydon's location of choice for her first real lesson, Tiaponine had to agree with Samuel this time—it was difficult to find much to like about the sparse expanse of ground. Outside of the intimidating view of the kingdom's massive southeastern stone wall, there was not much to get excited about. It was just dirt. And at the center of that dirt, an enormous kidney-shaped pit of mud. Not an ideal setting for an education on all things noble.

Yet, there they were, studying the history of the monarchy… for over three hours.

Tucking a loose strand of auburn hair behind her left ear, Tiaponine sighed.

True to his word, the prince had had her roused and readied just as the first rays of sunlight hit the horizon. She could not say that she had been an active participant as the maidservants dressed her and fixed her hair. She had, though, discovered that it *was* possible to sleep standing up. The maidservants would have plenty to laugh about later.

Samuel cleared his throat loudly, glaring at her from Breydon's side. Tiaponine snapped back to the present, blinking back her exhaustion.

She had already concluded that the servant hated her with every fiber of his being, but today he seemed colder than even she thought necessary. Since his hushed—and animated— conversation with the brutish-looking man in the hall that morning, he had been excessively irritable toward her.

"Where is your friend?"

At the sound of Samuel's voice, Tiaponine jumped. Her mind had been wandering again. "You mean VerGann?"

Samuel just nodded his head, annoyed.

"He'll meet us here later," Tiaponine answered, not inclined to give more explanation than was necessary.

"And what did he think of his night in the castle?"

For a moment, she was paralyzed. There was no way Samuel could have known VerGann stayed the night in the castle.

"I didn't know that VerGann stayed here last night," Prince Breydon said, suddenly interested in the conversation. He turned to Samuel. "I thought I said one guest chamber only."

Tiaponine's eyes darted from Samuel to the prince. While Breydon appeared only curious, she knew Samuel must have an ulterior motive for asking.

"He didn't," she answered. "He went home after dinner. He said he'd meet up with us later today."

"I see," Samuel said flatly. "So, how long have you known him? You two are rather inseparable, if you don't mind me saying."

"We are," she agreed, and turned back to the prince in an effort to end the discussion.

"So VerGann went home," Samuel continued, undaunted by Tiaponine's apparent unease. "And where is home? Draven? Some other kingdom?"

Tiaponine distracted herself with navigating around a mud puddle. She was done speaking. She had no intention of indulging the servant in whatever fact-finding mission he was on.

"Oh, come, Tiaponine," he teased, stepping around the puddle of mud to stand beside her. "We're all friends here. Why the big secret?"

Tiaponine laughed out loud before she could stop herself.

"*We*," she countered, her right index finger poking into his chest, "Are *not* friends."

The edges of his mouth pursed as he tried unsuccessfully to control his anger. "Why, you little," he started, his features contorting. "Do you know who you're speaking to?"

"Yes, I do."

Samuel froze, not expecting a response. "You do what?"

"I do know who I'm speaking to," Tiaponine retorted. "And you, sir, are at the bottom, not that far up from myself. You're part of the dirt people like him walk on each and every day," she said, pointing at the prince. "You may have your fancy clothes and live in his beautiful castle, but let me make this very clear." She stepped close to Samuel so that she was very much in his face. "I am not impressed."

Without another word, she turned and marched past both men. The prince appeared stunned.

"Nice," he grumbled.

"Little spitfire, isn't she?" Samuel hissed.

Tiaponine slowed to a stop. Although more aggravated than she could remember in recent history, she had to put her dislike for Samuel to the side. It was not fair to Prince Breydon. She must concentrate on the task at hand. Learning to be noble.

Taking a deep breath to calm her temper, she turned to the prince with a renewed sense of determination.

Concentrate...

Her attention drifted. She gazed at the swine behind the prince, the stench of mud permeating her nostrils. The eight pigs did look quite content as they rested at the center of the thick, cool, dark brown muck.

Forget concentrating. Her suffering was too much.

"It's so hot out here," she complained. "I'm almost tempted to join the pigs in the mud pit to cool down."

Breydon shot Samuel a quick look of warning, and the servant stopped short of speaking what was probably another sarcastic comment.

"We've only been at this for three hours," Breydon said, his tone almost pleading.

The prince was exasperated, clearly, and Tiaponine couldn't blame him. The lessons were exhausting, and her attention had been half there at best. It would be but a matter of days before he would have Gwenevieve forced on him.

Yes, Prince Breydon had all the motivation he needed to stay focused. No doubt he wished she shared in his fervor.

"But it's been a three hour history lesson." Tiaponine angled away from the prince, tugging the plummeting neckline of her bodice up. The plum colored dress was beautiful and elegant, but…

She tried not to focus on the less than comfortable low cut of the tight bodice, avoiding looking at Breydon. If he had noticed how conspicuous she felt in the garment, he had—thankfully—not mentioned it.

"I understand a lot more than you realize. I may need work on etiquette and such, but not the history," she sighed. "There isn't one person in this kingdom that doesn't know the history of the monarchy."

Breydon turned to the swine resting in the cool mud. "Fine, let's take a break."

"Thank you." Tiaponine fanned herself with her hand. However frustrated he was, at least Prince Breydon was reasonable.

Hearing a sudden, shrill scream pierce the otherwise peaceful calm of the countryside, Tiaponine spun around toward the EliSann Forest before glancing at Prince Breydon nervously. As she'd expected, he had heard it as well, and was squinting at the pines that made up the northern edge of the forest.

Pretending she had not heard a thing, she continued her walk along the edge of the mud pit, but her thoughts wandered. Thinking back to VerGann's promise of a walk by the ElinDann

River the night before, her spirits fell. In all of the craziness of the past day, she'd forgotten about his promise. And so had he.

"Ever been in there?" Samuel asked, joining the prince in scrutinizing the edge of the EliSann Forest.

Breydon cast another glance toward the forest before turning away. "A couple of times."

"It's supposed to be inhabited by demons," Samuel mused, lowering his voice as he crept behind Tiaponine.

"Give it a rest," Breydon admonished, laughing and waving him off with his hand.

"Perhaps scaring the girl will brighten my diminishing pleasant demeanor," Samuel countered; his head poking around Tiaponine's left shoulder as a wicked smile pervaded his features.

"You're superstitious," Breydon said. "And leave her alone."

"Don't you find it kind of peculiar that no one ever goes in there?" the servant pressed.

Breydon studied the vast forest a moment in silence and then, with another dismissive wave of his hand, turned his attention back to the swine.

"While it's true that the EliSann Forest isn't a place one just wanders into for a nice stroll on a bright sunny day," he said. "I'm not convinced that all the rumors are true, either. I've been there a couple times in the past, and can say with great certainty that I've never experienced anything that would give life to the ridiculous stories from the kingdom."

Tiaponine groaned in quiet aggravation. All hope of avoiding a conversation about EliSann was lost. Breydon did not seem interested. Samuel, though…

She was having a difficult time getting past Samuel's reference to the people of EliSann as demons. Although she'd never met anyone from the forest, except for VerGann, the word demon would never have entered her mind as a description for them. Outside of the delpins, it was rare for VerGann to speak of his people, and she respected him enough to never press him for information.

"And what about you?" Samuel asked, his attention returning to Tiaponine. "You ever venture into the EliSann Forest?"

She turned to the nosy servant. It was no surprise to find Samuel glaring at her with his fists resting on his hips. This conversation was clearly going to continue no matter what she said, so there was no point lying to the man.

"Yes," she answered, as if it were no big deal.

Prince Breydon and Samuel exchange doubtful looks.

"Really," the servant chided. "And when was this?"

"By yourself?" Breydon's voice was dripping with disbelief.

Tiaponine shrugged and turned away. The noonday sun was unmerciful, her gown hot and lacking in certain areas for her comfort. Engaging in another verbal confrontation would just add to her misery.

"I just hope you remember that you're not really going to marry him," Samuel said as soon as the prince's back was turned.

Tiaponine stilled, frowning. Was Samuel hinting that she carried some sort of attraction for Breydon? That was preposterous.

"What?" Samuel asked, feigning ignorance. "You've been ogling the prince all day. You know what I'm getting at." A wicked grin formed at the corners of his mouth.

"No, as a matter of fact, I don't," Tiaponine answered coldly. She so hoped the prince could not hear Samuel's desperate attempts to get under her skin.

"Come, Tiaponine," he persisted. "You like him."

True, there was something very likeable about Prince Breydon, but in the romantic sense? She had known him all of one day.

"He's all right," she answered.

"No. More than that."

Tiaponine huffed and tucked a wayward strand of auburn hair back into her umber colored headband. "No. That's it."

"Right," he said, snickering. "Just remember. He could never love you."

Shouldering him to the side, Tiaponine went to join Breydon along the side of the mud pit. She was determined to not lash out at the servant. That would make things worse, draw attention, and attention to *this* matter was something she could do without.

"Go ahead and tell him," Samuel yelled after her.

"Tell him what?" Tiaponine snapped, forgetting her resolve. "That you're the most annoying man ever born?"

Breydon gritted his teeth. "Samuel, I thought we'd agreed that you'd..."

"Your *Majesty*," Samuel interrupted, accentuating the title. "Like I said before, this isn't going to work. She's too stubborn to cooperate. It's hopeless. She's hopeless!"

"Leave her *alone*!"

"Fine," he grumbled, meeting her gaze again. "No account street rat."

She lunged at him. The servant may be big on words, but that was all he was big on. Verbal confrontations were a comfortable place for Samuel. Physical confrontations, not so much.

His eyes grew wide with fear, his mouth opening in surprise, and she could have sworn he screamed—although that may have just been the blood rushing through her ears. Tiaponine was more than satisfied.

Her enjoyment was short lived, though, as Breydon grabbed her shoulders, restraining her from making any actual physical contact with his servant.

She was so close, yet so far.

Stunned by the unexpected aggression and thrown off balance, Samuel started to fall backwards into the thick mud behind him. Breydon loosened his grip on Tiaponine's shoulders and grabbed Samuel's left arm.

Both men toppled into the mud. She was speechless as the thick muck engulfed the prince's entire body. This could not have been the ending he had imagined to his training session.

Feeling the slippery ground start to give way beneath her own feet, Tiaponine gasped. Her arms flailed as she attempted to gain her balance, to no avail.

The feel of strong hands about her waist pulling her back was unexpected. Tiaponine fell into her rescuer and looked up.

VerGann was but inches from her face, his features mirroring her sudden feelings of awkwardness. With a little assistance, she leaned forward to stand on her own two feet.

"Great," Breydon muttered, glowering at Samuel beside him as he struggled to sit up.

"Nice timing," the servant grumbled, his eyes fixed on VerGann.

He just didn't know when to stop. Tiaponine's anger was near boiling over.

"Sorry, VerGann. I just can't." She was beyond the ability to even describe to the delpin what had happened before his timely arrival. The best thing to do was to leave for a while. "I'll see you back at the castle later," she muttered, giving Breydon the slightest of nods.

"I'll count on it," Samuel shot back.

Forget restraint. Tiaponine was well beyond restraint. Reaching down to scoop up a handful of thick, grainy mud, she turned and threw it at the loud-mouthed servant. To her complete satisfaction, her aim was straight on, and she could not help but smile as the mud ball hit the servant square in his face.

"So will I," she spat. She gathered her skirt high above her knees with one hand, not caring in the least if it was proper or not, and mounted the nearest horse. Kicking the animal lightly, she left.

"It's a talent, isn't it?" VerGann mused. "I don't think I've ever seen her this angry, but you seem to know exactly what to say, don't you?"

The servant appeared ready to explode. Smirking, the delpin mounted a palace horse.

"That's my horse!" Samuel shouted, trying to rise from the mud, only to fall back into it.

VerGann glanced from him to the horse. "Yes, it is." He turned in the direction of the front gate.

"But that leaves one horse for two men!"

With one swift kick to the animal's side, VerGann headed toward the front gate.

Behind him, Breydon let out a frustrated breath. "Great. Just great."

"Tee?"

VerGann pushed the door to the simple attic space open. He smiled with a sense of relief.

As he had suspected, Tiaponine had returned home.

Given the current state of affairs, VerGann knew the castle was the last place she wished to be.

Letting the door close behind him, he grew quiet as he took in Tiaponine's motionless form. Stretched across a couple of rustic colored, worn blankets against the far wall, she was the vision of despair.

"I must say, that was quite the exit," VerGann mused, taking a seat beside her.

Rolling over onto her back so she could see him above her, Tiaponine let out a deep, frustrated breath.

"As I remember, Samuel was the one that brought up this whole idea in the first place," she spat. "One would think he could at least try to be somewhat pleasant. If he's trying to help the prince, he's failing. I mean, what if I just left? What kind of romantic trouble would our handsome prince be in then?"

"We both know that the prince's girl troubles aren't the real reason Samuel's being so helpful," VerGann said, gazing out the small window at his side. Even in the bustle of the afternoon activities on the streets below, the tiny two-roomed shelter felt safe. More to the point, it was far from the stress of Prince Breydon's charade.

"I know," Tiaponine agreed with a heavy breath, closing her eyes. "I think Samuel has his eye on a bigger prize; advancement in the king's service, an official title, perhaps." She adjusted the lump of blanket beneath her head. "I guess he was expecting me to do what I was told and be quiet. I'm muddying the path for him to get what he wants."

VerGann leaned his head back against the wall, the coolness of the stone welcoming in the scorching afternoon heat. "Perhaps Samuel doesn't like you because he knows that the prince does."

Opening her eyes, Tiaponine glanced at him suspiciously, shaking her head. "The prince likes me?" she repeated, confused. "He thought I was a thief."

VerGann again turned toward the window, an odd tension taking over his stomach.

"I don't think we've given Prince Breydon a fair chance," he offered, hardly able to believe he was defending the prince. "He may be concerned about things that we both find ridiculous, but that's the world he lives in. After your initial, unfortunate meeting with him, Breydon has been nothing but kind. Am I right?"

Tiaponine quieted, her stare distant. "I haven't really been around him much, but his attitude has changed from when we first met him, I guess. He hasn't offered to tackle me to the ground, anyway."

"True. I think he not only sees this plan as a real answer to his troubles, but also finds you and your feisty nature a bit to his liking." VerGann mentally kicked himself for saying so. "I doubt he comes across many girls like you."

Tiaponine giggled. "Girls probably just fall all over themselves around him. Remember how Lerra and Eva were talking about him?"

"I'd rather not," he muttered, forcing an uncomfortable laugh. "Anyway, I guess the prince finds you refreshing."

"That makes sense, I guess," Tiaponine agreed. "Feisty? You think that I'm feisty, VerGann?"

VerGann smiled. He had no doubt that he was correct in his choice of words, recalling Tiaponine's ball of mud hitting Samuel in the face earlier. "Don't get me wrong. Being a bit feisty isn't always a bad trait. I see how the prince might find it to his liking."

As soon as the last word left his mouth, the delpin wished he had not been so honest. Tiaponine was staring at him, his words causing an amount of confusion.

"Well, what's the plan for the rest of the day?" VerGann asked, moving on to another topic before his momentary embarrassment got the best of him. "While hanging around here and relaxing does have its appeal, I thought a little trip to make up for the missed walk last night might be in order. What do you think?"

Sitting up, Tiaponine smiled. "That sounds delightful. I was going to go back to the castle, though," she added, her excitement at once dropping. "It just doesn't feel right to walk out on the prince after one day. I told him I'd do this, and I intend on keeping my word."

"If that's what you want, you know that I support you," VerGann offered, his tone gentle. "Let's get away for a bit. We can return to the castle later this evening."

"But my dress," she said, tugging at the plum colored skirt lying in folds over her legs. "I had to borrow a blanket to cover myself even to get back here without too much notice. The only other two outfits I have to my name are at the castle." As if catching herself complaining, she paused, her shoulders falling. "You're right. Let's get away," she agreed. "But the castle, how will we get into…" She trailed off as VerGann grinned, and laughed to herself. She knew better than to question him.

"I'll take care of it," he said. "You'll be sleeping in that oversized bed tonight. I promise you."

"And you?"

After the events of the previous evening, he had no intention of leaving Tiaponine alone. She did not know of the assassin's attempt, and he preferred it remain that way.

"I'll be staying at the castle as well, from here on out." Noting her concerned expression, VerGann took her hand in his. "It'll be alright. Everything's fine." He stood, helping her up as he did so. "For now, all I want you to do is relax. I promised you a walk by the ElinDann River last night. I have to come up with something pretty spectacular to make up for missing it."

"Any sign of her yet?"

Breydon could not help but feel anxious that Tiaponine had not returned to the castle yet.

Glowering at Breydon, still sulking, Samuel shook his head.

If it had not been for the servant's continued harassment, Tiaponine would not have left, and Breydon would not have found himself with a thick layer of mud over his entire being. In the hot sun, the sloppy substance had hardened, becoming a rock-hard prison engulfing every limb of his body. The journey back to his eastern tower retreat seemed to never end. It was hard to miss the curious stares from the guards.

"No, Breydon," Samuel muttered. "The girl hasn't been seen since earlier this afternoon."

"I cannot believe this is happening," Breydon seethed, ignoring the sound of approaching footsteps in the tower stairwell. "It would've worked, Samuel. If you hadn't been so hard on her. When she returns…"

"If she returns…"

He spun around to face Samuel, his frustration growing. "You'd better *hope* that she does. I'm not going to be stuck with Santerine's princess the rest of my life."

"Breydon, I think that you're overreacting—"

"Find her," Breydon demanded. "Let me know the moment she gets back."

As the footsteps got louder, Breydon tugged free the top three buttons of his casual white linen shirt. "Who is that?"

Samuel hurried to the stairwell. "It's Princess Gwenevieve," he said as Gwenevieve's shadow rounded the stairs below.

"Great," Breydon muttered, edging Samuel out the door. "Tell her I'm not here."

"To see Hulbert's defeat will be my greatest triumph. Our kingdoms have been enemies too long. And your son—"

"My son is dead." Lundane squared his shoulders, his muscular frame casting a formidable shadow across the marble floor. While he appreciated King Sandis' hopeful tone, he knew better than to spend his time hoping for the impossible. "The pain of living in exile from Draven for eighteen years pales in comparison to the pain I felt at hearing of his death."

Sandis took another sip from his gold goblet, the red wine dribbling down his pudgy chin. "Lundane, you don't know this for certain. Breydon might still live."

"Your guard reported that he was killed shortly after my defeat." Lundane's jaw tensed. "His own blood. How could my brother kill his own nephew? How did I not suspect his scheming until it was too late?"

"But, my friend," Sandis pleaded. "We know a Prince Breydon does indeed live in Draven. He could very well be your son and not an imposter as you believe. Eighteen years you have been in hiding and to this date, no firm evidence exists that your son is gone."

Lundane did not respond, but pivoted on his heels, his back to Sandis. "Word of your guard? Have they reached Draven?"

"Fifteen hundred men are camped fifty miles to the east of Draven," Sandis offered, his tone suddenly reserved.

It was not his wish to disrespect the Tatrine king. Lundane took a deep, calming breath. King Sandis had offered him shelter and friendship at the lowest point in his life. Tatrus had taken him in, offered cover from his enemies for the better part of eighteen years. He was indebted to Sandis for all time.

"And the attack?" Lundane pressed. "All is in order?"

"We have three spies in Draven as we speak," Sandis said. "Hulbert is aware of our troops in the neighboring countryside. He has to suspect an attack is imminent. But for now, we're far enough away not to draw too much attention."

"Hulbert is no fool." Lundane's eyes narrowed. "My brother undoubtedly has spies of his own in Tatrus this very moment."

King Sandis took another big gulp from his goblet. "And that's why patience is of the utmost importance. We must wait to attack. Hulbert will be distracted at some point, and that is when we'll strike."

"Have your men move toward the EliSann Forest instead, the eastern side so as not to cross into Draven's territory." Lundane said. The stout Tatrine ruler's sudden confusion did not go unnoticed. "Make Hulbert think Draven isn't their destination."

"The EliSann Forest?" Sandis repeated. "What reason would we have to march on EliSann?"

"We aren't marching on EliSann, just camping to the east of it," Lundane added, the corner of his mouth turning up slightly in a grin. "Get the word out that Tatrus is there to investigate the recent uptick in raids on the smaller villages to the south of EliSann."

Sandis gripped his goblet with two hands, his brow furrowing. "Investigate? We know that the Magdina are likely the guilty party. Anyone traveling to the south of EliSann knows that an attack from a Magdina hunting party is a possibility."

Sandis made a good point. "Make it appear that Tatrus, no longer willing to tolerate the Magdina's lawlessness, are preparing to meet them head on. This will be our excuse for being stationed so close to Draven. Hulbert won't want a conflict with you if he can avoid it. I have to believe that's why he's left you alone all of these years. We know rumor of my hiding here has likely found its way back to him."

Sandis took another large swig of wine, an audible belch echoing in the castle hallway. "Your idea is sound. Hulbert will be alert to our presence but will likely leave us be." The Tatrine ruler turned to the servant on his right. "Fetch the captain of the castle guard. He'll send a message with his fastest rider this very night."

"This will buy us time," Lundane said. "That distraction you hope for had better come soon, though. I'm so close to taking back Draven's throne. I feel it with every beat of my heart."

"And perhaps a family reunion is in the near future as well."

Lundane straightened. "My son is dead and has been for a very long time." He heard Sandis' audible sigh at his side.

The stout little ruler's fingers tapped at the side of his goblet. "My apologies, my friend. Your son will not be mentioned from this day forward."

CHAPTER 6

Tiaponine took in the EliSann Forest with eager anticipation. The setting sun cast a warm glow over the ancient, twisted oaks as she and VerGann passed under a canopy formed by the tangled branches overhead. The calm gurgling of water over worn stone could be heard somewhere nearby.

She sighed at the beauty of it all.

She was not sure what they were doing there, but she was already excited, just as VerGann had promised. Draven had long since disappeared from sight, the noises of the city's bustling streets fading quickly behind them. All that was left was the great expanse of rich green trees, and her following VerGann as he effortlessly navigated the foliage.

"So, are you going to tell me where we're going?"

VerGann smiled slightly, studying the trees above and around him to get his bearings. "Not yet."

The walk had been a quiet one thus far. Tiaponine had never been this deep into the forest, and the new experience was beyond exhilarating, especially considering how few people were ever afforded such an opportunity. She was thankful that VerGann seemed to understand the distraction conversation would present, and was allowing her to enjoy the journey in relative silence.

After several more minutes, VerGann squared his shoulders, coming at last to a stop. "We're here."

They stood at the edge of an overhang, overlooking a large clearing framed on either side by the winding trunks of two ancient trees.

Tiaponine leaned in to peer down at the scene below her. The clearing was a bustle of activity. People of all shapes and sizes darted in between rows of long, thick wooden tables stacked with plates and bowls heaped full of colorful foods. Preparations for what appeared to be quite the banquet in the near future were underway.

A small grouping of young ladies clustered together, searching the opposite end of the clearing with eager eyes. In their simple, earthen colored, sleeveless dresses falling just below their knees, their hair pulled up in numerous ties accented by bright flowers, the young women were dressed for a very special occasion.

"What's going on? Are they waiting for something?" Tiaponine asked, her eyes moving from the girls to the empty forest they were so focused on. "No girl gets that dressed up without a reason. Usually it has something to do with a man."

She grimaced as she thought about her words. What would she know about dressing to impress a man? She glanced at VerGann, relieved to see him laughing.

"Well, they are," he chuckled.

"Waiting?"

"Waiting," he repeated. "This whole gathering is to celebrate the marriage of the nymphs and nardins."

Nymphs and nardins. Of course, Tiaponine knew the EliSann Forest was home to an entire community of beings. But seeing them up close, they did not look any different from her. She caught herself mid-stare and turned to VerGann. He seemed to be measuring her reaction, as if he could see what she was thinking. Yet, he did not seem offended.

"So, where are the nardins?" Tiaponine asked, noting the obvious absence of age appropriate men in the clearing.

"Passed out on the side of the ElinDann River, I would guess," VerGann lamented.

Tiaponine blinked in alarm. Whatever she had been expecting, that was *not* it. "What?"

VerGann shook his head, laughing. "I am just kidding, Tee. This celebration happens every two years. The nardins and nymphs who choose to participate make requests to the Seratine as to who they wish to pursue, or who they wish to pursue them. Who they would like to take as their mate," he clarified, noting her puzzled expression.

"Oh," Tiaponine responded, an instant feeling of awkwardness overtaking her.

"After a few long weeks of preparation for the final celebration, emphasis on the word *long*, the nardins compete in a game of sorts to catch their respective girl," VerGann continued, gesturing at the ladies below. "This is the end of that game. Once caught, the nymphs return to the clearing until all of the nardins can return at one time. Those girls down there are waiting for their men to return to them."

"And this… amuses you?"

"I'm relieved," VerGann corrected. "The weeks of over-the-top anticipation that we're all forced to endure are exhausting."

It was an awkward visual, but somehow appealing at the same time. Tiaponine felt a warmth spread through her face.

"After the nardins get back, there's a short break to give the young men time to clean up, and then they all meet back here for the marriage ceremony and the feast."

Tiaponine was not sure what to say. VerGann's description was like nothing she had ever heard. It sounded like a nice tradition, except for a few curious points. "You said catch. As in…"

"Yes," he mused. "The nardins chase the nymphs through the forest until they literally catch one. The girl he catches is the girl he marries."

Tiaponine's jaw dropped. She did not want to be rude, but this sounded barbaric.

"It sounds bad, I know, but it's not," VerGann reassured, squeezing her hand. "There's an understanding beforehand of which nardin will be pursuing which nymph. Trust me, everyone goes home very happy."

"And I take it that the nymphs aren't easy to catch," Tiaponine guessed.

"Quite the opposite."

The tradition held a certain romantic appeal. "To think that a man would go through all of that for his girl is sweet." Tiaponine's heart felt light. "Do the delpins ever participate?"

Not hearing an immediate response, she bit her lower lip, silently chiding herself. Her question was too forward.

"No, we don't," VerGann answered finally. He motioned back to the clearing in front of them.

Tiaponine followed his line of sight to seven young men—boys, really, by the looks of them—gathered at one of the wooden tables.

"It may sound strange, but the delpins just never have any real inclination toward relationships. At least, not the kind we're talking about." VerGann seemed to be avoiding her gaze.

Regretting that she had embarrassed him, Tiaponine nodded. "No, it makes sense, I guess. Given the circumstances, anyway. Has this changed at all for you as you grew? The lack of interest in relationships of that sort, that is?"

At her last word, her breath halted. She had done it again; she was being far too forward. She *must* learn to think about her words before saying them. What kind of answer could VerGann give to a question like that?

"I… I'm sorry," she apologized, stumbling over her words. "It's none of my business."

"I think it's fair to say that my appearance isn't the only thing that has changed," he offered vaguely, after a moment's hesitation.

Now it was Tiaponine's turn to stare at VerGann, struggling to put meaning to his words.

"So, does spending an evening at the celebration sound at all interesting?" he asked, seeming to move past the awkwardness with ease.

The question was a silly one. "Yes." She beamed with excitement. "Is it alright that I'm here, though?"

"It'll be fine."

A sudden commotion erupted below as a group of seven nardins, all appearing a little worse for the wear, entered the clearing. Without hesitation, the waiting nymphs ran to embrace their men.

Tiaponine breathed in deep, a dreamy feeling overtaking her. The innocence of it all was refreshing, a welcome change from the stressful situation she found herself in at the castle.

"Tiaponine?"

At the sound of the unfamiliar woman's voice, Tiaponine turned to see an older grey-haired nymph staring back at her with hopeful eyes. "Yes?" she replied hesitantly.

"Oh, how wonderful!" The nymph's voice was full of excitement. "You're *just* as I imagined you'd be." Grinning at VerGann, the nymph took Tiaponine's hand in hers. "If you don't mind, I'm going to steal the girl away from you for a while, VerGann, maybe find her something more comfortable to wear than this heavy dress from the city."

She could tell VerGann was studying her reaction to the request, but the elderly nymph had an inviting, trustworthy warmth about her. She had no worries about going with the woman.

"And VerGann, dear," the nymph continued, a motherly cadence to her words. "I'm sure the nymphs would be happy to have your help with some of the carrying."

"Of course." VerGann nodded respectfully. With one last look at Tiaponine, he turned and walked away.

"All right, dear, before I forget, my name is Zendra. It's an absolute *treat* to meet you, sweetheart. Now, let's see what we can do about this dress," Zendra said, fingering the flowing, plum colored material of Tiaponine's skirt as she guided her down a side trail toward the clearing. "Don't misunderstand me. It's very nice, but not at all suited for forest travel, and not at all comfortable on a hot evening like tonight. And that neckline..." She trailed off, wide eyed. Glancing at two nardins close by, the nymph took Tiaponine by the shoulders and turned her out of their sight.

"Well, it's *not at all* proper," she said firmly. "Why the humans insist on such silly discomforts is a mystery to me. Come, dear, I'm sure we can find something more appropriate."

Tiaponine's grin broadened. She was not offended.

Not at all.

"Please tell me they came back."

"*No*, Breydon," Samuel sighed, exasperated. "They're not back yet."

Repositioning himself against the hard cold stone frame of the tower window, Breydon cursed under his breath.

His hopes of getting rid of Gwenevieve were disappearing fast. He'd ignored two summons to meet with her already that evening, and his uncle was sure not to allow that sort of blatant disrespect to continue much longer.

"As I said, Breydon," Samuel said. "Marry Gwenevieve, make your uncle happy, and just be done with it. Who says that you have to be in love? Besides, you could do a lot worse than Gwenevieve. As far as women go, she's quite the beauty. Her figure alone makes up for any—"

"I'll see you tomorrow," Breydon interrupted, suppressing a groan. Princess Gwenevieve's shapeliness would *never* be able to make up for her many personality flaws.

"Until tomorrow," Samuel muttered, appearing a bit put out at being cut off as he shut the tower door behind him.

While VerGann had wanted to watch the simple marriage ceremony with Tiaponine, it was not to be. By the time he had finished carrying the last of the provisions for the feast, it was too late to join her.

Not a big deal, he supposed. He had checked in on Tiaponine off and on throughout the night. Helping the nymphs with the food, adding finishing touches to their hair and dress before the ceremony; she seemed to be enjoying every moment. The troubles awaiting her back in Draven were forgotten, if only for the evening.

VerGann could not suppress the smile invading his features. Mission accomplished.

Spotting Tiaponine across the clearing as a small crowd dispersed, VerGann felt an unfamiliar twinge in his stomach as his eyes drifted to the dress she wore. He had not really had the opportunity to notice earlier. Although very plain and simple, the tan leather dress the elder nymph found for Tiaponine was very flattering. He cleared his throat.

"I see Zendra found you something to wear," he offered as Tiaponine approached, her eyes twinkling happily.

Fingering the dark, leather laces along the sides of the form fitting, knee length dress, she flushed, her smile timid. "Such a dress would be viewed as too revealing for the city." She laughed. "Showing a woman's arms and legs is too revealing, but plunging necklines are quite acceptable. I must say, I prefer EliSann's definition of appropriate."

VerGann nodded in agreement, that awkward feeling creeping into the pit of his stomach again. Twice in one night. Curious.

"What is going on?" Tiapoinine turned her attention to the nardins sitting in a row on a bench as their giddy new brides stood in front of them. She bit her lip as she studied the scene.

"The nymphs and nardins are big on tradition." VerGann smirked. "This is the last of it, though. We are free to eat and relax after this."

"Oh," Tiaponine said, still watching the nardins and nymphs. "So what are they..." She broke off as each nymph moved to sit across the lap of her new husband.

After a quick community count-to-three, each nardin gave his new bride a gentlemanly kiss, a loud cheer of approval breaking out in the clearing.

Tiaponine's face flushed a bit, and VerGann smiled.

"Come," he said, taking her hand. "After all that work, you must be hungry."

They walked through a small crowd of elder nymphs whispering amongst themselves. VerGann did his best to ignore their curious stares as they passed. All were curious about the human girl from Draven. Bringing Tiaponine to the festival would be the talk of EliSann for a while.

Spotting four delpins sitting at a table just ahead, VerGann quickened his pace, Tiaponine in tow. He'd hoped the delpins would stay for the festival. He had spoken of them to her many times, but she had yet to meet them. This was his immediate family, for lack of better words, those he was most loyal to and those who understood him the best. Tiaponine was already an accepted part of their small circle, whether she realized it or not.

"This is amazing, VerGann," Tiaponine exclaimed, taking in the vast amounts of meat, bread and fruit along the center of the table. With the slightest of hesitation, she joined the table of quiet young men.

"Too bad the celebration is but every two years."

At the higher pitched female voice somewhere beside her, Tiaponine blinked down at the table. A tiny, winged woman, no taller than the cup she was leaning against, was staring back at her, grinning ear to ear.

"May I introduce you to Natimae," VerGann said. "A sprite."

"Natimae?" the pretty little sprite protested. "You may call me Natty. Everyone else does." Rolling her eyes, Natty shot him a cross look. "Natimae..." the sprite grumbled. "Really, VerGann. You make it sound like I am in trouble."

"You'll be happy to hear that Nat has managed to stay clear of trouble for quite a while now," the delpin closest to the sprite said. "After the last unfortunate episode with the nymphs being locked in the storage shed, she's been on her best behavior."

The sprite turned to the dark-haired delpin and waved him off with a playful swoosh of her hand. "As I told Marlott, it was an *accident*. It really wasn't that big of a deal. Anyway, where are your manners?" she chided, stomping her little feet on the table to get the attention of the four delpins at the table. "Were you planning on introducing yourselves?"

VerGann suppressed a grin as his four friends straightened, a bit uncomfortable with being put on the spot.

"This is KaiDinn," the sprite started, pointing to the delpin closest to her before any of them could speak, a slight twinkle in her eye. "And over here is Vrenler, Zeravin, and BriDonn. The other three had to leave for a while. There you have it. EliSann's best."

Tiaponine nodded to the young men. "I see," she said, flashing a polite smile. "Are there other sprites?"

Pulling a small piece from the cornbread on KaiDinn's plate, Natty laughed. "There are one hundred fifty-seven of us, to be exact."

"The sprites live in ErinDarr Hollow, not far away," VerGann explained. "It's rare for them to take part in the celebration."

"That's right," Natty agreed, taking another piece from the bread on KaiDinn's plate before finding a resting spot on the delpin's shoulder. "I just do my own thing."

"Thank you for bringing me here, VerGann," Tiaponine said, looking up at him with bright eyes. "This makes up for the missed walk many times over."

"Missed walk?" Natty asked with a dramatic gasp. "*VerGann?*"

VerGann gazed back at the sprite with forced calmness. "I'd promised a walk by the river last night, but due to... unforeseen events, I'm afraid it was missed."

Shaking her head as if she understood everything, Natty grinned. "I see. Well, this is a nice way to make up for it."

"Nat," KaiDinn admonished quietly, appearing embarrassed on behalf of the sprite.

VerGann stifled a laugh. "I'm so glad that you find this an acceptable second choice, Natimae," he said dryly.

"There you go again with the name. Although this time, I think I deserve it." The sprite drew imaginary circles with her foot in mock regret. Upon hearing the pleasant sound of a high pitched flute echoing through the clearing, all was forgotten, though. Natty sighed, her body falling against KaiDinn's shoulder.

"I think that a dance is in order here. Don't you, VerGann?" Natty glanced up at him, a mischievous glint in her eyes. "You cannot expect to take the girl back to Draven without first asking her to dance."

"*Nat*," KaiDinn pleaded again. "Are you sure the only thing you had to drink tonight was that berry juice? What's gotten into you?"

Natty frowned at KaiDinn. "What?" she hissed, genuinely confused.

VerGann stared at the sprite, not sure what to say. He knew that she was joking with him. The anxiety rushing through him was no joke, though.

He looked from the delpins to Tiaponine. It was not as though he had never joined in on a dance. On many occasions, he could remember dancing with a nymph at the celebration. Even the lower streets of Draven engaged in festivities once in a while. He and Tiaponine had danced quite a few times in the past. For reasons he could not explain, though, the current situation felt different. He offered his hand to Tiaponine.

Together, they joined the dancing couples. Letting his hands rest on the sides of her waist, VerGann pushed past his anxiety. This was Tiaponine, his best friend.

Feeling her hands reach up to his shoulders, her arms coming to rest against his chest, he started. This *was* different. This closeness was new, Tiaponine's obvious hesitation curious. Perhaps the romantic setting of the celebration was behind her nervousness. But what about his?

"Thank you for this evening," she said, breaking the long silence that ensued. "I think this distraction is just what I needed."

"So the frustration from earlier is gone?" VerGann asked.

"Yes," Tiaponine agreed, laughing. "Everyone's so happy." She paused. "Well, maybe not everyone. *He* doesn't look to be enjoying himself much."

He followed her gaze to see Dreesdin glaring his way and sighed in mild irritation. The evening had been such a nice one. At least the nardin had not tried to approach him yet. Thank goodness for small favors.

"What's his problem?" Tiaponine asked.

"Not problem… *problems*. He has quite a few." VerGann turned his attention away from the disagreeable nardin. "Right now, though, his problem is me."

"You?"

"His name is Dreesdin. He sits on the Council," VerGann offered, uninterested. "It seems that while I've been gone, EliSann has taken in a guest with, shall we say, questionable abilities. Dreesdin's angry that the delpins refuse to meet with his new friend."

"Is there a reason you won't meet with him?"

"Her," VerGann corrected. "And there are lots of reasons. The biggest one is, we don't trust her. Nelliah comes from a place that has a troubled history with my people. We're not going to be close friends."

"Dreesdin hasn't stopped staring at you since we started dancing," Tiaponine noted.

"I didn't even notice."

Shaking her head, Tiaponine laughed. "Sure you didn't."

VerGann bowed to her as the music ended around them.

"We should probably be getting back," he said. He was sorry to cut her fun short, but it was getting late.

"I know. Are you sure that we'll be able to get back into the castle?" Tiaponine bit her lip.

"Trust me; the guards will never see us." VerGann laughed to himself. He could have quite a lot of fun at their expense, if he wanted to. Perhaps he did want to.

"The celebration lasts all night." He ran his hand through his hair. "I'm afraid you wouldn't be much use to the prince if we stayed for the remainder of it."

"I suppose," Tiaponine agreed. "Back to the castle we go for another try, then…"

"We'll walk with you for a while," Natimae's familiar voice sounded as she and KaiDinn joined them. The sprite tugged on the material of Tiaponine's dress at the shoulder and began to pull her forward.

"Here," Zendra, the elder nymph from earlier, interrupted, hurrying to them. "You'll need this, dear." Placing a long, brown cape about Tiaponine's shoulders, the nymph nodded in approval. "We wouldn't want to draw attention from the outside. Not at all." Taking the heap of plum colored fabric from a nymph at her side, Zendra dumped the bundle in VerGann's arms. "Her dress, dear. But you do understand, this dress is not at all appropriate?"

So noted. He turned to Tiaponine, almost out of sight as she followed Natty into the depths of the forest. For reasons unknown, he could not take his eyes from her. The night had been a wonderful one…

"We'll let you know if anything changes with Nelliah."

VerGann tensed, realizing he was still staring Tiaponine's way, almost in a daze. He glanced at KaiDinn beside him. He did not say so, but it was clear he had noticed.

Nodding, VerGann looked over the clearing behind him, past the dancing couples and tables and music.

Marlott was staring at him from her seat at one of the tables. He had failed to notice her there before. For a brief moment, his eyes locked with hers.

VerGann knew in that instant that his seratine had also noticed his momentary lapse. Her carefully blank expression would have fooled most, but he had known her long enough to see through it.

She may not know the extent of his thoughts, but she was aware of his confused feelings. She did not appear pleased.

Mindful of his own expression, VerGann nodded respectfully to the seratine before turning to follow Tiaponine. He could feel her still watching him as he left.

CHAPTER 7

She could not have asked for a more perfect evening.

Tiaponine sighed contentedly as she and VerGann rounded the corner at the end of the hallway. Her trip to EliSann the night before had calmed her nerves. She was back at the castle, anxiety free, ready to focus on the task at hand.

"And... *he's* here."

Tiaponine stopped mid-step and looked at VerGann, whose face was drawn into a frown, eyes fixed on something on the ground floor. She followed his gaze to see just the top of Samuel's head as he stood at the bottom of the staircase ahead of them.

Her heart sank. She had forgotten all about the bothersome servant.

She descended the stairs with heavy steps. Thank goodness Samuel had not noticed her yet—he had his back turned to the staircase.

"Yes, I know I *could* find another girl to take Tiaponine's place."

Upon hearing Prince Breydon's voice, she stopped, peaking around the wall midway down the steps to see the prince pacing anxiously back and forth across the polished marble floor of the empty banquet hall.

"But I don't want another girl," he continued. "She's grown on me a bit."

Tiaponine straightened. This was unexpected. She turned to VerGann at her side in mild surprise, and found that she could not quite read his expression.

"Two days, Breydon," Samuel pointed out, disgust dripping from every word. "She's been here but *two* days."

"And your point is?" the prince countered.

Raising her chin high, Tiaponine continued down the stairs before Samuel could respond, and was gratified to see his eyes widen as he whirled around. She did not appreciate being talked about behind her back.

"Where did you come from?" Samuel blurted out, his face incredulous. "Better yet, how did you get back in the castle? The guards never mentioned—"

"It doesn't matter," Breydon interrupted. "She's here now. Keep your mouth closed this time." He shouldered Samuel as he walked by him.

Tiaponine was quite sure she had heard Prince Breydon breathe a sigh of relief at her sudden appearance.

Samuel retreated to a carved oak chair along the far wall of the room, silently seething.

Tiaponine felt the tension leave her shoulders. Perhaps it was just wishful thinking, but it appeared there might be a growing rift between the prince and his servant.

"I know we had a rough start yesterday, Tiaponine," Breydon began. "I take full responsibility for things ending the way they did. Maybe we could try to start again, *anew,* and avoid any further mud baths."

"Sounds good to me," Samuel scoffed. "I had mud in places I never knew—"

"We'll forget about events of the past," Breydon interrupted, drowning out Samuel's complaint. Focusing back on Tiaponine, he tugged at his collar anxiously. "Let's just start again."

Tiaponine took a deep breath, deliberately avoiding the servant's irritated glare. She would have to get past her annoyance at Samuel—it was worth it, in order to provide herself and VerGann with lifelong security and provision.

"All right," she agreed. "Starting over sounds good."

"And starting over right now sounds even better."

"*Now?*" Tiaponine asked. Although quite appreciative of Prince Breydon's apology, she hadn't guessed they would be diving into lessons so soon. "I suppose... We are in a bit of a hurry, aren't we?" she conceded.

"Right," Breydon agreed, distracted. He motioned VerGann off to the side.

Tiaponine looked from the prince to VerGann, now leaning against the wall beside Samuel. She wished she could put on a fancy dress, make an appearance, and be done with the whole charade. If one looked the part, why would anyone question it?

It was not that simple to Prince Breydon, though.

"Since the history lesson yesterday didn't go very well, I suppose I'll just have to trust you can hold your own if asked any questions."

It was difficult to miss the prince's underlying sarcastic tone.

"I can handle it," Tiaponine said coolly. "I'm not ignorant."

"All right. Let's work on presentation," Breydon announced. He surveyed Tiaponine's appearance with a critical eye. "You're still wearing the dress from yesterday."

She stared at him, dumbfounded. It was not that his tone was mean, it was just unexpected.

"At least she's wearing a dress," Samuel quipped. "Anything's better than the men's clothing."

Tiaponine shot him a poisonous look. "Alright, with this one wardrobe blunder aside, may we move on?" She twisted a lock of auburn hair around her finger, forcing herself to remain calm. New start… Lifetime of security…

"No one's going to believe you're from a privileged background if you don't act like it," Prince Breydon continued.

"Act like it?" Tiaponine echoed, unable to repress her laughter. "I can walk around with my nose in the air the same as anyone else frequenting the king's court."

Smirking, Breydon shook his head.

"That's not what I mean," he said. "Let's say that you're standing in a room full of handsome young men—handsome young *princes,* that is. One of them approaches you. What do you say?"

Before Tiaponine could give what she thought to be an obvious answer to a silly question, Prince Breydon strode forward. She stared in shocked silence—he now stood but inches away from her, at once dwarfing her. She felt tiny and frail.

Out of sheer instinct, she shoved the looming prince in the chest, forcing him back a step. Now with a comfortable amount of her personal space back, Tiaponine let go of the breath she was holding and glared at him.

"That would be what *not* to do," Breydon admonished.

"The question was what I would say, not what I would do. I was going to say that I would just tell the handsome young prince hello, very nice to meet you, or something just as normal. However, if the man came up to me the way you just did, I think that my response would be appropriate." Hearing Samuel's bemused laugh from the side of the room, Tiaponine shot the servant a piercing scowl.

"The idea was to make you feel the strong presence of a man in my position. I mean, what it would feel like to be close to someone that most women swoon over."

At the sound of a snicker from the side of the room, Prince Breydon glanced warily at VerGann, who looked amused.

"Tiaponine, women in your position—of your supposed title, I mean—are used to…" Breydon stumbled with his words. "I mean, females are often taken when around men like me. A prince, I mean. A woman has to know how to balance the attraction she feels with knowing her place. She cannot let him see the effect he has on her, and…" Breydon leveled his gaze on her. "She cannot push him away."

Tiaponine stared at the prince with skeptical eyes, unsure whether or not it would be appropriate to laugh.

"Well," she finally said dryly. "I can say with complete honesty that the only thing I felt was small and preyed upon. Am I to understand that every woman you meet feels some major attraction to you? Is that what you're saying, my *dashing prince?*"

Breydon's jaw tensed. "Not me, Tiaponine, I'm not talking about me, per se. What I'm speaking of is a normal part of an interaction between a man and woman, though."

"That a woman feels a certain nervousness due to the attraction she has toward the opposite sex?" Tiaponine scoffed. "Have you ever thought that, perhaps, a woman isn't attracted to every man she meets? I can guarantee that I've felt no attraction toward a lot of the men I've met. Quite the opposite."

Grabbing the back of his stiff collar, Breydon turned away from her in frustration. "I think you've missed the idea here, and we've drifted off point," he muttered. "Forget about the whole attraction thing. What I'm saying is that you have to know your *position.* An abundance of self-confidence goes a long way when you're in a position of title."

"You could've just said that in the beginning," Tiaponine grumbled.

Letting out yet another deep, guttural breath, Breydon focused on one of the many painted ceiling tiles.

"Your Majesty."

Breydon turned to the servant, just appearing in the doorway.

"Yes," he said uneasily. "What is it?"

"King Hulbert demands your presence in the Great Hall."

"For what reason?"

"I..." The servant hesitated. "I don't know, sire."

Breydon closed his eyes, defeated, his head falling back. "Let me guess, Princess Gwenevieve."

"I... I don't..."

"I'll be right there," Breydon answered, ending the servant's discomfort. The servant sighed audibly in relief and hurried away. Facing Tiaponine, her penetrating scowl leveled on him, he growled to himself, "I'll be back."

"I guess I'll just pick up where our esteemed prince left off," Samuel announced once Breydon was well out of sight.

Tiaponine exchanged looks with VerGann—he appeared unsure whether or not Samuel was joking.

She shook her head at the servant, also taken aback. If she was unable to grasp the lesson as given by Draven's handsome prince, there was no way she was going to find sudden comprehension when it was delivered by the poor excuse for a man standing in front of her.

"So, let's give this another try," Samuel continued, taking a step closer to Tiaponine.

"Back off," Tiaponine hissed, and he did, just as quickly as he'd approached. "I'm feeling a lot of things right now, but attraction isn't one of them."

"Well, you got lucky," Breydon grumbled, entering the hall once again. "It seems that I've been volunteered to escort Gwenevieve around Draven."

Tiaponine knew her attempt to hide her relief was not successful when Breydon's face dropped.

"I'll come for you later. Right now I have to appease my uncle a little while."

She felt a pang of regret as Breydon turned and sulked out of the room. Once again, her training session had ended on a sour note.

"Shall we?"

VerGann was motioning toward the door.

"Yes," she answered. "The sooner the better." Ignoring Samuel, his face still scarlet, she joined VerGann.

"Princess Gwenevieve must've asked for the extended tour." Adjusting the pillow beneath his head, VerGann smiled. His brief sight of Gwenevieve clinging to Prince Breydon's arm earlier as he showed her around the castle had provided him an immeasurable amount of amusement.

At least Breydon's misfortune had freed up the rest of the day for himself and Tiaponine. Even Samuel had not bothered them.

Hearing a deep grumbling sigh, VerGann glanced at the open window along the back wall. Tiaponine had been sitting in it, staring out at the kingdom below, since they returned to her room an hour earlier. No discussion. No complaints. Just distant thoughts.

"Wonderful," she said, rolling her eyes. "In other words, Prince Breydon is going to be in a great mood when he gets back. I cannot wait. This morning was bad enough."

VerGann crossed his arms and legs as he reclined on the chaise. "This morning was amusing, Tee," he offered.

"It was *not* amusing. Nothing about it was amusing in the least," Tiaponine asserted, shaking her head. "If the prince had just stuck with the lesson of me knowing my position, there wouldn't have been any problem." She narrowed her eyes. "But attraction, intimidation? I still don't see the purpose of all that."

Counting the individual squares on the ornate patterned ceiling above, VerGann sighed. A part of him hoped he had heard the last of the discussion earlier that day. This was not a topic he wanted to delve into. Couldn't they just make fun of the prince and move on?

"VerGann?" Tiaponine pressed.

That unfamiliar anxious feeling was returning. VerGann groaned. The prince had botched the entire underlying meaning of the exercise. Tiaponine was irritated and confused, and he was left to clean up the mess.

Forty-two, forty-three…

"Tee, the prince obviously failed to get his point across." He laughed. "Whatever valuable lesson he started out with was lost when the swooning women entered the discussion."

"So you thought it was as pointless as I did," Tiaponine said, her tone upbeat.

"Not… *necessarily*," VerGann said slowly, still counting the tiles above. He could not believe that he had managed to take some remnant of understanding from Prince Breydon's lesson.

"What?" Tiaponine sounded incredulous. "You just said that the prince failed to…"

"While I agree that Prince Breydon came across as a babbling fool this morning, I do understand the point he was trying to get across."

Fifty-four, fifty-five… VerGann grimaced. It was not as though he had first-hand, personal knowledge on the matter.

"And what point would that be?" Tiaponine challenged.

Sixty-six, sixty-seven…

VerGann could not look at Tiaponine. He felt ridiculous trying to explain the lesson.

"Think of a man in his position, Tee," he said. "He walks through the hallways of the castle and every servant girl looks at him as though he's her one true love. They don't know him, but they know he's a prince, a future king, and very rich. They want to be a part of it all. They want that happy ending."

"I guess if Prince Breydon was in a room with Lerra and Eva, I'd feel sorry for him." Tiaponine agreed. "I mean, I felt sorry for you, and you're not even a prince. The way they talked about you was…"

VerGann closed his eyes to block the scary images entering his mind.

"I was hoping to forget about that," he mumbled. "But yes, that would be a good example."

"So Prince Breydon is the recipient of a lot of unwanted attention," she reasoned. "I concede that this would be annoying, but what he was talking about, what he was trying to demonstrate? I don't see how one relates to the other."

"I wasn't finished," VerGann said, smiling to himself. He admired Tiaponine's spunkiness. "I think the bigger point Prince Breydon was speaking to was intimidation. Any girl at the prince's side has to appear confident. She has to know that that's her rightful place. Although he failed miserably, he was trying to demonstrate certain interactions between men and women that you must be conscious of if this *relationship* is to be believable."

VerGann took a deep breath. He had managed to state the point of Prince Breydon's lesson in the least awkward way possible. They could now move on to a more comfortable subject.

"Show me."

VerGann was sure he heard Tiaponine right but found himself unsure as to how to respond. He stared at her without comprehension.

"A man can intimidate a woman just by his very presence? An intimidation that I have to learn to ignore so I can impress the king? How can I ignore something that I don't understand in the first place?" Tiaponine jumped from the window ledge with a pronounced thud, arms crossed. "Show me what he's talking about."

VerGann could feel a lump starting to form in his throat. Show her? Show her what? This was new territory for him. He swallowed hard.

"Tee, I wouldn't know the first thing about..."

"You're a man," Tiaponine interrupted, her eyes traveling once over him head to toe. "According to Prince Breydon, every man has that intimidation factor. You can be intimidating, can't you?"

Standing, VerGann smiled. "I can be very intimidating, but I assure you, it has nothing to do with being a man."

"Well, this time let it be only about being a man," Tiaponine pressed. "Please, VerGann. I don't want to go through another session like this morning. Just do your best."

Running his hand through his tousled blond hair, VerGann took a deep breath. He knew he would feel like a fool even trying to appear as though he knew what he was doing. But Tiaponine was not going to let this rest.

Deciding on a strict educational approach, he turned to Tiaponine. Locking eyes with her, he strode toward her with purposeful steps.

Her eyes widened and she stepped back with a gasp.

Her reaction caught him off guard. She would not even look at him, opting instead to stare at a fixed point on the ground.

"At the risk of sounding as ridiculous as Prince Breydon did, there is something to be said about close interactions between men and women. Let's take this, for instance," VerGann said, taking a step closer so Tiaponine, having nowhere else to go, was forced to stare at him. "More often than not, a man is going to be bigger than a woman, stronger than a woman—both of these facts alone can create an intensity between them without either one ever really doing anything." Leaning in so that he had Tiaponine blocked, his arms caging her in on either side of her shoulders, VerGann stared into her eyes. He raised her chin with his left index finger. "While I agree that attraction was *not* the best word to describe it, Prince Breydon was right in the basic idea."

VerGann concentrated on Tiaponine not a few fingers length from his face, very conscious of his tall frame towering over her.

He was confused. Void was the instinct to push him away or offer some smart remark, as she had with Prince Breydon. Tiaponine didn't seem inclined to do anything but stand and listen. Her attention seemed to hang on his every word, her eyes fixated on his slightest movement.

"A lot of men in Prince Breydon's position feed on a woman's tendency to fall apart in their presence," VerGann cooed, exaggerating the melodic, sultry tone of his statement. A faint smile crossed his features. "Men like him expect it, and it makes them feel more masculine."

Tiaponine seemed to be holding onto her breath. Taking her right hand and holding it up in front of him, VerGann backed up, pulling her with him.

"Breydon doesn't need a girl to, as he so eloquently put it, *swoon* over him. If he hopes to trick his uncle, the prince needs a girl who knows who she is and what title she carries." Bowing to Tiaponine, VerGann moved to her side. He felt her hand tighten in his as he escorted her down the center of the room. "Someone who holds her head high and assumes everyone around her envies her."

Without thinking, he placed his hand at the small of Tiaponine's back and turned her to face him.

"Look the man in the eyes," he instructed, again raising her chin so she would meet his gaze. "Let King Hulbert know that Breydon is *your* prince, the man you want to marry, and stand at his side like you belong there."

"I... I could do that, I suppose," Tiaponine managed to say quietly.

VerGann was at a loss for words. And he had been doing so well. There was a new nervousness between them, although it wasn't quite a negative feeling.

"And whatever you do..." He smiled slightly, breaking the momentary silence. "Try not to swoon over him."

The spell had been broken.

"It'll be hard, but I'll do my best," Tiaponine joked, stepping a comfortable distance from him.

Hearing someone clear their throat, VerGann turned. Prince Breydon was standing in the open doorway, confusion etched across his face.

"Well," Breydon said, his voice a bit hesitant. "I'm back."

"And your day with Princess Gwenevieve?" VerGann prodded, smirking. "How did that go? Is love in bloom?"

"It's too painful to talk about," Breydon muttered. "You try spending a day with the woman and see how you feel."

"Tempting." VerGann lied.

"Anyway, as much as I dread it, we must finish our lesson from this morning, Tiaponine," Breydon said, taking a deliberate step toward her.

Tiaponine did not retreat from his advance. The prince appeared confused, like he had anticipated being hit again.

"I had some time to think about my approach this morning, and I think it would've been better if I'd..." Breydon began, trailing off as Tiaponine inspected him up and down once with an air of indifference.

"Consider the lesson learned," she said.

Such boldness. VerGann was speechless.

"But…" Prince Breydon began again.

"A man can intimidate a woman. I need to ignore it and be confident," Tiaponine said, her gaze flitting toward VerGann a brief awkward moment. "I've got it. Let's move on."

Prince Breydon stood paralyzed as Tiaponine strode toward the door. VerGann suppressed a smile. Her newfound self-assurance was masterful, and attractive.

He cringed. His recent foray into these types of thoughts was confusing. Where were they coming from?

Moving past his own awkwardness, VerGann walked toward the door, making sure to smirk at the dumbfounded prince, and joined Tiaponine.

CHAPTER 8

Breydon adjusted his back against the ice-cold stone wall, grimacing.

Almost five days had passed, and Tiaponine had made little to no progress in her lessons. Her lethal attitude made it almost impossible to get through the day without at least one argument.

Breydon sighed, his eyes traveling to Samuel a few feet away.

Tiaponine's attitude might be better if not for the servant's constant jabs at her.

"I just don't know what else to do," Breydon grumbled. "Tiaponine isn't even trying, and it's too late to recruit another girl. My uncle won't stand for any more delays. I was lucky to persuade him to hold off on a marriage announcement at all."

"Breydon, you made the king's day." Samuel offered, laughing. "And Gwenevieve's."

Breydon smiled. His performance before his uncle and Gwenevieve that morning had been top notch. His uncle truly believed he had given in and agreed to marry Gwenevieve, who seemed more than pleased with the attention he was giving her.

"I put a lot of effort into making it believable," Breydon agreed.

"Believable?" Samuel repeated, his voice echoing through the corridor. "King Hulbert found it believable. Gwenevieve looked like she was going to run down the hall, screaming *he's mine* to all she encountered. She may have even commissioned a banner stating just that."

Breydon glared at Samuel, shaking his head to ward off the distasteful image from his mind. "*He's mine?*"

"Wonder where they're off to?" Samuel asked, staring out the small arched window beside him.

"Who?"

"Tiaponine and her *friend*."

At once, Breydon was on his feet, pushing Samuel to the side. He leaned out the tower stairwell window to see two dots exiting the outer eastern gate and running south. There was no mistaking Tiaponine's auburn hair, or VerGann's tall form at her side.

"EliSann," Breydon said, thinking out loud. "They're going to the EliSann Forest." He frowned. They were supposed to stay in the castle—what could they be doing out so late? "Stay here."

"What?" Samuel protested.

"Just stay here."

Breydon rushed through the tower door, letting it slam closed behind him.

It felt like months since VerGann had brought Tiaponine to the EliSann Forest, instead of the mere days that had passed.

She followed him without a word. They would not see any of EliSann's inhabitants on this trip. Special permission had been given for her previous visit.

VerGann smiled. This time, it was just the two of them. Just like old times.

Studying the deep gully close by and the massive winding trunks of the age-old trees, he slowed. On those rare occasions when he did bring Tiaponine to the forest, they almost always came here. It was secluded and very peaceful, a place of rest and security.

"I'm in way over my head," Tiaponine blurted out, upon coming to a stop. "I mean, look at me."

VerGann turned. He had thought she had moved past her insecurities by now.

"An idiot could tell that I'm not what I'm supposed to be."

"Are you really trying?" VerGann immediately regretted asking—Tiaponine looked hurt.

"What do you mean?" she asked defensively. "Of course I am."

"I see," VerGann mused. "Call me crazy, Tee, but threatening to tear Samuel apart limb from limb may not be the best way to proceed. You may be giving the wrong impression." He forced back a laugh.

"That was two days ago," Tiaponine offered. "And I will *not* apologize for that." She walked by him with her head held high.

"And the dip in the mud that Samuel and Prince Breydon took?" VerGann pressed.

Tiaponine let out a deep, frustrated breath as she climbed onto a low hanging limb of the nearest tree, her eyes avoiding him.

"At the swine pits?" she asked. "It was an accident. I was aiming only at Samuel."

It was obvious that Tiaponine was trying to hide her guilt.

"And the prince's lessons—which have all ended in either someone stalking angrily out of the room or some other type of confrontation?" VerGann continued.

Tiaponine bit her bottom lip.

"Not that it isn't comical, but..." VerGann gazed up at Tiaponine sitting on the limb above him. "Tee, you know that

I'm on your side. I always have been. But we're dealing with people who don't know the first thing about us, nor will they take the time to find out. I also know that you're not putting forth your best effort."

Again Tiaponine's face dropped. He extended his arms above him to help her from the tree branch. "What was the prince having you practice last night?"

His hands circled her waist. Tiaponine grabbed his shoulders as he set her down on the ground.

Her expression dropped. "He had me walking the lower hallways of the castle with two books on my head while he held my hand out to the side as though he were leading a horse down the street. When I dropped the books, which was often, he would make me curtsy to pick them up—something about a lady needing to be graceful in all things. He got angry and left before we were done."

"Grace it is, then," VerGann announced. "We'll start there."

"All right," Tiaponine agreed, defeated. "Did you happen to bring a couple of large books with you?"

"I think we'll just let the books remain an ill-conceived idea on the prince's part." VerGann took her hand in his. "We don't need them. I like the more practical approach."

Tiaponine followed him down the steep embankment and across a gathering of smooth, oval-shaped stones at the center of the narrow creek. At last they came to stand on a medium sized, grassy island of sorts. He could feel Tiaponine tense in front of him. The island seemed much smaller with both of them on it.

"Grace?" Tiaponine asked, her voice a bit shaky.

Releasing Tiaponine's hand, VerGann stepped back and bowed deeply from the waist. He then looked at her, waiting for her response.

With a mischievous grin, Tiaponine bowed to him.

"Try harder," he insisted with feigned seriousness.

Tiaponine tucked a rogue strand of auburn hair behind her ear, and curtsied in the most regal manner she could muster.

VerGann smiled. Having to balance on such a small area to avoid stepping into the surrounding water was quite helpful. Tiaponine had to pay attention to every move she made.

Taking both of her hands in his, he stepped right and then left, as though dancing to an imaginary ballad. Tiaponine followed his lead without question. He was thankful for her forced concentration. It distracted them both from how close they were on the small island.

As if the imaginary ballad came to a sudden end, they both stopped at the same time.

Tiaponine grinned at him, obviously feeling very accomplished. She grabbed his right arm and began to drag him across the oval stones and back up the opposite dirt embankment.

"Up here," she ordered, refusing to give him a chance to protest. In no time, they were atop the beautiful, grassy, cliff-like area that overlooked the creek twenty feet below.

VerGann gazed out over the forest with calm reflection. From here, one could see the warm orange glow of the distant setting sun descending upon the trees.

"Isn't it beautiful?" Tiaponine said.

Leaning against a tree at the edge, VerGann crossed his arms. "I've found myself here before, when I needed time to think."

Tiaponine closed her eyes and leaned over the embankment, extending her arms out to her sides as if she were a bird riding an invisible wind. "Lucky. I wish—"

"Finally!" a familiar male voice bellowed, shattering the serenity of the forest.

Not at all prepared for the unexpected interruption, VerGann jumped as Breydon charged from the tree line.

Out of the corner of his eye, he saw Tiaponine's arms flail about as she lost her balance. VerGann's heart stopped as she disappeared over the ledge with a shriek.

"No!" Breydon yelled.

VerGann reacted without thinking. One second he was atop the cliff, and the next he was standing in the ankle high creek water with a very visibly jarred Tiaponine in his arms, her eyes wide and her hands scrambling to grab at his shoulders.

Prince Breydon peeked over the top of the ledge above, paling considerably once he caught sight of the two of them. No doubt, he'd expected to see the worst. Finding Tiaponine safe in VerGann's arms had to be confusing.

"*Sorry, VerGann,*" came Vrenler's apologetic voice. VerGann could almost feel his friend grimacing as he silently spoke. "*I thought they came with you.*"

"*It's all right,*" he responded, glimpsing Vrenler hidden in the trees above them. "*I would've known he was there if I were paying attention.*" He stepped out of the water and let Tiaponine down.

"Are you alright?"

"Yes, of course." She was still shaking, though. "There are bigger problems to deal with right now."

VerGann agreed. This was going to be an interesting conversation.

"All right, would someone mind explaining what just happened?" Breydon demanded, skidding down the steep path next to the embankment to the creek below. He was still very pale.

"*Finally* what?" Tiaponine demanded, her voice a bit shrill.

"I found you," the prince said, aghast. "Finally. Now, mind telling me what is going on?"

Tiaponine swallowed, although it was very subtle. "What do you mean?"

VerGann appreciated Tiaponine's coyness. There was a chance, be it very small, that Prince Breydon had not seen as much as he thought he did, and VerGann did not want to tell the prince things he did not need to know.

Breydon stared at Tiaponine a moment, his face shrouded in disbelief. "What do I mean?" he echoed. "Him." He pointed at VerGann. "That…" He shook his head, blinking rapidly.

"What?" VerGann asked innocently. At least he could have a little fun at the prince's expense.

Breydon narrowed his eyes in mounting annoyance.

VerGann vanished, and reappeared behind the prince a second later. Breydon's brow furrowed in confusion, and VerGann tapped him on the shoulder. A weak sounding gasp escaped the prince.

"*Your Highness,*" VerGann teased.

A few feet away, Tiaponine bit her lower lip again.

"What *are* you?" Breydon demanded. "You are *not* human."

VerGann took a moment to consider the prince's question. He turned back to him with a feigned look of complete shock and hurt on his face.

"I think I'm offended. I *am* human. With a little something extra." Brushing past Breydon, a cocky grin across his face, he glanced at Tiaponine.

She bit her lower lip harder, shooting him a warning look.

To describe himself as human was not accurate in the least.

"VerGann is a delpin," Tiaponine said.

VerGann waited for the prince's reaction. Such a revelation had to be shocking.

"They don't exist," Breydon countered dismissively, looking him over once.

VerGann took a seat on a nearby rock, enjoying the prince's discomfort.

"You were misinformed," he answered, matching Breydon's dismissive tone.

"All right, a delpin," Breydon conceded.

VerGann continued to stare at the prince.

"What?" Prince Breydon said, almost snappishly. "Cut it out! You've managed to unnerve me, alright?" He turned to Tiaponine. "How do you put up with this?"

"I don't know what you mean," she answered.

VerGann forced himself not to laugh. Tiaponine shot him a stern look that clearly said, *please stop*. They both knew Breydon was scared. It appeared she felt bad for him.

"I knew it!" another voice boomed from the forest. "I couldn't put my finger on it, but now it makes perfect sense," Samuel announced. "A delpin."

Running his hand through his hair, VerGann kicked at the pebbled dirt below in tired amusement. *They,* Vrenler had said. Breydon *and* Samuel. "Great, now the reunion is complete."

"You followed me?" Breydon yelled.

"Of course I did. So, what are you?" Samuel prodded. "Some sort of guardian? A human girl as your best friend? Tell me, what're you getting out of this, VerGann?"

VerGann stilled. The servant's sarcasm was not lost on him, nor was his insinuation. He was not amused.

"Kind of reminds me of a bug that just won't squash," VerGann said. "Tell me, *your Highness*, what root were you smoking when you decided to make *him* your best friend and confidant?"

"Cute," Samuel mumbled through gritted teeth.

"Prince Breydon, I owe you an apology," Tiaponine interrupted before Samuel could continue to speak. "I made a deal with you, but I haven't kept up my end. I promise you'll get nothing but the best from me from this point on, though."

VerGann smiled as Samuel blew out an exasperated breath. It appeared the servant had been hoping she would not be returning with them.

Breydon took both of Tiaponine's hands in his. "It's Breydon, and apology accepted. I'm sure that I myself have quite a bit to be sorry for. Tell you what. Let's just start over, for real this time. We'll both try harder." He glared at Samuel, still seething close by. "We'll *all* try harder."

Samuel gritted his teeth.

"Good," Tiaponine agreed.

VerGann knew he should be relieved that Tiaponine and Breydon were on friendly terms again. But something did not feel right—why? He studied both of them, and Samuel, but he could not put his finger on what was causing his hesitation.

"We should be getting back, Breydon," Samuel interrupted. "It'll be dark soon, and King Hulbert will be looking for you."

"No doubt," Breydon grunted, kicking a branch at his feet. He bowed to Tiaponine. His face brightened as she curtsied to him. "We're making progress already," he mused. "I trust that you know how to get out of here, VerGann."

Without waiting for a response, he turned with Tiaponine and headed north. She looked back at VerGann, appearing slightly surprised by the abrupt manner with which Breydon had left, but he nodded at her and she relaxed visibly.

"*VerGann.*"

Again hearing Vrenler's voice, VerGann paused in starting after Tiaponine, Breydon, and Samuel.

"*Another Council meeting has been called,*" Vrenler continued. "*Tonight. We all have to be in attendance.*"

"*Another Council meeting,*" VerGann lamented, fatigued. "*And so soon after the last one?*" He laughed. "*Let me guess. Dreesdin and his gifted nymph?*"

"*That's my guess,*" Vrenler responded, his words dripping with sarcasm.

VerGann straightened his shoulders. "*I'll be there.*"

Upon arriving at the underground Council chambers, VerGann was not surprised to find Dreesdin already seated and waiting, clearly pleased with having been given what he wanted yet again.

Taking his seat across from Dreesdin, VerGann leaned back in his chair. He glanced at the other members of the Council now making their way around the narrow, earthen-walled room to their respective seats. Clearly, no one else wanted to be there, either.

"*Troops from Tatrus are camped to the east of the forest.*"

VerGann's attention moved abruptly to Vrenler. "*For what reason?*" he asked silently.

KaiDinn leaned forward at the table. "*Rumor has it that they're on their way to confront the Magdina.*"

VerGann was at a momentary loss for words. The Magdina—the warrior women that resided to the south of the EliSann Forest—were among the most dangerous humans he had ever encountered. Their hunting parties were known to attack unsuspecting villages or travelers from time to time. The women and female children were taken to add to their numbers. The men usually did not survive the encounters. It did not make sense why Tatrus would suddenly feel it necessary to confront them, though. It was not as if their numbers posed a real threat to Tatrus.

"Going to war with the Magdina?" VerGann said silently. *"I don't believe it. It doesn't make sense."*

"I know," Vrenler said. *"The delpins are keeping a close eye on the situation. It's Marlott's wish that this information not be shared with the Council. The nymphs' monthly trips to Draven have been cancelled for the time being."*

VerGann nodded. A measure of caution did seem reasonable.

"Thank you, my children, for your attendance," Marlott greeted, appearing at the head of the wooden planked table.

"She looks about as excited as the rest of us," Vrenler noted, shaking his head.

"Good," KaiDinn said. *"This should be a short meeting, then."*

"Dreesdin," the seratine announced, motioning to the nardin seated toward the center of the table. "It's my understanding that you have concerns regarding the Stone of GraVinn, ones that we haven't been made aware of yet?"

Chuckling to himself, VerGann leaned back in his chair so that he was balanced on the two back legs. *"Well... she's getting right to the point,"* he mused. *"I think good old Dreesdin is getting on Marlott's nerves."*

"He is," KaiDinn agreed.

"He's been at her chambers every time Nelliah so much as sneezes," Vrenler added. *"Her patience with the whole thing has run out."*

"Thank you, my lady, for agreeing to call together the members of the Council on such short notice, and yes, the news I bring came to my attention but a few hours ago." Casting an accusing glance toward VerGann, Dreesdin straightened in his seat.

"Your concerns, my son," Marlott asked. "What are they?"

"Nelliah's visions are getting more specific, my lady. She knows that the human girl, Tiaponine, has the GraVinn." Dreesdin stopped. "Well, maybe not Tiaponine, exactly, but a female in Draven, nonetheless."

At Dreesdin's words, a nervous chatter broke out in the room. Letting his chair fall forward with an audible thud, VerGann focused on the nardin across from him. He did not believe for one moment that Nelliah had a vision telling her about Tiaponine.

"And how would the nymph know this?" Vrenler asked. "We've all been forbidden to speak of the stone or its whereabouts with anyone outside the Council."

"You're suggesting that I told Nelliah where the GraVinn is, and of Tiaponine's role," Dreesdin accused. "I did no such thing. It was revealed to her in a vision."

Shaking his head, fatigued, VerGann was not sure how many more times he could take hearing of the nymph's visions. He exchanged a knowing look with Vrenler and KaiDinn.

"*I think I'm going to hurt him,*" Vrenler said.

"*Fine by me,*" VerGann agreed. "*This is a complete waste of time. Once again, I've been called from Draven for… this?*"

"Do you feel that Nelliah is seeking the stone herself, Dreesdin?" Marlott asked.

"No, my lady," the nardin answered without hesitation. "Of course not. My concern is that the human, Tiaponine, is staying at the castle in Draven, right under King Hulbert's roof. I don't think I have to explain why there's considerable room for concern."

VerGann contemplated Dreesdin a moment in silence. It was curious how the nardin knew Tiaponine was staying at the castle.

"The girl is at the castle, VerGann?"

VerGann's gaze fell upon the seratine. It had not crossed his mind to tell Marlott of this development, as he had seen no harm in it. "Yes, my lady, she is."

"And you're not concerned?"

"No, I am not. Tiaponine is at the castle because the prince has asked her to be there. It was her decision." VerGann kept his gaze focused on the ill-tempered nardin across the table. "I'm not in Draven to tell Tiaponine what to do, but to watch over her."

"You are correct," Marlott agreed. "It's best not to limit her. I trust you to tell us if there's a problem."

"But Nelliah has also seen the human girl's death," Dreesdin blurted out. "Any measure of protection the GraVinn has from falling into the wrong hands will be gone the instant she dies."

At Dreesdin's words, the room fell silent.

VerGann managed a deep breath.

"Nelliah saw Tiaponine's death," he repeated slowly, staring down the nardin. Dreesdin was taking the discussion to a very dangerous place. "At whose hand? Hers?"

All in the room watched in stunned silence at the building tension between himself and Dreesdin. No one dared speak.

"She didn't know any specifics," Dreesdin answered. "Just that the human girl she saw in her vision will be killed."

"I see."

"It's obvious that this news troubles you," Dreesdin continued. "Perhaps now you'll agree to meet with Nelliah? Take her seriously."

VerGann had to force himself to breath. If Dreesdin was looking to get a reaction out of him, his chosen path was a dangerous choice.

"Take her seriously?" he echoed. "I don't trust her any more than I did before." He narrowed his eyes. "Unfortunately for her, she's got my full attention, though."

"So you'll meet with her."

"No," VerGann said. "And if I ever see the nymph in Draven, I'll assume that she's there to make her own vision come true. I will handle the situation accordingly."

Letting a nervous laugh escape, Dreesdin turned to Marlott for help. "Marlott, a threat against one of our own? Are we to sit here and let this go?"

"VerGann knows the laws well," Marlott answered. "This does fall outside of those laws, however, as Nelliah is not from EliSann. I trust that he'll use restraint in dealing with her if it should come to that."

"So am I to understand that the delpins will be watching Nelliah's every move?" Dreesdin asked, a slight scowl on his face.

"No, we have better things to do," VerGann said. "If the nymph leaves the forest, though, I will be told, and I will be looking for her," he added, the slightest hint of a smile crossing his face.

The silence in the room was incredible as his words sunk in. Never had the Council witnessed such an intense exchange between two of their own. Dreesdin knew VerGann was the most powerful of the delpins. It was bold to challenge him in this way.

"I find it curious that just the very mention of the human girl could elicit such a reaction on your part, VerGann. It stands to reason that you've formed a close friendship with her, but if I didn't know any better..." The corner of Dreesdin's mouth curled up in a vicious smile. "Well, I'd say that you care for her as much more than a friend."

VerGann had thought he was prepared for anything that would come up at the Council meeting.

He had been wrong.

"While it's true that the delpins don't involve themselves in the emotional relationships I speak of, as it isn't in their nature, it stands to reason that VerGann, now a full grown man, may have *tendencies* that weren't there before," Dreesdin continued, turning to the rest of the table.

VerGann felt the eyes of everyone in the room on him. He couldn't bring himself to look up at Marlott.

"*Tendencies?*" Vrenler repeated, dismayed. "*Please explain.*"

"*No, no—don't explain. I want to go home... now,*" KaiDinn said, shifting in his seat.

"I'll ask you right now," Dreesdin continued. "Do you have feelings for the human girl?"

VerGann stared at the nardin, unable to think of anything to say.

"VerGann is very aware that it is forbidden to find love in the human world." Marlott stood, her demeanor stern. "Delpins and seratines are held to strict standards in this matter, for good reason. Our power is great and our loyalty must remain to our people. Should one of us fall in love with a human, and that love be spoken, our power would cease at that very moment. We'd become human." Her piercing eyes never left VerGann.

Forcing himself to face the seratine, VerGann made sure to keep his reaction in check. "I'm well aware of the law, my lady," he said. "It is unnecessary to bring it to my attention."

"I trust you do," Marlott agreed. "And I apologize, my son, if I put you in an awkward position. This is a very serious matter, though."

An awkward position only began to describe what VerGann felt at that moment. "I understand." Feeling as though he had taken all he could from the meeting at that point, he was eager to leave. "If there's nothing more, my lady."

"No, you are excused. Your attendance here is appreciated," Marlott said, nodding once.

In the next moment, VerGann vanished.

CHAPTER 9

VerGann's muscles were beginning to cramp. He had been balanced atop the marbled banister at the base of the Grand Staircase for close to an hour.

An hour of waiting and thinking, the events of the previous night vivid in his mind.

In a way, he would have much preferred to be void of thought altogether. It would have been much more settling. What had started out as a relaxing evening with Tiaponine had ended with threats, embarrassment and half-truths. He was mentally exhausted.

Turning his attention to Samuel pacing in front of him, VerGann let out a deep breath he did not even realize he had been holding.

His misery knew no end.

"Is she coming?" Samuel made another pass in front of him.

"She'll be here," VerGann promised, refusing to elaborate. His patience would not hold out if he was forced into conversation with the servant.

At the sound of footsteps on the marble floor, VerGann looked up to see Breydon bounce into the corridor.

"Where's Tee?"

VerGann's eyes narrowed. True, Tiaponine and Breydon had agreed to start over, but the prince seemed to be taking quite a bit of liberty with this new start. Nicknames for one. *Tee*. Some unfamiliar bitter feeling tingled in the back of VerGann's throat.

"*Tee?*" Samuel asked, his top lip crinkling.

"What?" Breydon asked, defensive. "This is a new start. I thought it would be…"

He trailed off as his eyes moved to the top of the staircase.

VerGann followed the prince's gaze.

Tiaponine.

VerGann found it impossible to look away as she descended the stairs. With the brilliant sapphire-colored satin dress billowing around her with every step, auburn hair pinned up at the back of her head so it fell in elegant long ringlets down her neck, she was mesmerizing.

He forced himself to manage his reaction. She was looking right at him.

Breydon was obviously more than pleased with what he saw. Jealousy lanced through VerGann.

"You're breathtaking," Breydon said, stumbling over his words. He stepped forward and took Tiaponine's hand to help her down from the last step. "I don't know what to say."

"Yes," Samuel agreed. "What happened?"

"I told you I'd try harder," Tiaponine offered, her free hand brushing against the fine satin of her dress.

VerGann hid a smile as Tiaponine's hand came to rest at the base of her neck. Her dress was very different than the plain frocks she was used to, different even from the dresses she was given when she first arrived at the castle. Suffice it to say, much more revealing than Tiaponine probably wished. To have three men looking at her had to make her self conscious.

"Beautiful," Breydon said, admiring Tiaponine once again.

"VerGann?" Tiaponine asked.

VerGann felt a lump form in his throat. He hated that he suddenly felt nervous.

"You are beautiful," he offered.

The soft smile that crossed Tiaponine's features warmed him.

"We're going into the city today," Breydon announced. Squeezing Tiaponine's hand, he turned toward the front entrance. A pristine white carriage was waiting at the base of the stairs outside.

"The city?" Tiaponine repeated, alarmed.

VerGann was taken aback by Breydon's declaration as well. Breydon had said he had something special planned. But a trip to the streets of Draven?

"Um... are you sure that I'm ready for this so soon?" Tiaponine asked.

Undaunted, Breydon took a step toward the entry, Tiaponine in tow. "Perhaps the best way to learn is on the job training." He smiled. "You'll pick things up faster if you're forced into the situation. Am I right?"

Tiaponine hesitated, her hand at her neck again. "Yes, I suppose, but..."

"You look fine, Tiaponine," Breydon assured. Turning to VerGann, he shook his head, a crooked smile crossing his face. "You, however..."

VerGann stood silent as Breydon examined his attire with a critical eye.

In the very next moment, Breydon grabbed a pile of cloth from a nearby servant and tossed it at him. VerGann held one of the two garments up. It was as he suspected. Attire very similar to that worn by Samuel.

VerGann stared back at Breydon with resigned silence. He realized his present clothing was not up to the standards of someone in the prince's company. He was sure that he could get by without having to wear the more formal clothing in his hands, though. He inspected the dark brown jacket in his hands and frowned.

He loathed it.

"May I say something?" Samuel interrupted.

"Samuel…" Breydon grumbled.

"What I was going to say was that—"

"I think it would be better for all concerned if you said nothing," Breydon interrupted curtly. Bowing to Tiaponine, he escorted her out the door.

Samuel's lips pursed as a deep red hue flooded his face.

Looking out the window of the carriage as it lurched to a stop in one of the many ruts along the cobble-stoned street, Tiaponine pursed her lips. This was one of the busiest parts of Draven, the marketplace of the upper streets.

Breydon seemed very confident this would work. If the people that she had spent her whole life with could not see through her charade, then progress had been made. He was one step closer to avoiding a marriage to Gwenevieve.

Tiaponine, on the other hand, could not suppress her overwhelming anxiety.

Taking a deep breath for good measure, she took Breydon's outstretched hand as he stepped from the carriage. Together, they walked down the center of the narrow, crowd-filled street.

Not one person trying to sell their wares approached them. Breydon came ready to draw attention. His royal entourage demanded notice. There could not have been one person on the street that did not recognize who he was.

She glanced at VerGann and Samuel, following a few steps behind. VerGann appeared bored. Samuel appeared unhappy, as usual. She swallowed hard and continued ahead.

As they walked, Tiaponine realized that she was receiving most of the attention. Seeing Prince Breydon with a woman at his side would be the topic of conversation at many a dinner table that evening.

At last they came to a stop, the sweet scent of hundreds of wildflowers permeating her nostrils. Tiaponine sighed. Draven's upper streets always had the prettiest selection of flowers. They were even more gorgeous today than she remembered.

Recognizing the merchant, a grumpy old man that she had been unfortunate enough to tangle with on more than one occasion, staring at her, she felt on edge. They had not even been on the streets of Draven an hour, and already her true identity would be uncovered.

The merchant dug in between a grouping of orange and yellow tulips and pulled one bright orange flower from the bunch. He gave it to her and bowed.

Tiaponine tried to hide her relief as she took the flower. "Thank you," she said, nodding politely at the merchant.

Her relief faded as she turned toward the next stand, and more to the point, the four men standing in front of it.

No matter what her appearance, Drake and his three cronies would be able to recognize her. All four of them were staring at her.

Her blood ran cold, and she risked a glance at Breydon.

He would find nothing regal or refined about an interaction with Drake. Perhaps she should apologize for ruining the fine dress he had given her in advance.

"What is it?" Breydon asked.

Tiaponine's stomach tightened. "It's nothing," she lied, wishing her words sounded a bit more convincing.

"Do you know them?" Breydon pressed, studying the four young men.

She did not want to answer. She swallowed hard as a new thought entered her mind.

VerGann. Drake was sure to recognize him.

She turned, but the delpin was occupied a few stands further down the street. Crisis averted.

Her heart stopped as Samuel motioned Drake and his friends forward.

Tiaponine could feel her anger building. Samuel wanted to expose her unease.

"Prince Breydon," Drake greeted, bowing clumsily. His three friends followed his lead.

Tiaponine managed her reaction. Drake's show of respect was awkward, forced. She wanted to laugh.

"My lady," Drake said.

At the sound of the uncharacteristic gentlemanly tone of Drake's greeting, Tiaponine turned to him, dumbfounded. He had to be speaking to another girl—but no, he was looking at her. He bowed once more. Tiaponine could do nothing but stand in shocked silence.

"Do you know this woman?" Samuel asked, his tone suspicious.

Seeming to take a moment to think about Samuel's question, Drake looked back at Tiaponine, perplexed. "No, sire. I'd be sure to remember a lovely face such as hers."

Lovely? Tiaponine had never heard Drake speak to anyone with such respect. It was quite unsettling.

She breathed a sigh of relief as Breydon nodded to Drake to take his leave.

"You're sure that you don't know him?" Samuel pressed.

"I've lived here my entire life," Tiaponine said. "It's possible that—"

"So you *do* know him?"

She glared at Samuel, who suddenly seemed distracted.

His eyes were not on her, but... her necklace.

Tiaponine fingered the faceted aquamarine colored stone dangling from the thin leather cord about her neck. The very sight of it seemed to pique Samuel's interest.

Tucking the necklace beneath the hem of her bodice, she turned from the servant to speak to Breydon again. "Where to next?"

Seconds turned into minutes and minutes turned into hours. By the time the noonday sun was high in the sky, Tiaponine was ready to return to the castle. She cast Breydon a hopeful glance, relieved to find him motioning in the direction of the carriage.

"Well," he said, a slight bounce in his step. "I'd call this experiment a complete success."

Tiaponine smiled, rather pleased with how things had gone herself. She glanced at VerGann.

He smiled, but it did not reach his eyes.

"I think we're ready for the next step," Breydon continued. "Samuel, I want you to mention to my uncle that another woman has my interest."

"What?" Samuel asked, his jaw dropping.

Tiaponine nearly choked. "Oh—Breydon, I don't know if I'm ready for this. I mean, the king's full attention will be on me."

"You're ready," Breydon assured. "I wouldn't suggest this unless I thought you were ready. Do you trust me?"

Tiaponine could feel VerGann at her side. He said nothing.

"I suppose I..." she started. "I mean, yes, I trust you." She could not believe what she was agreeing to.

"It's settled, then," Breydon said. "Samuel, approach my uncle tonight. Report back to me immediately. I want to know his reaction."

"Breydon, this isn't a good idea," Samuel complained. "What am I supposed to say?"

Breydon looked back at Samuel and nodded. "Just do it. Tonight." He turned to Tiaponine and took her hand in his. "Shall we?"

"Pesky insects."

Taking aim at two fireflies landing on the thick woven navy fabric of his sleeve, King Hulbert scowled.

"How I hate these gardens," he griped. "They do nothing but take up space and attract bugs."

Samuel followed his king in silence. For most, the lush flower garden in the northern courtyard was a place of rest and refuge from day-to-day palace life. For King Hulbert, it was just another annoyance in a long list of annoyances.

Samuel continued two steps behind the king, his impatience growing. One brief moment of time, that was all he needed. Breydon's instructions were very clear. Mention to the king that Breydon was in love with Tiaponine—or, *Lady Christine*—and report back with the king's reaction.

Seeing King Hulbert stop, a long frustrated breath escaping him, Samuel dared not take another step. His stomach tensed as the king turned toward him.

"What is it?" King Hulbert demanded.

"Sire, it's Prince Breydon."

Hulbert straightened, his jaw clenching. "What about him?" he asked through gritted teeth.

"He…" Samuel hesitated, suddenly doubting his decision to approach the king right then. "I shouldn't say anything, but…"

"What!" Hulbert snarled, his eyes boring a hole through Samuel. "You followed me out here. You'd better have a good reason," he said, taking a swing at another firefly. "And it had better be something more than to tell me that Breydon's unhappy. I already know that."

Samuel managed his reaction. Spurring the king's anger by a flippant eye roll would not serve him well.

"Sire, Prince Breydon has found another girl to wed." Samuel held back a smile as Hulbert's face turned a bright shade of red. As expected, his last statement captured the king's full attention.

"Princess Gwenevieve will be Breydon's bride," Hulbert snapped, his tone dismissive. With a huff, he turned.

"Yes, Sire, but he's actively engaging in audience with another woman," Samuel pressed.

King Hulbert turned, his eyes narrowing. "Who is she, then?"

"Lord Draughton's only daughter, Lady Christine," Samuel answered without hesitation.

Hulbert's scowl intensified. "And who, may I ask, is Lord Draughton?" he roared.

As expected, he found the unfamiliar name suspect. The king knew of every person of nobility from the surrounding kingdoms.

"I'm not sure, Majesty," Samuel answered, trying to sound innocent. The last thing he needed was for the king to relate him to the deceitfulness that may come to light in the future.

"Breydon's continued resistance to the inevitable baffles me," King Hulbert seethed.

"Your majesty?"

"Where is he?" Hulbert demanded.

The king's response was more intense than Samuel had anticipated. The king would not tolerate his nephew's antics much longer. Blood relative or not, Breydon was losing favor fast.

And so was Samuel. It would be in his best interest to appeal to King Hulbert in a way to make himself indispensable. He could think of but one way to reach the king.

Tiaponine's necklace.

"Sire, I don't know where Prince Breydon is at this moment," Samuel advised, taking a deep breath as he thought about his next words. "There is one more thing, sire. I noticed that Lady Christine has a very unique taste in jewelry."

"The point?" King Hulbert snapped, turning from Samuel and starting for the garden's entrance.

"Unique enough that I've never seen a necklace—or, should I say, a stone quite like the one at the center of this necklace—but once. You've spoken of it many times in the past."

Hulbert stopped, seeming to mull over his words a moment. Samuel's breath caught in his throat as the king turned.

"The Stone of GraVinn?" Hulbert asked, his tone incredulous. "Lady Christine wears the Stone of GraVinn?"

"I'm sure of it. It's as you've described it. I don't think she knows of its power," Samuel added, studying the king. "She hasn't even mentioned it."

"I assume Lady Christine has a travelling party?" Hulbert asked.

Samuel had a good idea of where Hulbert was heading with his question. "Lady Christine has no travelling party. But there's a delpin accompanying the girl, sire."

Samuel could feel his spirits lifting. It was clear that Hulbert believed him. At the very mention of a delpin, the king's demeanor stiffened. If a delpin was at Lady Christine's side, there was but one conclusion to be made. She wore the Stone of GraVinn around her neck.

"Get Breydon," Hulbert hissed. "I want to speak with him. This stays between you and me. The delpin, especially, can know nothing." He leveled his glare on Samuel. "Understand?"

The king's tone was clear. "Yes, sire," Samuel answered. A grin stretched across his features as Hulbert left, stomping atop a patch of yellow colored daffodils on his way.

"For your sake, you had better," King Hulbert called back.

CHAPTER 10

"My dear? Are you all right?" Madame Farault rested her hand comfortingly on Tiaponine's shoulder.

Breydon studied Tiaponine. The massive carved oak entry to the Great Hall dwarfed her in a way that made her appear frail and weak. Her uncharacteristic mental detachment was concerning.

He understood, though. His uncle was a force to be reckoned with. And to those meeting him for the first time, he was... scary.

A few feet away was VerGann. Even the delpin looked worried.

"I'm fine. Just nervous, I guess," Tiaponine answered. With shaky hands, she smoothed the skirt of her dress. "I can't believe that King Hulbert wants to meet me so soon. I mean, it was just yesterday that Samuel told him about me."

Clearing his throat, Breydon tugged at the ends of his jacket. He could not deny his own anxiety at the surprising turn of events.

"I know. I never expected him to demand an audience with you the very next day." Breydon glanced toward the closed oversized doors. "He's going to put up a fight. I just know it."

"Perhaps he's come around," Madame Farault offered hopefully. "Perhaps this is an olive branch, if you will."

VerGann snickered. "Perhaps," he said flatly.

Although not appreciative of the sarcasm, Breydon could not disagree. "He didn't say that he was in favor of my new relationship, only that he wanted to meet the girl in question."

Tiaponine offered the meekest of smiles to VerGann, who nodded in return. Breydon felt a new sense of anxiety rush over him. VerGann would never stand by and let her be hurt. Not that he believed this *introduction* would take such a drastic turn, but just the knowledge that the delpin was watching was enough to spur his anxiety.

"Time to go, dear," Madame Farault said, her voice tender as she brushed a rogue lock of auburn hair from Tiaponine's face. "Remember to say very little."

"I'm right beside you," Breydon offered, taking Tiaponine's hand and squeezing it.

The oak doors to the Great Hall opened to reveal a small gathering made up of the king, several servants, a handful of guards, and one very angry princess named Gwenevieve.

"Great," Breydon muttered, starting forward.

The walk toward his uncle's throne seemed never-ending. A look of disgust, mixed with a good dose of outrage, had taken over Gwenevieve's features.

Breydon squeezed Tiaponine's hand tighter, a smile escaping him as Gwenevieve's frown deepened. At last coming to stand before his uncle, he took a deep breath to calm his nerves.

As Tiaponine curtsied to the king, Breydon thought his uncle's expression changed to one of intense interest—a peculiar sort of interest, like a child finding a lost toy. But by the time he registered the look, it had already been replaced by a cold, hard stare.

Breydon looked Tiaponine over once from head to toe. Nothing out of place. But he could not ignore the sick feeling forming in the pit of his stomach. Something was not right.

"I've never heard of a Lord Draughton," King Hulbert announced, motioning for Tiaponine to step forward.

"Most likely not, sire. He died when I was but a little girl, my mother before him," Tiaponine offered, curtsying again.

Breydon held his head high. She was doing a wonderful job.

"Where did you meet?" King Hulbert asked.

"Prince Sigrid introduced her to me at Gypsom's wedding last year. Lord Draughton was a family friend," Breydon said—he had to admit, he was very proud of himself for the spur-of-the-moment answer. Throw a couple of big names around, and anything sounded believable.

"Why have I not heard of this girl until now?" Hulbert asked, his eyes boring a hole through his nephew.

Whatever hopes Breydon had of avoiding an argument were gone in that very instance. "I didn't think it was a good time," he said, knowing full well that his answer would not be enough for his combative uncle.

"I understand that Lady Christine has been afforded accommodations here already."

"Yes, Uncle, I…" Breydon started.

"Show the Lady Christine to her room," King Hulbert ordered, motioning to a servant woman nearby. "Everyone out!"

Breydon stood frozen a moment. No discussion, no fight. Was it over?

That was quick.

The Great Hall was a flurry of motion as everyone present scurried to take their leave. Tiaponine was already halfway to the door, a servant girl pushing her from the room as fast as she could.

With one last scowl, Gwenevieve spun around and left in a huff, apparently keen on making a dramatic exit. Breydon sighed, refraining from rolling his eyes, and turned to leave.

"It was not a good time?"

Breydon's jaw tensed at the sound of his uncle's voice.

"Your marriage has already been arranged, Breydon," King Hulbert admonished. "This girl, this *Lady Christine*, will be welcome here as a guest for a short while, but then she'll leave and things will continue as planned."

"Have you been listening?" Breydon fumed, feeling his skin turn hot with rage. "I do not want to marry Gwenevieve. I can see why you've chosen her, though—Santerine is the largest kingdom, second only to Draven. My marriage would put you in a measurable position of power, wouldn't it, lest something *horrible* happen to Santerine's princess."

"This isn't up for discussion." King Hulbert chuckled, his grin not reaching his eyes.

"Uncle..." Breydon protested. He hated how desperate his voice sounded.

"This matter is closed." Hulbert snapped one last time before standing and disappearing through the door to his left.

Breydon stared at the shut door, seething.

He was going to find a way out of this if it was the last thing he did.

❧❧❧

"It could have been worse, VerGann, a lot worse."

Silhouetted against the night sky in the open window, VerGann sighed. There was no denying that the meeting with the king had been a failure. He was just happy King Hulbert directed his anger at Breydon and not Tiaponine. After the king had cleared the hall, the prince had the unfortunate task of staying behind to face his uncle's wrath alone. He almost felt bad for him.

Almost.

Watching as Tiaponine adjusted the plush rose-colored blanket on the grand four-poster bed in front of her, VerGann could not ignore his immense unease. They were back in

Tiaponine's room—no lessons, no pesky Samuel—the evening was theirs to relax.

But he could not.

He had seen a gleam, the type of gleam one had when they were up to no good, in Hulbert's eye as Tiaponine was presented to him.

VerGann uncrossed his arms. Paranoia was not a feeling he often entertained, but he was taking the curious gesture on Hulbert's part seriously. He would be a fool not to.

"VerGann?"

He turned to Tiaponine. She had noticed his distraction.

"VerGann, you haven't said a word since we left the Great Hall. Mind telling me what's going on?" She pulled back the embroidered top blanket on her bed and pushed the pillows to the side. "I know the meeting with King Hulbert was rough, but like I said, it could have been worse."

"No, it's nothing, Tee," VerGann assured her, gazing back at the warm glow of the kingdom below. What about Tiaponine would elicit such interest from Hulbert? There had to be a reason.

His head fell back against the window frame as an answer popped into his mind.

The Stone of GraVinn. What if the king knew Tiaponine carried it?

VerGann closed his eyes. His stress was hinging on unbearable. How could Hulbert know? It should be impossible. But if he *did* know, she needed to be aware of the danger she was in.

To mention the stone to her was forbidden, though.

"What is it? I know when something's bothering you," Tiaponine prodded.

"I've been called back for a Council meeting tomorrow," VerGann answered. He was not lying, just avoiding a more uncomfortable conversation.

"Another one? You've been called back for more Council meetings in the past few weeks than the past three years put together. Is everything all right?"

"Everything's fine. For the time being, anyway," VerGann said, aware that he was being vague at best.

"*VerGann,*" she pressed. "It's me. Everything is not fine. Just tell me."

He looked at her, their eyes locking.

He let his shoulders fall. He could not do it anymore. He knew he was risking a lot—there would be consequences when he returned to EliSann, and Tiaponine would be angry with him—but his mind was made up.

He could not let the girl he had come to care so much about go another day without knowing the truth.

"Tee, I'll get into a lot of trouble for what I'm about to tell you. I've been forbidden to speak of it. But..." He sighed. "It needs to be said. You need to know."

VerGann could feel a knot in his stomach already beginning to form. There was no turning back now. With one sure step from the window ledge, he landed on the marble floor below, the sharp thud echoing through the room.

"I couldn't help but notice how the king *looked* at you this afternoon," he said slowly. "Something caught his interest."

"You noticed that too," Tiaponine said, laughing. "I thought it was just my imagination. Like he was *studying* me. I couldn't be that interesting to him."

"There is but one thing I'd expect Hulbert to take any measure of interest in." VerGann stepped forward. Stopping, aware of Tiaponine's confusion, he reached forward to finger the thin leather cord about the side of her neck. He pulled the necklace away from where it rested against her throat until the brilliant bluish-green rock rested in his hand.

Tiaponine glanced from her necklace to VerGann. "My necklace? The king has a taste for jewelry, does he?"

"Not the necklace, just the stone."

"I've had this necklace as long as I can remember," Tiaponine said, laughing, but now she sounded slightly nervous, realizing that he was serious. "I always assumed it was a family heirloom."

With each sentence, VerGann felt his anxiety increase. He was about to change how she viewed him, how she viewed her life thus far.

"It's not a family heirloom, Tee. You are meant to have it, though." He sounded tense, even to himself. He was nervous, and Tiaponine could tell.

"Meant to have it?" she repeated, her words hesitant. "How would you know that?"

"The stone in that necklace has a name. It's the Stone of GraVinn."

"The Stone of GraVinn?"

"There are stories of how it came into existence, but I cannot say that I believe any of them." VerGann shrugged. "It doesn't matter. Its creation wasn't an accident and not out of pure intention. It's amazing what can come from dabbling in things one should not."

Studying the stone in his hand, he paused. He had never held the GraVinn before, and it felt *wrong*. But as long as Tiaponine was wearing it, it was harmless. "This stone possesses a power so great that it has been sought by all walks of life, be them human or... not."

He resisted the urge to look at her. "No one knows what would happen if it fell into the wrong hands. I can assure you, though, it would be nothing good." He ran his finger over the stone. Now came the hard part.

"The story of the GraVinn begins a long time ago. Many years had gone by without even a mention of the GraVinn in EliSann. A select few of us knew where it was all along, but felt that it was secure; the couple that had come into possession of it was poor and wouldn't garner much notice. Their home seemed the perfect hiding place. We were wrong."

Looking up at Tiaponine, he let the necklace fall back. "I don't know how, but King Hulbert, new to the throne, discovered the GraVinn's location. He went to the couple's home, searching for it. He burned their entire village and killed almost every person there. He didn't find it. It seems that an old man fleeing the destruction with his infant granddaughter had wrapped the baby in a shirt he found. The GraVinn was in the pocket of that shirt. Anyway, Hulbert soon found the old man and killed him."

"And the baby?" Tiaponine asked after a tense pause, her voice barely above a whisper.

"He would've killed the baby as well, if not for Marlott," VerGann continued, trying hard to sound more detached from the story than he felt. "It wasn't in her power to destroy the GraVinn herself. She was, however, able to limit its use and thereby insure its destruction one day. Marlott placed the stone in a necklace around the baby's neck. As long as it stayed with the girl, the power would lay dormant. It would remain so, unless the girl willingly gave it to someone else. At that point, the Stone of GraVinn would be as powerful as before."

"Willingly," Tiaponine repeated, thinking out loud. "What if it's not given willingly?"

"If someone takes the stone from her by force?" VerGann asked. "The GraVinn should be rendered powerless. It'll be nothing but a rock. It would be easy to arrange for it to be taken, but Marlott isn't completely sure we'd get the desired result."

VerGann stopped as the possibilities ran through his mind. It was not something he preferred to think about. "It's too dangerous. It was decided that it would be better to keep watch over the GraVinn so that we knew where it was at all times. Marlott put a delpin in charge of the stone's keep."

"That baby... I'm that girl. Aren't I?" Tiaponine's voice trembled. "And you..."

The hurt in her face was something he would never forget.

"The numerous Council meetings have to do with concern over King Hulbert perhaps being aware of the GraVinn's location," VerGann admitted.

There was a long moment of tense silence, during which Tiaponine's expression flickered between hurt and something else—denial, maybe—before settling on anger. She examined the necklace, glancing from the stone to him and back again. Her fist clenched around it.

"You're in Draven with me because the seratine ordered you here," she said, her voice kept carefully blank. "And... and the awkward tension between us... it had to do with this necklace and nothing else."

Awkward tension. VerGann was without words.

"It was nothing but a delpin playing a part in order to keep watch over the GraVinn." Pulling the leather cord of the necklace over her head, Tiaponine thrust the loathsome object in her hand toward him.

"Here, take it," she said icily.

VerGann could not take his eyes from the Stone of GraVinn. He took several steps back, and Tiaponine recoiled slightly. Good. His response should frighten her.

"*Help me,*" he pleaded silently.

At once, two delpins appeared. Vrenler and KaiDinn glanced at one another, concerned, and then at VerGann.

"Tee," VerGann said, taking another step back to put additional distance between himself and the GraVinn. "I cannot take that. I cannot even touch that. If you aren't wearing it, there's no limit to its power, and... I'm *not* someone that should have access to that power, trust me."

Paralyzed, Tiaponine stared at the three delpins a moment. Her fingers closed around the Stone of GraVinn. "I'm tempting you," she said, her words regretful. She placed the necklace cord back around her neck. "I'm sorry. I didn't mean to..."

"I know," he said. "I'm sorry that..."

"No," she interrupted, the immense hurt she felt dripping off every word. "There's no reason to be sorry. You were just doing what was requested of you."

He winced. "Tee..."

"*No*," she interrupted again, her tone short and matter-of-fact. "I really don't think I can take much more truth tonight. I'll keep this *stone* close to me. You don't need to worry about it."

Glancing at Vrenler and KaiDinn, VerGann could tell both delpins were as nervous as he was. Tiaponine was hurt, and he was the reason for her anguish. It was an uncomfortable place to be.

He stepped forward, but stopped as Tiaponine took a deliberate step back from him, shaking her head. The conversation was over. She did not wish to continue.

"I need some time alone," she announced.

He stared at her, her eyes displaying a detachment that paralyzed him. He wanted so much to take the pain he had caused from her. The damage was done, though, and there was no turning back. The least he could do at this point was give Tiaponine what she wanted.

Some time alone.

Away from him.

Following Vrenler and KaiDinn's lead behind him, VerGann disappeared.

❧❦❧

"Yes, your majesty. You called for me?"

Not seeing anyone at first, Samuel let the library door close behind him. Except for a single glowing candle along the opposite wall, the room was dark.

Samuel's jaw tensed as his eyes adjusted. The shadowy image of Draven's monarch sat at the small wooden table near the candle, staring at a book open to a drawing of the Stone of GraVinn.

"I have a message for you to relay," King Hulbert ordered, watching the light from the candle flicker over the page.

"Yes, sire?"

"Three nights from now, a grand banquet will be held," Hulbert continued, his gaze never leaving the book. "The entire upper kingdom is to be in attendance."

Samuel watched the king with mounting curiosity. "A banquet for what occasion, sire?"

"To introduce the kingdom to their future princess."

"Princess Gwenevieve?"

"No, you fool," Hulbert snapped. "Lady Christine."

"Lady Christine?" Samuel could feel his upper lip curl. "Your grace, why…"

"That's not your concern," King Hulbert growled, pounding his fist on the table. "Your duty is to do what I have ordered."

"Yes, sir," Samuel said, dropping any hint of disgust he'd been inclined to show. "Right away."

He turned to leave.

"Finally!" the king roared behind him as he hurried down the corridor.

⁂

The thin rays of moonlight from the many tiny holes in the ceiling accented everything they touched with a mysterious beauty. VerGann took in his tiny underground home with quiet reflection. It was the perfect place to gather his thoughts.

He unbuttoned his embroidered, dark brown jacket with resigned annoyance. Breydon had demanded he wear the uncomfortable, stiff attire when Tiaponine was introduced to King Hulbert.

His stomach knotted as his last conversation with her repeated in his mind.

It was painful to think Tiaponine was even the slightest bit angry with him. As much as he hated it, though, she needed time to herself. And so did he.

Throwing the jacket onto the simple bed at the center of the room, VerGann ran his hand through his hair.

"Finally, I get to meet the *elusive* VerGann."

Turning, VerGann took in the small framed, dark-haired young woman standing in his doorway. He had to be distracted, not to notice her approach.

He carefully kept his face void of emotion. He was unfamiliar with this nymph. And for her to just walk into his home unannounced was concerning.

This had to be the nymph Dreesdin spoke of. Nelliah.

"Elusive," VerGann repeated, turning away and adjusting the loose fitting undershirt about his shoulders. "Not elusive. Just unavailable to those that I have no desire to speak with."

"It's strange to see a delpin as a full grown man," the nymph admitted. "Strange and... captivating. Physical maturity has been very kind to you."

Turning, he glared at the nymph.

Straightening her shoulders, Nelliah stepped forward. "I apologize, I should have introduced myself."

"I know who you are," VerGann interrupted. After the events earlier that evening, he was in no mood to oblige the nymph with forced politeness.

"Do you?"

"A nymph from the BarLonn Mountains with several weak-minded nardins wrapped around her little finger." He returned to the buttons on his shirt.

"I can assure you, I've parted ways with the BarLonn," Nelliah said. "They aren't a representation of who I am, of what I believe."

Smiling, VerGann shook his head. "I see," he laughed. "Well, what I know to be true is that the BarLonn hate everything about EliSann. Their children have spent a lifetime hearing of how the seratine, with the evil delpins at her side, saw to their expulsion those many years ago, and how all of EliSann must be held responsible for that injustice. I don't think it's hard to understand why I might question your loyalty."

VerGann was sure he saw the briefest scowl cross Nelliah's face.

"I understand your concern," Nelliah assured. "Again, I say to you that I left many years ago, and, as such, I've been free from any ill words regarding your people for that time. I come here for the sole purpose of offering help to EliSann by means of my gift. My *visions*."

Upon hearing the unmistakable rattle of stones being dropped on the wooden table at the bedside, VerGann clenched his jaw.

"I'm sure that Dreesdin has informed you that I believe the girl you watch over in the city may know where the Stone of GraVinn is," Nelliah said, replacing her leather pouch at her side, her gaze shifting from one stone to the next. "For Marlott to place a delpin as powerful as yourself at the girl's side all of these years, well, it stands to reason that you're not simply providing her with companionship."

"The reason I'm in Draven is of no concern to you," VerGann answered, his tone icy.

"And if I were to tell you that I saw the girl in a vision?" Nelliah pushed.

Grinning to himself, he looked at the nymph. "Yes, I've heard what you have seen in your *visions*," he said. "Everything."

Again he noticed a measurable amount of nervousness rush over the nymph.

"My visions always come true, VerGann."

Very aware of how uncomfortable he was making the nymph, VerGann nodded his head and smiled.

"But Dreesdin has told you of what I've seen," Nelliah continued. "It would be wise to listen to your fellow Council member."

"And I'm sure Dreesdin has told you what I had to say about it," he shot back. For the briefest of moments, his eyes locked with Nelliah's. Judging by her fearful expression, his message was understood. There were no words she could offer to make him trust her.

"You don't know me," Nelliah shot back. "I'm not who you believe me to be."

"You are exactly who I believe you to be," VerGann said, glancing down at the smooth black stones on the table. "You know it, and so do I."

"But…"

The nymph had outstayed her welcome. Not that she had one in the first place.

"It's time for you to go. Take your *rocks* with you," he said, waving to the stones littering his bedside table.

Pushing the candle on the table to the side, the nymph leaned over to study the stones spread across the wooden surface.

Almost at once, the entire assortment flew from the table and, without a sound, disappeared through a small hole in the ceiling to land somewhere in the forest above.

"Uh-uh," VerGann said. "Not here."

Nelliah stared back at the delpin in stunned silence.

"And just so there's no misunderstanding," VerGann said, turning his back to her as he started through the rounded opening in the earthen wall leading to a small room at the back of the dwelling. "My home is off limits to you. I may be gone more than I'm here, but trust me, I will find out."

"A grand banquet. Preparations are already underway."

Lundane slowed, his eyes darting from the castle guard to Sandis. "In Draven?"

The guard took another deep breath. "Yes," he panted, his raspy intake of breath causing gray clouds to form in the night air. "A big announcement of some sort. All of the upper kingdom is to be in attendance."

Lundane crossed his arms, his thoughts racing. His eyes darted around the Tatrine garden. No one else was nearby. "What would call for such a lavish event?"

"My friend, does it matter?" Sandis asked, a sudden excitement in his words. "This is the distraction we've been waiting for. True, we won't be in place to march on Draven before then, but Hulbert won't be prepared for our attack in the days following. That's a chance I want to take."

The stout little ruler did have a point. There would never be a more perfect time.

"Gather the rest of the troops. We march toward Draven tonight," Lundane ordered. "Send word to the Tatrine guard outside of EliSann of our approach. We'll meet up with them, and then…"

"We attack," King Sandis finished.

"We attack," Lundane repeated.

CHAPTER 11

"New candles on the head table, ladies! Fresh flowers lining the court!" The high-pitched voice rang out over the commotion in the castle hall.

VerGann's eyes drifted over the flurry of activity around him. Something was up. Every servant in the king's charge scurried back and forth, each with a specific mission.

He walked with heavy steps and a heavy heart. He had not slept a wink the night before, unable to stop worrying about Tiaponine. Afraid of how angry she might be with him.

But, as uncomfortable as it was, he had to come back. After all, Tiaponine's safety was important to him, and he was still in charge of watching over the Stone of GraVinn. Having to explain his time away from Draven to the EliSann Council was not something he was willing to deal with at the moment, either. They would have little understanding for his personal troubles with his best friend. Dreesdin would relish the opportunity to bombard him with questions. He did not have the strength to handle it, right now.

"Quick now, girls!" a maidservant called out. "The king demands nothing short of perfection for Prince Breydon's bride-to-be."

VerGann halted midstep, unsure whether he had heard that correctly. Breydon had decided to go ahead and get married? He hadn't expected the prince to surrender so easily, after setting up such an elaborate charade to worm his way out of this.

"Fresh linens to Madame Farault! Lady Christine must look her best when introduced—"

At that, VerGann's blood ran cold. *Lady Christine.*

Breydon was marrying… Tiaponine?

He pushed past the nausea beginning to overtake him and turned down a side hall. The sudden change of heart on the king's part was curious, not to mention troubling. The last time he had seen Hulbert, it was very clear that he had no intention of entertaining Breydon's new love-interest. But now…

"VerGann, a moment of your time, please."

Hearing Breydon behind him, VerGann sighed.

"*Sire*," he greeted.

"Sire," Breydon repeated, annoyed. "Just leave the formalities to my uncle." Noticing the sidelong gazes of several servants passing by, he retreated into the nearest doorway off the hallway. "In here."

His already less-than-good mood rapidly souring, VerGann followed the prince through the door. Looking around the storage room, he noticed that not a single shelf was lacking a sword, battle axe or crossbow.

"Problem?" he asked, raising his eyebrows at Breydon.

"No," Breydon answered, frowning. "You appear not in the best mood, VerGann. Mind sharing what—"

"You had a question."

"Uh, yes." The prince cleared his throat. "I was just thinking about something you said earlier. About Tee."

"Tee?" VerGann repeated. He was even *more* uncomfortable now with Breydon's use of Tiaponine's nickname, given their upcoming marriage. The dagger had been placed in his heart. The prince was twisting it. Was he aware of that?

"About you being her guardian."

Chuckling to himself, VerGann shook his head. "I don't recall saying anything like that."

"All right, not those exact words. But you're a delpin… accompanying a human girl."

"Very observant of you," VerGann sighed. He knew Breydon meant well, but why must he be so curious? He did not want more reminders of the reason Tiaponine was so upset with him.

"I did some checking," Breydon continued. "Rumor has it delpins never grow past adolescence. Yet you appear to be at least my age. Why is that?"

"You don't think I'm a delpin?" VerGann raised an eyebrow. "Should I prove it again?"

"Um... No." Breydon cleared his throat. "I don't doubt that you are, but a delpin living outside of the EliSann Forest? You've lived here with Tiaponine for almost seventeen years as best as I can tell. Why?"

He had thought quite a bit about this. "And all of this makes me some sort of guardian, in your eyes?" VerGann asked.

"*VerGann...*" Breydon grimaced, appearing fatigued. "It's just irregular. There has to be a simple answer for it."

VerGann studied Breydon, conflicted. When it came right down to it, he liked the prince, even if the idea of Tiaponine marrying him shattered him inside.

"Sure," he said. "I prefer not to think of myself as a guardian. Let's just say that something specific was requested of me a long time ago. Watching over Tiaponine happened to fall in line with that. I grew with her because that's what humans do. They grow up." He allowed a cocky smile to cross his face. "I assure you, I'm much more than twenty, though."

"All right," Breydon said, lowering his voice as two servants passed in the hall outside the door. "Watching over her for what reason?"

VerGann clenched his jaw, unrelenting. It was dangerous enough that Tiaponine knew about the Stone of GraVinn. He was not going to give the prince that information.

"Why Tiaponine? Is something going to happen to her? What does she need protection from?"

"I'm not sure, Breydon," was all VerGann could say.

Breydon studied him for a long moment, a layer of disbelief etched in his expression. But he sighed in defeat, evidently deciding there was no hope of getting VerGann to explain any more. "Very well. I'll leave you alone now." He turned to leave.

"Wait," VerGann said, catching the prince's attention before he got to the door. "In the beginning, it may have been the case, but now…" He swallowed. "It would be a lie to say that I stuck around all these years simply because I was ordered to."

Even that simple statement hurt him. He supposed it was almost too close to the truth—which he was not allowed to say, to himself or to Tiaponine or to anyone.

Breydon nodded. "I'm sure you've heard that my uncle has agreed to my marriage to Tiaponine. He's going to introduce her to the kingdom tomorrow at the banquet."

The prince appeared nervous. His words felt like another knife twisting in VerGann's chest.

"Yes," VerGann said, forcing a smile. "That's how it was supposed to go, wasn't it? It won't be long until Gwenevieve is on her way back to Santerine."

Breydon opened his mouth as if to say something, but then just shook his head, turned, and left.

Taking in the weaponry behind him, VerGann let out a deep breath. His brief time back in the castle had been just as exhausting as the previous night. The next matter of business was to find Tiaponine and hope she would not turn him away.

He left the room with an even heavier heart than when he'd entered it.

Without VerGann, Tiaponine felt even more lost than before, and that was quite a feat.

Of course, his news had hurt her—the fact that he was in Draven because he was ordered to protect her felt like a slap in the face. But that didn't change the many years they'd spent together, relying on each other—there was no denying that their relationship went far beyond just an amiable existence.

If he'd faked his entire friendship with her, he was the most skilled actor ever born. She just did not believe it.

Hearing the light chirp of a cricket along the lush floral-lined path, Tiaponine snapped out of her reverie. It was Breydon who had suggested they take an evening walk through the garden in the western courtyard. Silvery rays of the moon cast an eerie, yet calming, glow on everything they touched.

She glanced at Breydon, walking at her side. He had not uttered a word since they entered the garden, yet she was well aware that he was watching her. It was almost as if he was afraid to say something.

She steadied her nerves. There were many reasons for her to be uneasy about Breydon's silence. He had changed recently. Not a bad change, by any means, just a concerning one.

His plan had worked. She was marrying him, and a very unhappy Gwenevieve was sure to be on her way back to Santerine within a few days. The charade was almost finished— an overwhelming relief.

That's what it should be, anyway. But the unfamiliar thoughts and emotions disrupting her nerves recently were incredibly distracting. Stepping over a wayward rock that had rolled from the side of the path, Tiaponine risked another glance at Breydon.

Those unfamiliar thoughts and emotions had nothing to do with Draven's handsome prince, though.

"You're amazing."

"What do you mean?" Tiaponine asked.

"Look at you," Breydon said, grabbing at the back of his neck and grinning. "I'd never have guessed it was possible."

"Oh." Tiaponine focused on the dirt path at her feet awkwardly.

"No," Breydon stammered. "I'm sorry. That didn't come out right. Let me try again. You're a very beautiful girl, Tiaponine."

Tiaponine laughed to herself.

Every girl in Draven dreamed of hearing Prince Breydon say such a thing to her. So why did it not affect her the way it should?

"I'm not sure if you believe me," he added gently.

She sighed. She knew Breydon meant every word he said. She just did not want to encourage him.

"Breydon…"

"No—please—just think about it," he interrupted. "This beautiful person has been hidden from the world by a cover of rags and a quick tongue. I think back to the first time I met you, and…" Moving to step in front of Tiaponine, he looked her directly in the eyes. "Tiaponine, it's as if you're a different girl. I really like this girl."

"It's just a dress, Breydon," she mumbled, tugging at the copper colored skirt beneath her fingers.

"That isn't what I mean."

Tiaponine didn't respond, and Breydon shifted anxiously. She was afraid she knew where he was going with this, and he seemed to sense her hesitation.

"I… I know that all of the frills of living in the castle aren't to your liking, but I don't think living on the streets is, either. Don't you want to stop running?" His voice had gone soft. He took her hands in his, waiting for her to look up at him before continuing.

"I can… I can do that for you," he whispered, and then hesitantly leaned in to kiss her.

And she turned her cheek.

She felt Breydon's momentary pause. She felt him kiss her cheek and take a step back. She could hardly bring herself to look at him.

"Well," he said softly, a small smile crossing his face as he let her hands fall to her side. "Tomorrow night you'll see what the rest of us see." There was a flicker of something pained in his expression.

"Your uncle changed his mind very suddenly. I just cannot help wondering why," Tiaponine said, pushing past the awkwardness between them.

"I know. But nothing makes sense where my uncle's concerned, frankly." Breydon laughed, though his smile quickly disappeared. "Are you having second thoughts about this, Tee?"

The question caught Tiaponine off guard.

"No," she said, trying to ease his mind. "I made a promise, and I'll keep it. This means a lot to you."

"Yes," he agreed. "But I also want you to be happy."

"Happy," she repeated. "How could I be anything but happy? Food, shelter… Things I could never count on until now. When this is over, VerGann and I will have everything we could ever want or need."

"VerGann…" Breydon's face fell. "Yes, you will. You deserve it. These are things that you should never have had to worry about, even before you agreed to all this. And VerGann. What can I say? You're… very lucky to have him as a friend."

Tiaponine smiled. She could tell Breydon's last statement was not quite heartfelt. "Yes, lucky."

"Well," Breydon said, holding his right arm out to her. "It's late. Shall I escort you in?"

His hopeful expression only made her feel more guilty. The prince's feelings for her complicated things.

"No, I think I'll walk a while longer," Tiaponine said, looking down at the calming trickle of water over a few smooth stones in the stream alongside the path. "Thank you, though."

Kissing her on the cheek once again, Breydon nodded. "Good night, then."

Instead of watching him leave, Tiaponine found herself concentrating on the stars. Her eyes stung with tears.

She was in way over her head. The banquet, the king, Breydon's feelings... and no VerGann. Where was he? The overwhelming confusion was only amplified by his absence. She glanced from the stream to her beautiful, embroidered dress and gritted her teeth.

It would be frowned upon for a lady to be found wading through the stream, but she wanted to do something a little bit reckless right now. It would not be the first time her behavior had been called into question at the castle.

Kicking off her uncomfortable—and, undoubtedly, expensive—shoes, Tiaponine raised her skirts just enough that they would not get soaked. She stepped into the cool water, and felt a wave of contentment wash over her.

At least until she noticed her reflection in the water.

Even aside from the fact that the ripples dancing on the surface of the stream distorted her image, she was unrecognizable. The perfect-looking dress, her hair tamed and flawlessly curled, her posture... None of it felt familiar. She kicked at the image, which of course did nothing but disrupt it until the water settled back into its slightly rippled surface. She tensed as another image joined her reflection.

There he was...

"Disrupting the flow won't make the reflection change," VerGann noted.

Tiaponine's head dropped. "It already has," she sighed. "I've been disrupting things since the day I entered the castle."

"Different clothes, different surroundings..." VerGann said. "Same you."

"*Not* same me," Tiaponine said. She appreciated VerGann's attempt to make her feel better, but she knew the truth. She was but a shadow of the person she was before.

"It's as Breydon said. I'm a different girl." She took a deep breath. Her bodice suddenly felt constricting. "He said I was beautiful, VerGann." With one foot, she kicked at a rock on the bed of the stream. "What am I supposed to say to that?"

"He's correct," VerGann offered. "But that doesn't come from fancy clothes or the company you keep." Pausing to think about his words, he looked at the ground. "If I'm being honest, I think he knows that."

For a brief moment, Tiaponine heard something like sadness in the delpin's voice.

"What have I gotten myself into?" she asked, not expecting an answer. "Breydon, he..." She paused as the image of the prince leaning in to kiss her entered her mind. Snapping out of her dreamlike state, she was surprised to see VerGann staring back at her as if he could see the images in her mind.

With the side of his finger, he wiped a tear from her cheek. "Tiaponine, I'm sorry. I know that you're hurt and angry, and you have every right to be. Forbidden or not, I should've told you the truth about everything long ago."

"I'm not angry," Tiaponine admitted, avoiding the delpin.

"But you are hurt."

Letting out a deep breath, Tiaponine turned her focus to the calming stream once again. "I guess I always assumed that you were in Draven because... *of me*. It frightened me to think that you were only here because you were ordered to be."

"When Marlott asked me to go to Draven, it was understood that my primary duty was to keep an eye on the GraVinn. Any contact I had with you was to be limited. I grew so it would be easier for you to relate to me. The point was that you would feel comfortable around me, to make my job easier."

Again, Tiaponine could feel the tears starting to collect at the corners of her eyes. She straightened her shoulders, determined not to let them fall.

"Tiaponine..." VerGann said, raising her chin with his index finger so that she was forced to look at him. "I couldn't do it. I liked being with you, and despite concerns from Marlott, I continued to pursue a friendship with you. The GraVinn became far less important than my relationship with you. And as the years went by... I realized that..."

He stopped.

His words were heartfelt, honest, and not as surprising as she knew they should be. This alone gave her pause as she dwelled on the array of her own confusing feelings. She let a slight smile brighten her face.

"Much better," VerGann mused. Taking her hand and stepping onto the dirt embankment at their side, he helped her step from the water.

Walking at VerGann's side as they followed the stream deeper into the garden, Tiaponine was happy to see that all seemed to be returning to normal between them. The night was beautiful, the breeze cooling and the sound of the frogs along the bank was...

Tiaponine jumped as a frog leapt from its hiding place among the cattails and into the water, splashing a fair amount of mud all over the hem of her dress. She was speechless.

"There," VerGann offered dryly. "This is a little bit like old times."

Tiaponine's jaw dropped. "Great," she muttered, wiping at the fresh muddy splotch on her skirt—in vain, as it had already left a stain. Sighing, she reached down to take a sizeable amount of mud from along the bank in her hands, and let the thick substance fall down the front of her dress.

"Oh, your maidservants will *love* that."

She wiped her mud-covered hands down the front of VerGann's shirt and looked up to see his reaction. Shock at first, and then…

A mischievous grin crossed the delpin's face. Tiaponine's eyes grew large. In the next instance, she was running through the garden, VerGann giving chase behind her.

Her heart beat out of her chest as she peered out from behind the overgrown, twisted tree where she had taken cover. VerGann was no longer in sight.

The sudden force of a sizeable mud ball hitting her from behind sent Tiaponine running again, but not before she was able to return a mud ball of her own. She laughed in delight as VerGann stepped into the stream and ran his fingers through his now-muddy hair, sighing.

Without warning, Tiaponine launched herself onto VerGann's back. The delpin desperately tried to remain standing.

It was useless. He fell back into the stream, Tiaponine still clinging to his back.

Shocked at how deep the water was, Tiaponine righted herself and stood up in the waist high water. She could not have known that the sizeable ledge existed on the creek bed. "VerGann?" she asked, spluttering a bit.

She gasped as VerGann sprung up in the water, right in front of her. Losing her balance, she fell back onto the muddy bank. The thick brown mud oozed around her, seeping through every piece of fabric on her body.

The cold left her in shock for a few moments. Now she wished the game had ended earlier.

Standing, VerGann offered his hand to her. She took his outstretched arm and pulled him back into her. She was not going to be the only one to take a mud bath that evening.

VerGann fell forward to land over her on the muddy bank, one arm braced on either side of her shoulders. Dazed, he raised his head.

Tiaponine swallowed hard. He was not three inches from her face. They had never been this close before, and it should have been enough to send both of them scurrying away, embarrassed, but… it was not.

Their eyes locked.

Time seemed to slow.

"Lady Christine!" a voice called from the garden entrance.

"They're looking for you," VerGann said, his head turning toward the outline of Madame Farault in the garden entrance.

Tiaponine felt numb. She stared at him, then looked away as he turned back to her.

"I'm expected back in EliSann tomorrow night," he said, rolling to her side. "I'll return to the forest in the morning."

Composing herself, Tiaponine stood.

"You mean you're going to leave me on my own at the banquet?" she complained. "I'm sure that'll go well."

"I don't have a choice, Tee," VerGann apologized. "You'll be so busy, I doubt you'll even notice."

He stood, his clothing soaked through with mud. Tiaponine again hoped he did not catch her staring at him. "Will I see you later?"

"Yes." He grinned, pulling her up from the mud beside him. "But I seem to have a little cleaning up to do first."

With one last defeated grumble, Tiaponine walked toward Madame Farault. It was no surprise to see the maidservant's jaw drop at seeing her in bare feet and covered in mud from her neck down.

When she turned back to the garden, VerGann was already gone.

Taking a quick glance around the familiar surroundings of his underground home, VerGann felt calmer than he had in days. It was amazing how so much anxiety could be dispelled in a single night.

Peeling the mud-soaked shirt away from his chest, he laughed to himself. He was an utter mess. No doubt Breydon would have taken quite a bit of enjoyment from his appearance.

At the sound of a very long sigh, he whirled around. It only took a moment to find the source of the noise– a sprite nestled under a cloth on his bedside table.

VerGann put his finger to her side to nudge her awake. He laughed as she stretched a moment, her delicate wings spreading out wide.

"Nat," he whispered. "Natimae."

At once, the sprite was on her feet, her breath coming in short spurts.

"It's just me, Nat," he soothed.

"What're you doing here?" the sprite asked, embarrassed.

The question seemed odd, given that they were standing in the middle of his bedroom.

"I was about to ask you the same question," VerGann said. "What's going on?"

"I volunteered to stand watch," Nat said. "I don't know what you said to Nelliah at your little meeting, but by the great oak, she was angry. She refuses to speak to the delpins."

"I'm sure they care," VerGann said, turning his attention to the dresser along the back wall.

"Oh, they're *crushed*," the sprite answered with a dramatic eye roll. "Anyway, with the delpins so busy, I volunteered to stay back here, in case she decided to stop by again." Putting her hands on her hips, she stomped forward. "What happened to you? I'd say you're making a mess of everything, but it seems rather pointless seeing how this *is* your room."

For just a moment, VerGann had forgotten his reason for returning home in the first place. "It's a long story," he said, once again peeling the mud-soaked shirt away from his chest and running his hand through his muddied hair.

"And one that I have time to hear."

"Nat."

Hearing KaiDinn's unexpected reprimand from behind, Natty sighed. "Good timing," she muttered dejectedly.

"I'd say perfect timing," KaiDinn answered with mock displeasure.

"Come on," Natty complained. "You *know* you want to hear what happened."

With a slight chuckle, VerGann turned to KaiDinn. "Nat says the delpins have been busy."

KaiDinn appeared uncomfortable.

"Yes… It's come to our attention that Nelliah often goes missing," he said. "No one knows where she is during these absences, just that she isn't *here*."

Troubling news, but not surprising. "Have you been able to follow her?"

"No," KaiDinn said, extending his hand to Natty. "It's hard to know when she's gone unless we watch her every move. We'd be noticed at some point."

"And Marlott?" VerGann pressed.

"She's concerned," KaiDinn said, exchanging knowing looks with the sprite now on his shoulder. "Nelliah speaks of the Stone nonstop, and each vision is more detailed than the last."

"Dreesdin said she believed a girl in Draven had the GraVinn. After our last meeting, I know for a fact she suspects Tiaponine," VerGann said. "Perhaps she's seen Tiaponine on one of her *outings*."

"Nelliah hasn't been to Draven, of that much I'm sure," KaiDinn said, shaking his head. "I think she's still just looking for information, since we didn't confirm her suspicions earlier."

It was then that KaiDinn seemed to take in VerGann's mud-splattered appearance, head to toe, and raised an eyebrow.

"So she's seeking information for the BarLonn." VerGann opened the top drawer on his dresser. "They want the Stone of GraVinn."

"We've looked, VerGann," KaiDinn said, sounding exasperated. "There's no one in the forest that shouldn't be here, not that we've found. We spend most of our time on guard, recently."

"And does Marlott believe Nelliah is separated from the BarLonn?"

"No," KaiDinn answered. "But she wants us to be discreet about figuring out what she's up to."

Taking another glance down at his mess of clothing, VerGann nodded. "Understood."

"So *are* you going to tell us what this is all about?" Natty asked, waving her hand in the direction of VerGann's entire person. "I *know* there's a juicy story behind all the mud..."

KaiDinn looked at the sprite with a look of disapproval. "Nat."

"KaiDinn."

"Goodnight, Natimae," VerGann said, casting the sprite a look.

"*Natimae*," the sprite repeated, resigned. "Goodnight, VerGann."

CHAPTER 12

It would be fair to say that Madame Farault had found more humor in Tiaponine's appearance after her impromptu mud bath than the servant girls responsible for assisting in her clean-up did. Although she'd insisted she could clean up on her own, Madame Farault would not hear of it, and had put the maidservants to work filling a bath and finding dry clothes.

Tiaponine stared at the empty chaise along the opposite wall. Having a bit of *clean-up* to do himself, she did not expect to see VerGann any time soon. It was just her and her thoughts.

And she happened to be having quite a few confusing ones at the moment. Perhaps thinking was not the best idea right now. She needed a distraction.

Moaning, Tiaponine rubbed her stomach.

Distraction identified. She was hungry.

It was not even the darkest of night yet. No harm would come from sneaking a light snack. Unlike everyone else in the castle, she was very capable and willing to find something to eat on her own.

Mission at hand, Tiaponine left her room.

The upcoming banquet was the talk of the entire castle. The entire kingdom.

Everywhere he went that day, Breydon could hear whispers. *Where had he met the Lady Christine? Why had no one ever*

L. C. Watkins

heard of her before now? Many daughters of the nobles were especially troubled by the sudden announcement. *How would this affect their own future romantic interludes with the prince?*

Breydon steeled his gaze ahead, the darkness of the corridor closing in around him. A nighttime walk had seemed like a good idea, but now he wasn't so sure. He felt like the weight of the world was upon him.

He rounded the corner into the banquet hall. Tomorrow night, it would be filled with nobles and curious onlookers. Spying Madame Farault's shadowy form stacking linens along the far wall, he allowed himself a small smile.

"So tomorrow's the big night," Breydon said, his voice echoing across the hall. As Madame Farault turned to see him, she smiled.

"Yes, I'm very happy for you, dear," she said, folding the last linen in her hand.

"You look worried," he noticed. "What is it?"

She hesitated, her fingers running over the top of the pile of cloth on the shelf. "Do you love her?"

Breydon shifted uncomfortably. "Tiaponine?"

"Yes."

Yes, he almost said. *Of course.* But he hesitated, and the maidservant raised an eyebrow at him.

"I… don't know. I…" he stammered. "I thought I had it figured out. *Us,* I mean."

"You may find a confidant and dear friend in Tiaponine," she continued. "But do you love her?"

"It wouldn't all be pretend," he admitted, casting a glance around the otherwise empty room. Madame Farault was the only person he would ever share such personal things with. "There *are* feelings."

"But there are different types of love, dear," she reminded gently. "It doesn't make you a bad person, or Tiaponine any less important, if you don't love her in that way."

Breydon looked down. She was right.

Hearing the *clack, clack, clack* of heels on the marble floor, he turned. He groaned as he saw the shapely shadow approaching them, his shoulders sinking. Unfortunately, Gwenevieve had yet to take her leave back to Santerine.

"You're a very hard man to pin down," her shrill voice interrupted, breaking the heartfelt moment. "If I didn't know any better, I'd say you're avoiding me." Her attention turned to Madame Farault. "You, I want fresh bread brought to my quarters at once."

"Yes, my lady," Madame Farault said, curtsying.

"No, Madame Farault," Breydon interjected, glaring at Gwenevieve. "One of the girls will bring her bread. Go and get some sleep."

Gwenevieve sucked in her cheeks. "Apologies. I didn't realize I'm not permitted to give a *servant* an order."

"Not her," Breydon answered coolly.

Not saying a word, Madame Farault turned and left, though she did cast a curious look Breydon's way, taking in the confrontation.

Eyeing him with disgust, Gwenevieve smiled. "Are you always so familiar with the help?"

"I have to go," he grumbled, turning toward the entry. Again, he heard the annoying *tip, tap* of her shoes on the marble floor as she rushed to catch up with him.

"Prince Breydon," she said, stepping in front of him to block his retreat. "I'll just skip the niceties and get right down to the truth of the matter." Pushing her finger into his right shoulder, she forced him to take several steps back until he was almost against the wall. "I know something's up. This Christine girl comes out of nowhere, and you just give away your heart and want to take her as your wife?" Gwenevieve laughed, her eyes growing wide. She looked rather deranged. "I'm not buying it, Breydon. She's not even your type."

"And what would my type be?" Breydon asked.

Pushing him back so that he was pinned against the wall beside the door, Gwenevieve locked eyes with him. He clenched his jaw, incredibly uncomfortable—she was far too forward.

"You need someone more refined, a girl that knows what she wants," she cooed. "And I am that girl. There's no question about my background, and I know *exactly* what I want." She smiled. "Like it or not, our lives have been decided. I *will be* your wife."

With those words, she leaned in. Breydon recoiled slightly, not at all sure what to do. Was it appropriate to push her away? He had never met anyone like this before. She appeared satisfied with his discomfort, more so than his uncle, which was saying something.

And then she kissed him. Forceful, deep and seductive. She kissed him.

He stared as she released him. He already knew she was pushy, shallow and irritating, but at that moment, it became clear that he needed to add one more description to his mental list.

Insane. She was insane, and it was terrifying.

It was not that he disliked forceful women—he had entertained a few in his time—but this was different. He wanted no part of what was being offered to him. Forcing himself to regain his composure, he pushed Gwenevieve back by her shoulders.

"Look, take offense if you wish, but… no. It's not going to happen. A friendship, the marriage… any of it." Breydon leveled his gaze on the princess, narrowing his eyes. "I'll make sure some bread is brought up to you, as requested." Without another word, he turned to leave.

No *tip, tap* of shoes behind him. Thank goodness for small favors. The rest of the evening could be best spent alone in his eastern tower.

With the door locked.

The castle was large—very large.

Tiaponine grimaced. Fetching a snack had taken longer than she intended. She navigated the darkened corridors with a sense of purpose. VerGann would be back soon, and she didn't want to miss his return.

Feeling the hint of warmth in her cheeks, she cleared her throat. What was wrong with her? She was acting a bit like Lerra and Eva. VerGann was sure to be embarrassed, should he know her thoughts.

"Tiaponine."

Tiaponine froze at the sound of Breydon's voice. It was not her intention to have him find her roaming the halls alone.

"Breydon," she greeted. "I didn't expect to find you here."

"Well, it appears that I'm not the only one who's taken to late night walks by myself," he said, laughing.

A faint smile crossed her face, and she looked down, embarrassed. "I was hunting down a snack."

"And VerGann?"

"He went back to EliSann." Tiaponine smiled wider as the image of VerGann's mud-soaked form in the stream entered her mind. She looked at Breydon, who appeared confused. "He had to take care of something."

"I see," he said. "Well, I'll leave you for now. Big night tomorrow."

Tiaponine forced a smile. There was still an amount of awkwardness between them, after their interaction earlier. She was happy he was keeping their meeting brief. "Yes, big night. Until tomorrow."

Waiting until Breydon had disappeared around the corner, Tiaponine at last turned. Back to her room. With any luck, VerGann would be there.

Stepping into a long corridor lit by a handful of candles, she scurried off, unaware of the young woman hiding close by.

Princess Gwenevieve smirked, retreating further into the shadows as Tiaponine passed.

Be discreet.

VerGann had been mulling these words over and over in his mind since his return to the castle an hour earlier. He took a steady breath.

There was much to be concerned about. Never in his memory had Marlott put the delpins on watch in the forest. They were always on guard, but that did not mean spending hours at the forest's edge. Now, however…

Adjusting the pillow behind his head, VerGann glanced at Tiaponine, fast asleep on her oversized bed. Her night without him must have been an eventful one. She was already asleep when he returned from EliSann, very uncharacteristic for the perpetual late-to-bed, late-to-rise girl.

VerGann took another steady breath. He must sleep. He had not had much rest in days.

Suddenly aware that he was no longer alone, he opened his eyes.

"VerGann," Vrenler whispered, taking notice of Tiaponine a short distance away. "Nelliah's missing."

"Marlott wants us to find her," GaeLenn added, appearing beside Vrenler.

Sitting up, VerGann looked between the two delpins, narrowing his eyes. "Missing," he repeated. "Any ideas?"

"She couldn't have gone far," GaeLenn said. "We've checked the forest, and she's not there. She hasn't been gone long enough to make it far beyond EliSann. That should make our search a little easier."

Vrenler smiled dryly. "Marlott wants this taken care of, *now*. When we find Nelliah, she is to be notified immediately."

VerGann contemplated Vrenler's words. Nelliah was playing a dangerous game, and Marlott had clearly grown tired of it. She was bound to find trouble at some point.

Having all of the delpins in the EliSann Forest searching for you was the worst kind of trouble.

Five additional delpins appeared in the room.

"Will Tiaponine be all right here by herself tonight?" KaiDinn asked.

VerGann looked at Tiaponine, still slumbering across the room. For the moment, the castle was the safest place for her.

"Yes," he said, nodding. "She'll be fine."

"All right," Vrenler announced quietly. "TraviDenn, BriDonn and I will take the areas south of the ElinDann River. Zeravin, Kemperis and GaeLenn, take the north and west. VerGann and KaiDinn, you take east of the forest. Nelliah has to be close."

"Nelliah would stay clear of the west and north. She knows I was expecting trouble from her, and those are the most visible areas from Draven." Turning to KaiDinn, VerGann crossed his arms.

"To the south of the forest is nothing but trouble," KaiDinn said. "A Magdina hunting party, thieves hiding along the main road, the distance from any populated city."

"Especially for a woman. The area due east of the forest would be ideal for hiding, though." VerGann smiled. "And it also just happens to be in the direction of the BarLonn Mountains. A two day ride by horse, at best."

"But we've searched." KaiDinn kicked at a branch on the ground as he paced back and forth. "For over an hour we've searched."

"Not everywhere," VerGann said.

KaiDinn halted midstep, looking up in mild disbelief.

"The SaranDinn Valley?" he asked. "That's the most inhospitable terrain around. Do you really think she would risk it?"

"Yes, I do. Take the south end of the valley," VerGann said. "I'll take the north. Meet in the middle. Stay to the upper ridges of the cliffs."

Nodding, KaiDinn vanished.

In the blink of an eye, VerGann was standing in the shadows of a deep cove nestled in the heavy thickness of the forest's outer eastern reaches—the SaranDinn Valley.

He studied his surroundings. The play of moonlight against the many dips and ridges of the cliff side offered an array of confusing and mysterious shadows. If Nelliah was there, she had picked a curious hiding place, for sure. Anyone else would have been terrified.

With deliberate, silent steps, VerGann made a path through the dense foliage, careful not to lose footing on the uneven ground. Tall, jagged, rocky protrusions lining the length of solid cliff slopes, trees so thick that they seemed to form an impenetrable wall at the breaks in those cliffs, an endless array of bottomless shadows from the caves and crevices scattered throughout—the valley was as uninviting as it had always been.

He paused, squinting into the depths of the shadowy cliff edge with cautious interest, taking particular interest in a rocky overhang.

The shadows under the ledge appeared darker than those around them. Perhaps they concealed more than a jagged cliffside beneath them. A small cave would go unseen to the untrained eye. A small cave that...

VerGann stood motionless. Although faint, there were voices—whispers—coming from the shadowy area under the ledge.

In the next moment, he was at the outer edge of the suspect cave.

He cocked his head to the side to listen. It was possible that some wayward travelers were there seeking shelter for the night. If that was the case, he had no interest in scaring them half to death.

"The girl," a deep male voice somewhere in the darkness sounded. "Are you sure the girl in the city knows where it is?"

"VerGann's with her," the familiar voice of Nelliah answered. "There has to be a specific reason Marlott sent him there, and it has nothing to do with keeping her company."

"I've seen her," a second male voice interrupted. "They call her Tiaponine. She's at the castle as we speak."

"But the question is, how to get to her?" yet another male voice said. "You said that when you saw her, VerGann was with her. We have to assume he's close by at all times."

"True," Nelliah agreed. "But she's also his weakness."

"Oh, come, now," the first male voice exclaimed. "We're talking about the most powerful of the delpins! The human is his weakness?"

"Dreesdin has said on more than one occasion that he suspects a relationship with the girl, beyond the rules VerGann is forbidden to break." Nelliah laughed, and VerGann gritted his teeth. "I have to agree. At the very mention of her, he becomes protective. He tries to hide it, but I can see it, plain as day. It seems that one of Marlott's dear delpins has broken the laws of EliSann. Poor, poor Marlott. Good for us, though."

"Distract VerGann and the rest of the delpins," the third male voice growled. "We'll take care of the girl."

"Once we have the GraVinn, EliSann is ours." Nelliah continued laughing. "As it should be. Marlott and the delpins will regret their sins against our people."

"Of course, to get VerGann's full attention, you must do something that would put you in a great amount of danger," the second man said.

"Leave the delpins to me. They don't trust me, but they aren't allowed to touch me, either. I think another vision is in order, perhaps one that affects all of EliSann. That would get Marlott's attention. She'd have the delpins confined to EliSann in a heartbeat if she thought her people were in trouble."

"What are you talking about?" the third man asked.

"A group of nymphs goes to the ElinDann River every morning with a delpin escort. If the delpin weren't with them, they'd have no defense against an attack. Furthermore, no one would even know there was a problem until the attacker was long gone."

"And what makes you think that the delpin won't be with them one morning?" the first male voice asked.

"He'll be gone," Nelliah answered. "Don't ask me how, but I'll make sure of it. You just be ready. Two days from now, be at the river at Blotner's Pass. Leave no one alive. VerGann's attention will be on the EliSann Forest as they search for the attacker. At that time, you'll go to Draven and take care of things there. We'll have the GraVinn before anyone is the wiser."

"All right," the first and loudest of the male voices said. "Make sure you take care of the delpin escort."

"No need to worry. It'll be my pleasure," Nelliah laughed.

VerGann looked at KaiDinn, who had appeared at some point on the other side of the cave entrance. He had arrived in time to hear most of Nelliah's plot.

At the loud crack of dead branches being pushed to the side as the small group of traitors prepared to leave the hidden cave, VerGann straightened.

It was but moments later when the first of the BarLonn nardins emerged from the cave. As expected, he was quite startled to find two delpins there waiting for him.

VerGann stared at the nardin, whose face paled considerably. Nelliah and a second nardin joined him moments later.

"VerGann," Nelliah greeted after a long moment of uneasy silence.

VerGann said nothing. The second nardin swallowed audibly.

"I'm glad that you're here," she continued, clearly floundering for words. "These men are here to help us." Motioning to the two nardins behind her, she smiled. "I apologize for the secrecy, but we had to be careful. You see, they're from the BarLonn Mountains and, as such, are wanted men. The BarLonn don't take well to being crossed by one of their own."

"There's one missing," KaiDinn noted.

Spinning to look at KaiDinn, Nelliah frowned. "VerGann..." she pleaded, a measurable amount of concern creeping into her words.

At the sudden appearance of five additional delpins, the nymph swallowed hard. Her game was up.

"I'll go look for the third nardin," KaiDinn said.

"No need," Vrenler answered, appearing amongst the small gathering. "He's right here."

In the next instance, the third nardin flew from the cave and fell to the ground in front of Nelliah, thrown by invisible hands. He was not dead, but injured and in a lot of pain. How Vrenler had managed that, as silently as he had, was beyond VerGann, but it did not matter.

Nelliah turned back to the group of delpins, hatred seeping from every pore. "Am I to believe you're here to kill us? Is this what your dear seratine has ordered? Have the delpins become her personal assassins now?"

"No," Marlott answered, her voice cold.

Nelliah and the three nardins from BarLonn gasped as the seratine appeared.

"The delpins are forbidden from taking a life, as they have an advantage, and such an action would be... unfair," Marlott said. "I have no such restraints."

Any remaining color drained from Nelliah's face. She recoiled, drawing closer to the nardins standing behind her.

"Leave this place, my sons," Marlott ordered, her words void of emotion. "VerGann and Vrenler, you are to return here in an hour's time and keep watch for any further trouble. I will return to our people in a short while."

VerGann

VerGann glanced at the others. It had been a very long time since any of them had seen the seratine like this. Her silence, her very presence, was frightening.

"Go," she repeated.

The order had been given. No one would question it.

With one last look at Nelliah, VerGann disappeared.

CHAPTER 13

The day had started with a three hour final fitting.

Tiaponine frowned. She thought her dress for the banquet had looked perfect the day before. Why was it necessary to wake her an hour before the sun was even up?

Shutting her bedroom door, she sighed. The banquet was quickly turning into a thorn in her side. She could not wait for it to be over, and it hadn't even started yet.

"I would ask how it's going, but..."

Tiaponine spun around, a smile brightening her face as she saw VerGann sitting on the chest at the end of her bed.

"Let's just say, I've had a long morning," she lamented, shaking her head and pulling her skirt out in front so that she could walk unobstructed. She studied the delpin's tense expression. He was clearly distracted.

"Anyway, I'm more interested in what's bothering you," Tiaponine said. "You didn't stay here last night?"

"I was here," VerGann answered, his voice distant. "For a short while, anyway."

There was an unusual level of detachment in his mannerisms. Tiaponine could not remember the last time she had seen him like this. "VerGann?"

"I'm sorry, Tee," he apologized, running his hand through his hair and leaning over. "Nelliah went missing from EliSann last night. The delpins were ordered to find her, which we did, and then..." He trailed off.

"And then..."

"I can only guess," VerGann said. "Marlott came. She ordered us to leave. That was it. Nelliah and the three nardins from BarLonn with her haven't been seen since."

The words left an uncomfortable image in Tiaponine's mind.

"Did Marlott…"

"Tee, Nelliah was making plans to come here." VerGann let his shoulders fall. "For you. They had been watching you."

Tiaponine felt sick to her stomach. A nardin was no delpin, but even so, she knew she could not stand a chance against one—let alone three of them.

"And to answer your question, yes, Marlott…" He stopped, letting out a deep breath. "She got rid of them."

"Rid of them?" Tiaponine repeated slowly.

"The only thing she said was that those from BarLonn would not be returning." VerGann grasped the back of his neck, and sat up. "They're dead, Tee. How it happened, I don't know. No one will ever ask."

Tiaponine was stunned into silence, although she knew Marlott had made what she thought to be the best decision. She'd just never thought of the seratine as someone capable of that—VerGann always spoke of her with the utmost respect.

"I suspected something like this all along," he continued. "I just never imagined it would end like this."

Tiaponine looked away, glancing down at the stone around her neck. "Making plans to come… here."

"They wouldn't have gotten far," he assured her. "A fight with me would have put an immediate end to the whole affair."

VerGann was serious—very serious. She felt her cheeks begin to warm, and rushed to try and change the subject.

"Alright… So, we've covered Nelliah. Is there anything else?"

VerGann laughed mirthlessly, leaning forward to stare at the marble floor. "Let me see. There's still the Stone of GraVinn—just having it near King Hulbert makes the Council nervous. Oh, and the trouble I seem to be taking giant strides toward at home…"

"Wait, you're in trouble?" Tiaponine interrupted. "What for?"

He tensed. "Well, I'm not *in* trouble. Not yet," he said, his tone dismissive. But she could hear that it was forced. He was nervous.

"It has to do with you being here, doesn't it?"

He glanced from Tiaponine back to the marble floor. "Yes," he agreed, after some time. "There are concerns as to whether my time here is being used in the best way. Whether I'm as focused as I should be."

It was hard to think that anyone would question VerGann's ability to do what was asked of him. "What would be taking your focus from your duty?" she asked.

After an uncomfortable pause, he managed a smile. "I am focused, Tee. The GraVinn just makes them nervous. That's all."

For the time being, she was going to have to accept that answer, although she knew there was more to it.

"I have to be going. I'm supposed to be on guard with Vrenler, and Marlott will notice my absence soon." Puffing out his cheeks, VerGann let his breath escape slowly. "And then there's the Council meeting tonight. Just the thought of having to sit across the table from Dreesdin is enough to give me a headache."

Watching VerGann, still leaning forward as he rested his elbows on his knees, defeated, Tiaponine could not help but feel sorry for him. He'd always been calm, unbothered by anything— until recently. She could only guess how stressful the full extent of his situation was.

Reaching out to him, Tiaponine ran her hand through his tousled blond hair and down over his cheek. He flinched at her touch. She locked eyes with him.

"Don't worry about it," she reassured him. "Go and take care of what you need to at home. Take as much time as you need. I can manage this silly banquet on my own. You know, *smile a lot and say very little.*"

Finally, he offered her a small smile. A real one.

In the next instance, he was gone, and her fingers were closing over nothing but air.

❦

Taking his seat in the all too familiar chair at the center of the table, VerGann leaned back.

He felt restless. The Council room was already buzzing with quiet chatter of Nelliah's noticeable, sudden *absence* from EliSann.

Even VerGann could not remember a time when Marlott had taken such extreme action. Discipline in EliSann consisted of admonishment, perhaps exile in rare, extreme cases. Nothing more.

He tapped his right index finger on the table. Nelliah and the three nardins had not been verbally disciplined. They had not been exiled. They had been… *eliminated.*

He looked at the two delpins with him. Not one of them had said a word since they arrived. And then there was Marlott. The seratine sat at the head of the table in silence. She seemed to be studying those around her. The air in the Council chamber felt thick, foreboding.

"VerGann."

VerGann inwardly groaned as Dreesdin took his seat across from him. He offered the slightest of nods to the nardin.

"I see the delpins found time away from their pressing matters to attend the meeting," Dreesdin said. "Your recent absence has not gone unnoticed."

"Absence?" Vrenler spoke up.

Dreesdin crossed his arms, a frown forming. "No delpin could be found last night. Where were you?"

"If you were meant to know, you would have been told," Vrenler answered, with a rather cold look in his eyes.

VerGann smiled to himself. The nardin looked ready to explode.

"My children," the seratine began. "This meeting was called to discuss the ongoing issue of the Stone of GraVinn. It came to my attention recently that measures were being taken to secure the GraVinn by those it was most important to keep it from."

Her words were slow and deliberate. VerGann listened carefully, knowing what was coming next.

"The nymph Nelliah, being found with three nardins from the BarLonn Mountains, making plans to murder our citizens and steal the Stone of GraVinn, was eliminated. At my request, the delpins have scoured the forest and surrounding areas. I can assure you that no other threat from BarLonn exists at present."

The room was silent.

VerGann let his eyes travel over all sitting at the table. This was the last thing any of them had expected to hear when they walked in the door.

"Eliminated?" Dreesdin questioned, his voice tight. The nardin's jaw tensed at Marlott's revelation. News of his precious gifted nymph's demise very clearly did not sit well with him.

"The BarLonn were seeking the GraVinn. Nelliah was helping them," Marlott stated, her eyes never leaving Dreesdin. "I have no tolerance for such treachery. All four of them were eliminated."

VerGann had to admit that the often-reserved seratine's words sent a chill through even him. Marlott was the strong silent type, patient and understanding. Her present emotionless—*cold*, unfeeling—manner was terrifying.

"The Stone of GraVinn," Dreesdin said, still uneasy. "What news of it now, my lady?"

"No one knows of the stone's location in Draven," Marlott said, "Not even the human girl that wears it. All has been returned to the way it was."

VerGann glanced briefly at KaiDinn. The seratine had happened onto a subject that he was not at all comfortable with, and KaiDinn knew it.

"The human girl doesn't know of the stone, correct?" Dreesdin questioned, catching VerGann's sideways glance and seizing the opportunity to put him on the spot.

At once, the entire room was silent as all attention turned to him.

The thought to lie came to mind, but it would only make matters worse. He had gone against the orders of the Council. Against Marlott's orders. The damage was done.

"Tiaponine knows of the GraVinn." He had to force the words to come.

An audible gasp spread through the room.

"VerGann," Marlott asked. "You are aware that you were expressly ordered not to tell her?"

"Yes, my lady."

"Yet you chose to disregard this command?" Marlott continued, narrowing her eyes slightly. "I find such disobedience surprising from you. Did you not worry about the consequences of your actions?"

VerGann stared back at the seratine in silence.

"I must know your reasons, my son," she pressed.

He hesitated. He knew his reasons. How to best put them to Marlott and the entire Council without drawing further questions was another matter.

"In placing the Stone of GraVinn in the necklace Tiaponine wears, we put her in danger, and she had no choice about her involvement in any of this," he began. "With her presence at the castle, so near to Hulbert, I felt it right that she be made aware of it. My hope was that with this knowledge, she would take care not to let Hulbert know of the stone's location."

"And why was the Council not informed of your decision?" Marlott questioned.

"It wasn't something I planned to do beforehand, and as such, I didn't have time to place it before Council for discussion." VerGann managed his breathing. He was uncharacteristically nervous. He must not let it show.

It was clear that Marlott was deeply troubled by this news. He just hoped that any disciplinary action would be handled at a later time. Dreesdin would love nothing more than to have a front row seat to any punishment handed out. The very thought was sickening.

"Although concerning, I believe we can all understand that such decisions have to be made at times," Marlott said, after an uncomfortable pause. "I trust that you made this decision with great caution." She looked back over those at the table. "My children, take comfort in my words—should it come to pass that Hulbert takes the Stone of GraVinn, we have to believe it'll be destroyed as I designed."

"And then VerGann will return to us?" an elder nymph asked.

Marlott nodded, a warm smile crossing her face. "Yes, my children. The end of the Stone of GraVinn also signifies the end of the great task I requested of VerGann so many years ago. We'll all be happy to see his return."

Resting back in his chair, VerGann sighed, a whole new wave of dread settling over him. He had never given thought to a time when he would be returning to EliSann for good. Alone.

He wasn't sure he wanted to.

No matter. As long as the GraVinn was kept secret, he had nothing to worry about.

Crossing his arms, VerGann settled in. This was going to be a long meeting.

Rounding a corner in yet another dimly lit corridor, Samuel frowned. Why did castles have to be so dark and cold?

Guests for the banquet were already gathering upstairs. He would be expected there soon. Not that there was anything for him to be excited about, though.

The thought of Breydon marrying that street urchin, Tiaponine, made his stomach turn, his blood boil.

Stepping into the darkened staircase of the northern tower, Samuel gasped as someone stepped in front of him.

"Princess Gwenevieve," he greeted, an amount of annoyance in his words.

She looked irritated herself as she moved closer to him. When she spoke, her voice was just as tense as his own. "Just the man I was looking for."

Samuel frowned. "Is something wrong?" he asked, trying not to laugh. He knew Gwenevieve was unhappy, not to mention embarrassed. Breydon had dropped her like a cannonball. He just did not care. His heart was cold and dark on the subject.

"Is something *wrong?*" she repeated, infuriated. "Yes, I should say so. Who is she?"

At once, the thought to expose Tiaponine crossed his mind.

"Lady Christine?" Samuel asked with feigned innocence. "She's Lord Draughton's daughter. Prince Breydon's one and only true love."

"Oh, be quiet," Gwenevieve snapped. "I've heard all I want to hear of these lies." She pushed past him. "You know what? That's fine. More fun for me."

More fun for. . . She had his full attention now.

"What do you mean?" Samuel asked. His frown deepened as she leaned in close to him.

"The pleasure of exposing this little trick you're playing on the king," she said, grabbing his shirt front.

"A trick, you say," Samuel repeated.

"Don't play stupid with me. I overheard Breydon and Lady Christine in the hallway, you idiot," Gwenevieve shot back. "Or, should I say, Titaninny."

It was just too painful.

"Sorry?" Samuel said slowly.

"Tiatany."

"Tiaponine," he corrected.

"Whatever," Gwenevieve said, waving him off. "Point is, she's no daughter of a lord. She's not even nobility. Curious how I didn't notice before. The simpleton—she sticks out like weed in a bouquet of roses."

Samuel contemplated his next move. Tell Gwenevieve the truth, or risk the king's anger.

The choice was an obvious one.

"Lady Christine doesn't exist. Breydon created her."

"So who's the girl?"

"We took her from the streets," Samuel admitted. "You can put the finest cloth and jewels in the kingdom on her, and she'd still be nothing but street trash." He laughed. "Breydon put this whole thing together to get out of the marriage."

"He doesn't want to marry me?" Gwenevieve's jaw dropped.

Samuel stared at her. He would have thought this fact was apparent from the very first time Breydon had spoken to her.

"I don't even want to get in the middle of that," he said finally, rolling his eyes. "You'll have to take it up with your handsome prince."

Walking past him, Gwenevieve twirled her hair between two fingers. "Breydon marries…" Stopping, she turned to Samuel. "What's the dear's name?"

"Tiaponine."

"Breydon marries Tiaponoon," Gwenevieve continued. "And I'm sent on my way. Tiaponoon is princess."

Samuel smiled. Visually, Gwenevieve may have been every man's dream of the perfect woman, but she was dumb as a rock.

"Think about it," he pointed out. "She'd be above you in station."

Gwenevieve whirled back around to face Samuel.

"I will not bow to the likes of her, *ever*," she seethed. "If Tiaponooty thinks she'll be above me, she'd better think again."

Samuel laughed, turning back toward the stairs. "I'm sure."

"What're you getting out of this, anyway?" Gwenevieve demanded.

"I have my reasons."

"I see," Gwenevieve said. "You're going to help me get rid of her."

Samuel stopped in his tracks. "No. I'm not."

"It's better to side with those who will benefit you the most." Gwenevieve held her head high. "At present, that would be me."

"Not going to happen."

"You know I can make your life unbearable." The edges of Gwenevieve's mouth curved up in a wicked grin.

Samuel swallowed hard—swallowed his pride—every last bit of it.

"So what's the plan?"

King Hulbert tried to take the stone seventeen years ago... We have no reason to believe that he knows of the stone's whereabouts at the moment...

Letting out another deep breath, VerGann adjusted his back against the wood of his chair. This Council meeting was excruciating. He had heard it all before. Who had not?

He leaned forward over the table. His recollection of the past hour was limited, at best.

Dreesdin had made a point to stare at him for the better part of the meeting. While flattered, VerGann was sure the nardin's actions had a more aggressive motive behind them. Any other time, he would have been up for the battle of wills, but he was just not in the mood.

For now, he would ignore the building desire to push Dreesdin's chair out from underneath him for no other reason than to amuse himself.

Closing his eyes to clear his mind, VerGann ran his hand through his hair. He stopped. In that very instance, that brief moment of habit, the image of Tiaponine came flooding into his mind.

VerGann shifted in his seat—him sitting on the trunk at the end of her bed, her hand running through his hair and down over his cheek– he could still feel it. Unbeknownst to her, Tiaponine's innocent attempt at comforting him had served to do quite the opposite. Things were changing between them.

Whether she felt the same was unclear. But he could not ignore it anymore. The days of rationalization and excuses for confusing thoughts and emotions had passed. He knew exactly what to call it, and…

It scared him.

Telling Tiaponine of the Stone of GraVinn paled in comparison to the trouble he would find himself in if he acted on his feelings. Marlott would not be forgiving on this matter.

"VerGann."

His breath halted as he looked at the seratine. His suspicions were confirmed. She had noticed his preoccupation.

"My children," she announced. "We will adjourn for now."

Marlott's timing couldn't be better. With a cocky smile, VerGann nodded to Dreesdin and pushed his chair back. He stood.

"The delpins will stay," Marlott continued.

VerGann tensed. This could not be good. What did she need to address with them that the rest of the Council could not hear?

"Your thoughts, VerGann," Marlott said, watching the last nardin exit the room.

He could not bring himself to look at Marlott. He knew what plagued him. How best to explain it was the issue. No matter what he said, she would not be understanding this time.

The best thing to do was apologize for his lack of attention and move away from the topic.

"I realize that you've come to care for this human girl," Marlott said after an extended silence. "But you knew the time would come when your task would end."

VerGann felt paralyzed. It was worse than he thought. Marlott had not only noticed his preoccupation, she somehow knew the cause of it. It made him anxious to think he was that easy to read.

At his side, KaiDinn and Vrenler both appeared almost as uncomfortable as he felt.

"You've done well," Marlott continued. "At some point, however, you will return to us. You must have thought about this—how nice it will be for you to return to your previous life. Your people look forward to it."

"And Tiaponine?" VerGann asked, his words more abrupt than he had anticipated. "I mean, if the end of the GraVinn is closer than we realize?"

"She'll remain in Draven." Marlott answered without hesitation. "It's my understanding that she's been spending a lot of time with the prince. Perhaps she could remain in his company, should the GraVinn be destroyed in her lifetime."

The seratine's words were cold. VerGann managed his reaction.

"You've become very familiar with the outside world. This I realize. But our worlds can never coincide." Marlott paused. "You know this."

At once, VerGann's guard went up. It did not make sense why Marlott would not consider allowing Tiaponine to live in EliSann. She'd allowed it before, albeit rarely. Unless…

She suspected his feelings for Tiaponine.

There was no point in concealing the truth at this point.

"Their world isn't what's on my mind."

He glanced at Vrenler and KaiDinn once again. It was not his wish for them to see him as such an emotional mess, and clearly they did not wish to see it, either. Vrenler crossed his arms, tapping his foot anxiously, and KaiDinn suddenly seemed very interested in the ground, standing perfectly still with his lips pursed.

"Their world doesn't interest me," VerGann admitted, as calmly as he could manage. "It's no different than ours, in many respects. But Tiaponine... She's not something one becomes accustomed to and then discards. I cannot do that. I will not do that."

KaiDinn's gaze snapped up at VerGann's sharp words, his eyes full of anxiety. Vrenler's expression shifted in warning.

"VerGann," he pleaded.

"You have feelings for this human girl?" Marlott questioned, her tone icy.

He came close to saying it. But that would change everything—his entire life.

Averting his gaze away from Marlott, he remained silent.

"VerGann," Marlott continued. "You are not human. This isn't permitted—"

"I know," VerGann interrupted sharply, at once regretting his show of disrespect. Both Vrenler and KaiDinn winced as the temperature around Marlott seemed to drop a few degrees colder. He forced himself to stand a bit straighter.

"The delpins have been among the few to venture into the outside world," Marlott began again. "Even then, their experiences don't compare to what you have been exposed to with Tiaponine in the city. You aren't that boy of fourteen anymore. You belong here."

"I..." VerGann began, finding himself scrambling for the right words. "I understand our laws," he managed. "I've watched over the Stone of GraVinn as commanded and will continue to do so, as is my duty. I've also watched over Tiaponine, as her involvement in this was by no decision of her own. In watching over her, our friendship has become strong."

He stopped.

"But now, things are different. I... we..." Closing his eyes a moment, VerGann tried to gather his thoughts. He was very close to making a mistake he would not be able to mend. He could feel it at this point, actually *feel* it.

"Tiaponine isn't like the others I've met there. She knows me better than almost anyone. You have to have seen this."

"VerGann," Marlott said, her voice taking on a more authoritative tone. "You don't know the first thing about what you speak of. About the love of a human... a relationship... the closeness that comes when—"

"No," he interrupted, exasperated. "I know that I don't. How could I? This is all new. I've never experienced anything like this before, but that doesn't mean I don't want to learn." He swallowed before continuing. "I've watched thousands of people pass through their lives, within my own life, and I cannot say that I gave much thought to any of them. I've decided that Tiaponine is not someone that I want to see just pass through." He glanced at Vrenler and KaiDinn.

Both appeared shocked, perhaps on the verge of panic. That shouldn't surprise him—delpins never gave much thought to what he was speaking of. The fact that he *had* thought of it... That alienated him from them in a way that none of them had ever come close to.

And he understood their panic. He felt it, too.

"VerGann," Marlott said, her voice lowering, her stare cold. "No." She strode past him toward the door, then paused to look back at him for a long moment.

She touched the side of his face with her hand.

"I love you, my son."

CHAPTER 14

How she managed to keep from fainting was a mystery.

Tiaponine steadied her breathing, focusing on Breydon ahead. It was just a short walk until she would be at his side.

She felt everyone's gaze fixed on her, and tried to distract herself by examining the room. Banners fluttering, torchlight burning from every wall, the scent of wildflowers permeating her nostrils; the banquet hall was breathtaking. It was hard to believe this elaborate staging was all for her.

Gliding past the nobility of the kingdom, Tiaponine smiled as she at last came to stand before Breydon. Taking his outstretched hand, she curtsied to the king and turned to face the crowd.

The room resounded with the fanfare of trumpets as the king waved to his guests.

"People of this esteemed kingdom," King Hulbert announced. "We come together tonight to celebrate Prince Breydon's engagement! I give you Lady Christine, daughter of Lord Draughton, and your future princess!"

At once, the room erupted in cheers and clapping. Tiaponine looked at Breydon. Never before had she been the center of attention like this. He sent a reassuring wink her way as he led her a few steps toward the crowd. The cheers grew louder, and Tiaponine's spirits soared. She never could have imagined this going as well as it seemed to be going.

She wished VerGann was there to see it. Pushing past the small *pang* in her heart at that thought, she took a deep breath and straightened.

"Sire!"

The outburst stood out from the crowd's cheers. People began lapsing into puzzled silence as a lone figure pushed her way to the front of the room.

A knot formed in Tiaponine's stomach as Princess Gwenevieve's cold gaze met hers.

"This girl is not who you believe her to be." Gwenevieve approached Tiaponine and Breydon slowly, confidently. "There is no Lord Draughton, sire. She's been deceiving you and your nephew for her own gain."

Tiaponine risked a glance at Breydon. He appeared dumbstruck for a split second before gritting his teeth.

"Think very carefully about what you're doing," he muttered to Gwenevieve.

"Oh, I have," she snarled. "Believe me, I have. The servant named Samuel can testify that what I say is true."

Samuel. She'd known that he hated her, of course—she'd just assumed he cared more about his reputation. At the sound of his servant's name, Breydon's grip tightened around her hand.

"Breydon!" Hulbert roared. "Do you know what she's talking about?"

Breydon's audible growl did not get by her. Tiaponine stood frozen as the prince turned toward the king.

"No," he said shortly. "Of course not. These are the words of a scorned woman—angered that I chose someone else to be my bride."

"You're going to carry this charade to the very end, aren't you?" Gwenevieve spat.

Breydon's eyes narrowed.

"Samuel!" King Hulbert bellowed.

Tiaponine's anxiety grew as Samuel stepped from the crowd. The smug look on his face told her all she needed to know.

"Yes, sire," Samuel said, bowing to the king. "What Lady Gwenevieve says is true. The girl is nothing but a street urchin masquerading as nobility."

Tiaponine found herself searching the room for the closest way out—there were people blocking every door, but the urge to flee was overpowering. The sudden turn of events seemed unreal; she felt like she was in the middle of some kind of fever dream.

"This is a disgrace to my kingdom and my father's good name," Gwenevieve complained. "He'll be outraged at my treatment here!"

Tiaponine felt Breydon's hand leave hers.

"I admit Lady Christine's heritage was known to me," Breydon said. "As it was to Gwenevieve and Samuel. Lady Christine isn't responsible for this mess."

Tiaponine caught her breath. The king was staring at her, as though captivated—it was making her paranoid. She shrank back, desperately wishing she could disappear, and when he spoke again, she thought, distantly, that she must be having a nightmare.

"Bring her to me."

She didn't see the guards; they came up behind her, roughly grabbing her arms and pushing her forward, toward Hulbert. For a moment, she couldn't seem to move at all; she stumbled as their grip on her tightened, and though she wanted to cry out, her voice didn't seem to be working.

"What's that necklace?" Hulbert demanded, his eyes fixed on the thin leather cord just visible around her neck.

Tiaponine's mouth went dry; she still didn't seem able to speak. It occurred to her at that moment that this had been Hulbert's intention all along, with or without Gwenevieve's outburst. He knew she wore the Stone of GraVinn, and he was going to take it.

She gasped as one of the guards holding her grabbed the leather cord and pulled until the GraVinn was visible for all to see. King Hulbert stood not two feet in front of her.

"A thief also," he seethed, though his eyes glinted with something like joy. "You're a girl of many talents."

"I'm no thief, sire," Tiaponine pleaded. Her voice was quiet, shaky—too fragile. "This is all a misunderstanding."

"That necklace was in my possession until just a few days ago," Hulbert snarled.

"A gift from my mother, please," Tiaponine lied. "I've had this for years. I didn't take it from you, your majesty." She looked around at Breydon for help—her heart fell.

He looked from her to the necklace and back again, suspicion clearly etched in his face. He said nothing.

"A cloth of this fine design is more than you deserve," Gwenevieve hissed, stepping forward and fingering the embroidered sleeve of Tiaponine's dress. With one firm tug on the material, the sleeve was left to hang in shreds, exposing her bare shoulder.

Tiaponine cowered as Gwenevieve continued the assault. Soon her gown was nothing but a tattered length of material. Holding the material of the dress up to her in a futile effort to take away the vulnerability she felt, Tiaponine cried out as the guards shoved her into the center of the room.

"My father will hear about all of this!" Gwenevieve screeched. She spun on her heels and left the hall with her nose in the air.

Again, Tiaponine looked to Breydon, hoping he would step in. Again, he did not move, instead appearing conflicted.

Her blood ran cold as Hulbert took the GraVinn into his hand. A wicked smile invaded his features.

VerGann's warning echoed through her mind. Putting her hand over the king's as he held the stone, she began to back away, but found Hulbert moving right along with her. He tightened his grip on the GraVinn, its aquamarine surface reflected in his eyes.

He pulled the cord roughly, and she careened backward, still trying to get a good grip on the stone.

"*VerGann*," she whispered.

The leather snapped.

His arms crossed on his knees, his forehead resting on his arms, VerGann was too exhausted to do much else.

Never had he shown such disrespect to Marlott, and never had he felt so exposed in front of her—and KaiDinn and Vrenler had witnessed the whole thing, too. That was some small comfort—at least the scathing verbal admonishment was confined to the privacy of his two friends and not the whole Council. He could not have handled Dreesdin after such a scene.

VerGann let his head fall back against the wall. Marlott knew exactly what she was doing. Letting him sit for hours on end in the darkened silence of his room, recounting the argument over and over—it was part of her plan. Or part of his punishment. She was succeeding on both accounts.

Something in the room shifted, like a breeze that couldn't quite be felt. VerGann opened his eyes. He could just make out Marlott's form in the shadows. She stared at him emotionlessly.

As the first wave of nervousness washed over him, turning his stomach, VerGann tensed. Marlott's intense gaze was focused on him—it became clear that either she was forcing these feelings upon him…

Or she was opening him up to what someone else was feeling at that very moment.

"VerGann."

VerGann froze at the whisper in his mind.

Tiaponine.

His eyes darted back to Marlott. She showed no outward sign of having heard the whisper, but continued to stare at him intently.

He disappeared.

❦

Mere seconds later, VerGann stood at the center of the banquet hall, straight and alert. The people around him screamed at his sudden appearance, the crowd pushing back to cower along the walls. He searched the room for Tiaponine.

He found her just as King Hulbert ripped the necklace from her neck, and with his free hand, struck her across the face. She fell to the ground from the force of his blow, curling in on herself.

The stone erupted in a blinding burst of lime light, and another collective scream resonated through the hall—whether it was just the terrified nobles, scrambling away from the center of the room, or the deafening sound of the blood rushing in VerGann's head, he couldn't tell.

When the blinding light died, Tiaponine still lay motionless on the floor, and VerGann stepped toward her.

He stopped as all seven delpins appeared beside him.

"Not yet," Vrenler cautioned silently, casting him a warning look.

It was all VerGann could do not to run to Tiaponine. Not to break every bone in Hulbert's body. But he heeded Vrenler's warning. The delpins were his family, but this time he was certain they would side with the seratine.

VerGann's eyes drifted to Breydon being restrained by two nearby guards. All three men looked puzzled, still blinking rapidly after the explosion of light.

But the king, apparently satisfied, eyed the GraVinn in his hand, smiling. It had turned a darker color than usual, and unlike the last time Tiaponine had taken it off, VerGann felt no power emanating from it—no invisible pull for him to move past and ignore. Nothing.

Before anyone could fully recover, every candle along the walls extinguished, plunging the hall into complete darkness. An auburn light began to swirl above the heads of those gathered.

The display of lights circled the center of the hall, gathering to form the silhouette of a woman.

"You have claimed your prize, King Hulbert of Draven," Marlott said, and a hush fell over the room, a strange, tense silence.

"Yes," Hulbert snarled, his eyes narrowing. "I've found what you stole from me those many years ago." He clutched the GraVinn tighter. "At last, the Stone of GraVinn is mine."

"You may have it. It's worthless now."

The seratine sounded sure of herself. VerGann carefully looked over the stone– less than formidable. Could it be that the enchantment had worked? The GraVinn had been destroyed?

"Worthless?" Hulbert hissed. "What do you mean, worthless?"

"Once removed from the girl, the power of the Stone of GraVinn ceased."

He gripped the stone so tightly his knuckles turned white. "Liar," he muttered, staring at it—as though expecting it to light up again, expecting any response from it at all. It remained dark; in fact, a low cracking noise could be heard echoing across the hall, and black lines webbed their way across the GraVinn' surface.

"Liar!" Hulbert repeated, louder this time. He flipped the stone over in his hand. "What have you done to it?" The dark lines expanded even more—it now looked ready to fracture into pieces. "What have you done?"

"It's powerless," Marlott said. "As you can see. But do you plan on breaking your prize, after all you've done to get it?"

Apparently seeing the damage he was inflicting on the stone, Hulbert tore his gaze away from it and glared at the seratine. "You've destroyed it!"

VerGann had heard enough. He started toward Tiaponine's still-motionless form on the floor. Marlott cast a sharp look his way, and he slowed, his blood chilling.

She wouldn't stop him... Right?

He took another step, and the cold feeling inside him grew. He felt as though he were wading through water, pushing against a strong current. He tried to picture himself at Tiaponine's side, tried to make himself disappear—and went nowhere.

Marlott's gaze remained leveled on him, her face void of emotion.

"Stop—the urchin belongs to me!" Hulbert seethed, motioning for a nearby guard to approach. The guard seemed to snap out of a daze as he started forward. He hesitated as he made eye contact with VerGann, but seeing that the delpin had stopped advancing, he scooped Tiaponine up.

"Stop..." The voice was quiet at first. Breydon cleared his throat and spoke again, louder this time, pulling against the grip of the guards restraining him. "Stop! Leave her alone, please—"

VerGann gritted his teeth. He couldn't even speak; the words would not come. But he remembered, distantly, that Breydon had been here this entire time. Had he *really* done nothing until now?

Hulbert scoffed, cutting off the prince. "Take both of them away," he said, dangerously quiet. His eyes were still locked on the fractured stone, blazing with fury. "Everyone out!"

This last part was a yell, and the nobles scrambled to obey; the doors were flooded with people pushing their way out of the hall, and as VerGann struggled to catch sight of Tiaponine again—with no success—his panic mounted.

They were not leaving her, were they? Marlott couldn't expect him to abandon her...

But Marlott maintained eye contact with the furious king, hardly even glancing at the delpins arrayed behind her.

VerGann felt himself trembling. *He could not, would not, leave without her...*

He could hear the confusion of the delpins at his side; in his head, their voices were hesitant and bewildered.

Why didn't we take her? We're not leaving yet, right? KaiDinn glanced from VerGann to Marlott and back again.

Stop fighting, VerGann, Vrenler said firmly. *You won't save her here without Marlott's help.*

If Marlott was aware of the conversation, she made no indication of it.

"We take our leave now, King Hulbert of Draven," she said, as Hulbert's knuckles turned white from gripping the GraVinn so tightly. "Enjoy your reward."

The delpins hesitated, their unease palpable. Then, one by one, they disappeared.

We'll find a way to get her back, Vrenler said quietly before he left.

Now, only now, did Marlott turn to look at VerGann. He glared back at her, but the barest trace of sadness in her eyes caught him off guard.

She would not leave until he did. She did not trust him.

Clenching his jaw, VerGann disappeared.

Among the crowd pouring out of the palace was a lone soldier.

He wore a navy blue Draven uniform, but if one were to look closely, they would notice that it did not quite fit—just a little too short in the sleeves and trousers.

He was inconspicuous enough, though, and he slipped through the panicked and shaken nobles with no trouble whatsoever. Leaving the palace grounds, he walked briskly through the upper streets until he reached the middle kingdom.

Here, he came to a solitary house and knocked at the door twice. Upon receiving no response, he knocked again.

This time the door opened, revealing another man frowning deeply at the soldier.

"Long live King Sandis," the soldier said, saluting. At this, the second man opened the door a little wider.

"Yes?"

"Hulbert is deranged. If we were waiting for the moment to strike, the time is now."

CHAPTER 15

"Sire..." Samuel studied Hulbert's still, shadowy form, alone in the banquet hall, with a measured caution. "You asked to be kept informed of the Tatrine troops' movements?"

The king was silent for a long moment. He still held the Stone of GraVinn in his right hand, its dark, cracked surface reflecting the limited light in the room.

"What is it?" he asked finally.

Samuel swallowed thickly.

"The city walls have been infiltrated."

He waited for the explosion of temper. It did not come immediately, like he had expected, although Hulbert's eyes flashed and he turned to stare at the servant.

"How?"

"It appears that Tatrine troops were already inside the city, sire. The gate fell before anyone knew what was going on."

Hulbert gritted his teeth. "And?"

"Their armies are in the lower streets as we speak. Your troops await your orders."

The explosion finally came. Hulbert slammed his fist against the wall, and Samuel jumped.

"The orders are, *fight back*, for goodness' sake! Get them out of my city."

"Y-yes, sire." Samuel bowed stiffly. "Of course." He turned to leave.

"Wait." The king turned toward Samuel. "I want the prison guard to double patrols. Those... Those... *things* from EliSann, they may return for the girl."

The girl. Samuel resisted the urge to roll his eyes.

"Sire," he began, forcing his tone to remain even. "No disrespect, but I don't understand why the girl still matters. You have the GraVinn—"

"This, you mean?" He came forward, waving the stone in Samuel's face. "Worthless! Worthless! A rock, nothing more!" He grabbed Samuel by the collar. "You would be wise not to speak. You're to blame for this, as much as the girl and my nephew."

Samuel froze, forgetting for a moment how to breathe. Hulbert eyed him distastefully, as though he were a bug or something equally insignificant, and Samuel wondered if he might be right about that.

After what seemed like an eternity, Hulbert's eyes narrowed. "Get out," he spat. "Before I part your head from your body!"

Gasping as the king released him, Samuel bowed once more. "Yes, sire." And he turned and made for the door, fighting to control his trembling.

The first thing Tiaponine noticed as she came around was the throbbing pain in her head.

She winced as she turned her head slightly, trying to figure out where she was. She remembered the attack—King Hulbert had been standing in front of her. She could see her necklace in his hand... and his other hand...

She sat up slowly, squeezing her eyes shut against the dizziness that followed. The king...

She opened her eyes, blinking as she grew accustomed to the dim lighting in the tiny room. Shivering, she pulled her arms closer to ward off the cold dampness around her. She touched her cheek gingerly, and winced again.

Yes, the king had slapped her across the face. There was sure to be a bruise there.

But where was she now? She blinked at her surroundings until they came into focus. There was a dark wall in front of her, and a set of bars. Somewhere in the corridor there must be a candle; a faint orange light highlighted a worn, damp, stone floor strewn with bits of hay.

She shuddered again—was she really where she thought she was? Everything had been going so well... And then, a few short hours later, here she was in a dungeon?

"Tee?"

VerGann? She felt her hopes rise, until she found where the voice had come from—a cell identical to her own, directly across the corridor. The shadowy form of its inhabitant belonged not to VerGann, but to Breydon, pacing back and forth slowly.

She recalled his look of suspicion when the king had accused her of theft, the trace of distrust in his eyes, and her heart sank.

"Tiaponine, are you alright?" He spoke again, and she winced.

"What..." she began instead of answering. Her voice came as little more than a whisper, so she swallowed and tried again. "What happened?"

"What happened," echoed Breydon. He sighed and sat down. "What *didn't* happen? Gwenevieve and Samuel—"

"Yes," Tiaponine said quickly. "I remember that very well. What else?"

The prince hesitated, and she could just see a hint of unease in his expression before he continued.

"Right," he said. "I don't really understand what happened myself, to be honest. VerGann was there, a handful of teenage boys were there, and a woman in the air..."

"VerGann was there?" Tiaponine couldn't keep the hope out of her voice. And then the apprehension—*if he had seen what had happened, why was she here? Was he alright?* "Where is he now?"

"It… It was strange." Breydon sounded troubled. "I think something kept him from intervening. But I didn't see where they all went."

Tiaponine was silent for a few moments. It wasn't realistic to worry about VerGann's whereabouts; he could take care of himself, of course he was safe. But if something had been keeping him subdued—what did that even mean?

She remembered what he had said, just a couple of days ago, when she had asked if he was in trouble. *Not yet.* Apprehension surged inside her again.

"Tiaponine," Breydon began quietly. "Are you—"

She clenched her jaw and cut him off. "And my necklace? What happened to the stone?"

Breydon winced visibly.

"The stone…" He trailed off. "That's what it was all about, wasn't it? He just wanted that stone… Why?"

Tiaponine did not reply. It was not as if she had a definite answer, anyway.

"It changed," Breydon said uncomfortably, registering her silence. He shook his head. "My uncle went insane."

She breathed a sigh of relief at that. If Hulbert was upset, then the enchantment on the GraVinn had worked—that was a good thing, at least.

"Could I… talk to you?" the prince began quietly. "About what happened up there?"

Tiaponine remembered the suspicion in his expression again, and clenched her jaw.

"I don't think there's much to talk about."

"Tee, listen." Breydon faltered slightly, but kept speaking. "I know you must be upset with me. I know I should have stepped in—I should've stood up for you up there." He swallowed. "And I understand if you don't want to forgive me for all of this. I'm sorry, I'm *so* sorry…"

Tiaponine stared at him for a few seconds in stony silence, her memory reaching even further back—to the day she'd met the prince, the chase through the lower streets of Draven. It might as well have been another lifetime. Her heart panged a little more at the thought.

"Have you—have you thought, this *whole time*, that I was a thief?" She could not keep her voice even this time; the fear and anger were audible even to her. "Really?"

"No! No," Breydon leaned forward, as though trying to see her more clearly from across the corridor. "No, I know you aren't. I just… I'd never seen that necklace before, and everything was changing so quickly—"

"I didn't steal it," she said crisply.

"I know. Tee, I know. If I'd thought about it for just a moment more, I would have reacted differently. But I didn't, and I cannot go back and change it. So I'm just sorry." He swallowed. "Will you forgive me?"

Tiaponine studied him carefully. He maintained steady eye contact with her, and she could see the desperation in his expression. He was still leaning forward, waiting for an answer.

She sighed. "I wasn't quite myself, either." Seeing that he was still tense, she rolled her eyes, allowing herself a small smile. "Of course I forgive you, Breydon."

He relaxed visibly. "Thank you. And anyway, considering my uncle's behavior…" He scoffed. "There was no chance of mixing up guilty parties after that spectacle."

Tiaponine winced, which did nothing for the dull aching in her cheek.

"I still don't understand, though, why he even *wanted* the stone." Breydon studied her, as though searching for an answer in her expression. "Why so desperate for it?"

A few seconds of uncomfortable silence passed before he clarified, "You *were* wearing it. Do you know anything about that?"

She drew in a deep breath and blew it out slowly, gathering her thoughts. VerGann had never explained to her specifically what the GraVinn did—she was not sure *he* even knew—and discussing it somehow felt dangerous.

"I know it is—it *was*—extremely powerful," she said at last. "Many have sought it in the past."

"And what is it supposed to *do*?"

Tiaponine worried at the hem of her skirt. "I don't know, to tell you the truth. I think it's beyond our ability to comprehend... I only took it off once, but..." She recalled how VerGann had clearly recoiled from the stone when she tried to give it to him, how nervous he'd looked. "It was dangerous. That's all I know for certain."

Breydon nodded, although he did not appear fully satisfied by this response. Tiaponine had no other to offer.

"And why did you have it?" he asked.

She shook her head. "A fluke. It's complicated. I'll explain later, if..." She trailed off as a sound reached her ears, echoing around the damp corridor. Footsteps—someone was approaching.

Breydon's mouth tightened as light bounced off of the walls, and someone started whistling. When the owner of the whistle came into view, a knot formed in Tiaponine's stomach.

"Good evening," the guard said, bowing to her in mock politeness before turning to sneer at Breydon. "*Your majesty.* How are you this fine day?" He made a show of glancing around the cell. "Not well, I see. Shame."

Breydon drew his shoulders back and stood up taller. "Excuse me," he said. "What's going on? What's the king playing at, keeping us down here?"

"Oh, calm down. You're very lucky, you know—the king wants to give your crimes the full attention they deserve, when the time comes. Not all prisoners get their own personal guard, see?" The guard smiled wide, a malicious satisfaction glinting in his eyes. "Just to make sure you stay safe and in one piece while he figures things out in the city."

Figures things out in the city. Tiaponine frowned, narrowing her eyes.

"What do you mean? What's wrong in the city?" she asked.

The guard turned on her in mild surprise. "What was that? Did you say something?"

She stared up at him defiantly. She was not going to repeat herself.

After a few moments, his face fell. "You aren't any fun at all. Yes, Tatrus has managed to worm a few troops into the city. *I* suspect that you two may have had something to do with that." He smirked at Breydon. "All this, just as the king is preoccupied with you and your *Lady Christine*? I'm sure he'll find the timing very interesting."

Tiaponine met Breydon's gaze across the corridor. He looked just as puzzled as she felt.

"Tatrine *troops* in the city?" he muttered.

There were, in fact, Tatrine troops in the city of Draven. There were many more than *a few* of them.

Earlier that evening, the streets had been alive with movement as the king's banquet guests fled his fury. Now, they echoed with the sound of metal on metal, pounding feet, screams and cries of pain. The streets filled with Draven blue rushing to meet Tatrine green, like a tide crashing against the shore.

Shops locked their doors and blew out their lanterns. Families huddled in houses, peering out fearfully from behind curtains and half-closed doors. Those unfortunate enough to have no home crouched in alley corners, making themselves as small as possible, hands clapped over ears and eyes squeezed shut. Dogs barked, horses whinnied in agitation, and the setting sun turned everything under it red and orange.

And the battle continued all night.

CHAPTER 16

VerGann paced the length of his room restlessly, clenching and unclenching his fists. KaiDinn, sitting on a chair nearby, shifted uncomfortably.

A few hours after returning to EliSann, the seratine had sent no word regarding a plan to take Tiaponine from the king's custody. At VerGann's insistence, Vrenler had gone to seek an audience with Marlott.

Another few hours later, there had been no response. Now, two days had passed. Between Vrenler's silence and the low hum of aggravated, jumbled thoughts emanating in waves from VerGann, KaiDinn was getting nervous.

Natty, sitting on his shoulder, sighed and leaned back on her hands. "I can *see* the anxiety in this room," she muttered. If VerGann heard her, he made no indication of it.

KaiDinn tapped his fingers on the table in front of him. "I'm sure they're coming up with something..."

"Must be quite the plan," Natty remarked unhelpfully. "For the amount of time it's taking Vrenler to get back."

VerGann paused to glance at her and then resumed his pacing.

KaiDinn knew what he feared—after yesterday's Council meeting, Marlott might think it a bad idea to have anything more to do with Tiaponine at all.

There was too much about this situation that he did not understand. He did not understand the true nature of VerGann's attachment to Tiaponine. He also did not understand how Marlott could leave Tiaponine in the palace in the first place, worried or not for VerGann's well-being. He *also* did not understand how pacing for hours on end could be comforting in any way, shape, or form. It certainly did not comfort *him.*

"*Vrenler, what's going on?*" VerGann's mouth did not move, but KaiDinn heard his voice clearly in his head, fraught with frustration.

He had asked the same question a couple of times before, and received no response, so KaiDinn wasn't expecting one this time. To his surprise, though, Vrenler finally broke his silence.

"*There's a battle going on in the city. Tatrine troops are making progress toward the palace. Marlott believes it's too dangerous for us to venture into the middle of a war zone.*"

VerGann made a sound of dissent and slammed his fist against the wall. Natty jolted.

"What just happened?" she asked, sounding faint.

KaiDinn repeated Vrenler's words to her quietly, wincing as the other two's argument threatened to scatter his thoughts.

"*We have to get her anyway!*"

"*What do you think I've been doing? I went to the city, looked around—there are too many people around the palace.*"

"*They have her in the* dungeon*! Marlott—*"

"*Is right, for now. It's too dangerous.*"

"*But—*"

"*We'll get her as soon as we can, alright? With or without Marlott. But there is already enough chaos.*"

With that, Vrenler fell silent again.

Seeing VerGann's eyes flare, KaiDinn cleared his throat.

"Well… If Hulbert's busy with the troops from Tatrus, then she's safe for now, isn't she?"

VerGann was obviously not reassured. He shook his head, almost to himself. "I'm done waiting. I'm going to get her tonight."

"Wait!" KaiDinn said before he could vanish, sitting straight up. Natty toppled over backward, grabbing his shirt collar before she could fall off of his shoulder. "You heard Vrenler—there's a battle going on. Marlott might give you permission once things calm down a bit—"

"Yes," VerGann said through gritted teeth. "But Tiaponine's there *right now.*"

"If you get to her, how will you get out? You'd have to lead her right through a battle." KaiDinn could not keep the confusion out of his voice. He had rarely seen VerGann as worked up as he was now. "If you wait, it'll be all of us together. Maybe even Marlott. Isn't that safer?"

"I'll just have to figure it out as I go." VerGann's expression was one of determination—clearly, his resolve hadn't waned. "Should I assume you'll be notifying the others of this the moment I leave?"

KaiDinn's nerves mounted some more. Next to him, Natty's eyes were wide.

"I—I—no," he stammered. "But why... I don't understand..."

He thought of VerGann's sharp words after the Council meeting yesterday. *Tiaponine is not someone I want to just see pass through my life.* What did that even *mean*? How did that equate to needlessly throwing oneself headlong into danger?

"I don't understand," he repeated. "To be honest. I know you... care for her, but..." He shook his head. "But even though I care for you and the other delpins like brothers, if one of you were in Tiaponine's position, it wouldn't make sense to pull you into more danger when an alternative was available—"

"KaiDinn!" Natty exclaimed, hitting his shoulder.

"*What?*" He frowned at her. "It's *true!*"

Something in VerGann's eyes softened, just a bit.

"I know that," he said. "But this isn't about what makes sense. She had to go through everything that happened yesterday all alone. I should've been there, and I wasn't. Now..." He swallowed. "Even if things *are* dangerous, I must be there to support her."

With that, he vanished, leaving KaiDinn blinking at the spot where he had just stood, as perplexed as ever.

VerGann reappeared in a dim stone corridor, lit only with the occasional torch along the wall.

He was somewhere underground. The network of tunnels stretching underneath Draven's castle was elaborate and extensive, housing forgotten nobles' tombs and old family heirlooms. The dungeons were part of the network, too, separated from the tombs and vaults to prevent escapees from accessing them.

Tiaponine should be somewhere down here; he just had to find her.

And then... somehow lead her back out to safety. Meaning they would have to find a way out of the dungeons. And then... make their way through the city, which was in chaos— Vrenler had been right, the battle with the Tatrine troops had reached the castle grounds.

If he'd been Marlott, he could simply transport both himself and Tiaponine out of here. But he wasn't Marlott.

VerGann crept along the corridor, listening carefully around each corner before proceeding. A few times, he saw movement in the distance—the silhouettes of guards walking along their patrols—but each time, he pulled back into the shadows of the hall and went unnoticed.

The hallways began blending into each other—one grey stone wall indistinguishable from the next—and he lost track of how many turns he'd made. And then, finally, he heard someone whistling a horribly out-of-tune melody.

The sound spilled out of the corridor ahead of him and to his left. He peered around the corner to find a guard situated right outside a pair of barred iron doors, facing each other across the hall.

Given the silence of the rest of the tunnels, this looked promising. It was a special prisoner that warranted a personal guard.

VerGann pulled back, out of sight, thinking. How to get rid of the soldier?

His eye twitched as the man whistled another out of tune note. But then an idea struck him, and he had to smile to himself.

He started quietly—a soft countermelody underneath the guard's whistles. The sound seemed to come from the far end of the corridor. A few seconds later, another whistle joined the mix, slightly louder this time. Another one—another one—

The guard's whistling faded as he realized that he wasn't the only one whistling anymore.

"Who's there?" he called out into the dim corridor. "Who's making that noise?"

The ghostly sound continued, getting louder all the time. It issued forth from the walls now, from the stones in the floor.

"What the..." A man's voice came from one of the cells—Breydon.

"Quiet!" The guard drew the sword at his belt and shouted down the corridor. "Who's doing this? Show yourself!"

VerGann vanished from his spot at the corner and rematerialized directly behind the guard. Tiaponine—she was in the other cell, knees pulled to her chest—shrieked at his appearance.

He winked at her. Then he tapped the guard's shoulder.

The guard shrieked even louder. He whirled around, blade swinging toward VerGann, only for the delpin to vanish into thin air and reappear behind him. He stumbled, turned, and swung the sword again, his movements reckless.

VerGann grabbed the man's sword hand, wresting the weapon from his grip, and struck him over the head with the hilt. The guard crumpled, eyes rolling back into his head.

Immediately all the whistling stopped.

Two wide pairs of frightened eyes stared up at him, one from the cell on either side of the corridor. Tiaponine got over it first.

"VerGann!" she said, and then repeated it as she scrambled to her feet. "VerGann, you're here! Oh..." She swayed and fell forward, grabbing the cell door before she could hit the ground. Now that she was closer to the torchlight from the hallway, VerGann could see the grey-green bruise forming on her cheek. He felt sick.

Breydon stood in the opposite cell, hands clapped over his ears. "Why must you do things like that?" he asked dourly. VerGann thought he might be trembling.

Good, he thought, a little maliciously. *He's part of the reason she's here. Perhaps he should stay a little longer.*

"Because it's fun," the delpin replied, monotone. He bent down and grabbed the key ring the fallen guard carried on his belt, and unlocked Tiaponine's cell door, leading her out into the corridor. She regained her balance quickly, to his relief. "We've got to go—it'll be hard enough to get back home without anyone trying to find us."

"Home?" Tiaponine turned her head to the side. "Draven?"

VerGann realized his mistake. "EliSann," he corrected. "Come on—let's go."

He started walking, gently pulling Tiaponine along, but she stood firm. He looked back at her in puzzlement.

"But…" She gestured in Breydon's direction. The prince did not look at all surprised as VerGann glowered at him; in fact, he appeared almost resigned to the thought that he would be staying here, in this cell, in the dungeon of his own castle.

"We can't leave him," Tiaponine said. "You *know* we can't."

He rather thought they could, if they so pleased. But she grabbed his hand, pleading eyes wide.

After a moment, he sighed. "Very well." He strode over and unlocked Breydon's cell door. "You're lucky she's good enough to intervene for you."

The prince maintained direct eye contact with VerGann. "Believe me," he said with a sincerity that surprised the delpin. "I know."

"Good." VerGann turned on him and reached for Tiaponine's hand again—she took it readily. "Now, we need to find a way out of this dungeon."

CHAPTER 17

By the time the guard came around, the prince and the girl were gone. He had no clear memory of the third person— *creature*-only a hazy image in his mind of a tall man, gone as soon as he appeared, and the eerie sound of whistling from a hundred unseen corners.

He stared at the open cells in front of him for a long moment, his head throbbing. He was so disoriented, he did not hear the footsteps approaching.

"What's going on here?"

In the entrance to the corridor stood the captain of the dungeon guard. He glared from the guard to the open doors on either side of the hall.

"Sir." The guard forced himself to sit up, although his vision went dimmed as he did so. "The prince... He's escaped..."

"The prince." The captain's voice was steely. "The king is not concerned with the prince at the moment. Where's the *girl?*"

His words echoed around in the guard's head without being understood. "The girl?"

The captain made a growling sound in the back of his throat and retreated into the corridor he'd come from. "Get down here!" he called to someone in the halls beyond him. "We have an escape situation. Tell all patrols you see—search for the girl and that EliSann creature!"

"We've already been this way," Tiaponine sighed as they reached another intersection between two corridors. The exhaustion in her voice was clear. "We're walking in circles."

Breydon studied the hallways before him. Personally, he couldn't distinguish where they had already been from where they had not—all he saw were narrow, dimly-lit halls of damp stone and mildew. But he suspected that Tiaponine was right. At this point, they had been wandering the dungeons for at least forty minutes. He would have expected to reach a staircase by now, or a supply room at the very least. All they had encountered were more cells, most empty, some occupied by prisoners who tracked their movements with dull, weary eyes before drifting back to sleep.

He led Tiaponine and VerGann into the corridor in front of them. "Let's try going straight this time. We'll find the end of the network eventually."

VerGann made a sound that Breydon suspected was a hastily-disguised scoff. "Brilliant," he said. "I'm glad you know where we're going."

Something in Breydon snapped. He was not sure how much more of the delpin's snide commentary he could handle. He knew VerGann was angry, probably *furious* with him, and understandably so, but still—

"How in the world would I know where we're going?" he retorted in clipped tones. "Do you think I spend much time down here?"

"Stop it," Tiaponine snapped before VerGann could respond. "Both of you." He didn't miss the sharp glance she shot VerGann's way, and the delpin actually looked chastised. "Bicker like children once we're all safe."

They lapsed into silence for a few minutes, until they reached another junction between hallways.

"It's true," VerGann said, his voice shattering the silence even though he spoke quietly. "We should eventually reach a way out if we just head straight."

It was a concession of some sort, albeit a very begrudging one. Breydon did not reply, but nodded and plunged ahead.

No sooner had they left the junction behind than a gruff male voice from the intersecting corridor called out. "Hello? Who's down there?"

Tiaponine gasped and froze in her steps, almost causing VerGann to run into her. All three of them stared at each other with wide eyes, holding their breath as they listened for signs of the stranger's movements.

"Sir!" the voice called out a name that Breydon did not recognize. "There are people out of their cells down this way."

As he spoke, footsteps started pounding toward them. VerGann moved first, grabbing Tiaponine by the hand and starting to run, Breydon on his heels.

He knew the moment the guard rounded the corner—it was accompanied by shouting, and then the corridor was echoing with the deafening sound of many pairs of boots pounding against the stone floor. How many guards were back there? Breydon did not dare turn back to look.

"They have a straight shot at us," he gasped as he raced to keep up with VerGann and Tiaponine. "We need to get out of this hallway."

Tiaponine was already ahead of him on that count, though—at the very first junction, she threw herself into the hallway to the right, and then left at the next possible turn. Breydon had forgotten how quick she was—now he remembered, as he and VerGann both fell behind her.

They kept running. The sounds of the guards' footfalls and shouts were more distant now, thankfully, but Breydon still forced himself not to look back—if he did, he would slow down too much. As it was, he struggled to keep his pace, and he suspected that VerGann was intentionally holding back to stay next to him. A small kindness—one that could get them all caught—but Breydon appreciated it nonetheless.

Tiaponine ran past another junction, then skidded to a stop and backed up, looking off to her left. The relief spreading across her face felt like a breath of fresh air to Breydon.

"Staircase," she panted. "Stairs."

Then she was dashing into a narrow stairwell, and Breydon and VerGann followed her up, up, up, until they reached a door.

Tiaponine had stopped moving. Her hands trembled as she tried the door. "It's—it's locked."

The yells behind them were still distant, but they grew slightly louder with every passing second. They would be found if they stalled here for long. And they had just cornered themselves against a locked door.

Breydon tried the handle himself. "Great," he muttered. It was a heavy door, several inches thick, on crude iron hinges. "VerGann, do you think we can force this open if—" He broke off with some irritation, catching VerGann's signature eye roll. "*What?* What have I done wrong now?"

"Relax, princeling You forget what you're dealing with very easily." The delpin set his hand against the door nonchalantly. "Step back, please."

Tiaponine pulled Breydon back toward the wall. There was a sickening cracking sound, and then the door began splintering out from VerGann's hand, the wood falling to the ground in pieces. In seconds, all that remained was a pile of what might be useful as kindling, but certainly served no purpose as a door.

Breydon realized that he was gaping, his mouth hanging open. *First the whistling in the dungeon, now this.* But then he saw VerGann's smug look, and tried to compose himself.

"Well, then." He cleared his throat. "Good." He plunged past the delpin into the cool fog of the early morning.

He almost did not see where the ground gave way in front of him. He staggered to a halt, then threw his arm out to keep Tiaponine from falling.

"What—" she began.

"It's the moat," he explained. Yes, he could hear it now— the sound of water somewhere below him. Not a long fall, by any means. If the dungeons had let out where he thought they had, they stood on an overhang only fifteen feet or so above the moat.

By now the guards were surely making their way up the stairwell to the surface. A dirt path led from here around the castle grounds, Breydon knew, eventually leading to a bridge used by the guards to cross the moat. That was where he, VerGann, and Tiaponine would be expected to go, most likely. So they needed a different way off of the grounds.

He squinted down at the grey water below him. It moved quickly, and it would be cold and unpleasant, but...

VerGann was at his side. "Where to now?"

Breydon started, not expecting the delpin to be so close. "Can't you just take us out of here?" he asked. "You appear and disappear all the time, so..."

VerGann shook his head. "Not all of us."

Breydon stared—somehow he had never considered that VerGann's power might have limits. "What was that at the banquet hall, then? You just popped a bunch of people in and out again—"

"That wasn't me." VerGann's expression was earnest, for once. "Unless you'd like for me to abandon the two of you, I'm stuck here, too."

He said it as though it were a viable option, but he glanced at Tiaponine as he spoke. He would never actually leave her behind, even if he was fully capable of escaping himself. That small observation, somehow, was enough to make Breydon's heart *pang*.

The echo of footfalls on stone reached them from the stairwell. Breydon shook his head, forcing himself to think clearly.

"We'll go this way," he said, turning to his left—away from the guard path. "Just a little ways, we need to be lost in the fog. And then we'll cross the moat."

He started ahead, and the other two followed at a brisk pace. Even VerGann looked tired of running at this point—he took lurching steps forward, his even gait gone. No one complained about the prospect of diving into freezing cold water. What waited behind them would probably be worse.

The fog, thankfully, held as they moved along the overhang. It wasn't long before the faint light from the stairwell faded behind them. The guards had reached the moat, by the sounds of it, but their voices drifted further away as they followed the guard path to the back of the castle grounds.

Something was still off, still not as it should be, though Breydon could not quite place what the disturbance was. Tiaponine furrowed her brow as they walked, tilting her head slightly.

"Do you hear the yelling?" she asked quietly.

"Yelling?" Breydon blinked, realizing what was wrong. The guards pursuing them were gone, but the air *was* still full of sounds—the rushing waters of the moat, and beyond that, distant voices yelling, the clinging of metal on metal. As he listened, the sound grew louder.

He muttered a curse under his breath, recalling the guard's taunts from earlier. "Tatrus. I forgot."

"Ah, yes." VerGann gave a long-suffering sigh. "They weren't this close to the castle when I arrived."

Tiaponine paled. "So now we'll be wading through a moat and then through a battlefield?"

Neither of them responded. They only looked at her with expressions that matched the exhaustion on her face.

She took a deep breath, rolling out the tension in her shoulders. "Very well. Might as well get on with it."

She backed up, got a running start, and jumped over the edge of the overhang.

"Tee—" Breydon began to protest, but too late. A *splash* from below told him she'd hit the water.

VerGann met his gaze and shrugged. Then he jumped after her.

Breydon shook his head to himself. He had not been anticipating walking through a battlefield today—Tatrus had completely slipped his mind in the panic of their escape from the dungeons. But there was no help for it.

He braced himself for the cold, took a deep breath, and dove into the moat.

❦

Tiaponine had thought she'd prepared for the cold. She had been wrong.

The chilly morning water closed over her head, and the cold seeped straight through her clothes, her skin, her very bones. She froze there for a moment, feeling the current carry her, and then forced herself to start kicking her feet.

She surfaced only moments later, thankfully, and found VerGann spluttering as he came up for air next to her. Breydon was just seconds behind, his teeth chattering.

Tiaponine did not have time to make sure they were all truly alright. The current was stronger than she had expected, and already it had carried them away from where they had jumped. If they did not cross the moat quickly enough, they could very well end up meeting the guards on the other side of the castle grounds.

She kicked her legs and propelled herself forward, swimming toward the far bank. Without the current, it would have been easy. As it was, her head kept being forced underwater, and she had to put all of her remaining strength into pushing ahead, ignoring the chill seeping through her.

When her feet hit solid ground, she practically sobbed in relief. She hauled herself onto the bank and collapsed there. She did not move as the other two climbed up after her.

The sounds of the battle were almost directly overhead now, but Tiaponine could not bring herself to care right at that moment. She lay there and shivered and stared at the lifting fog and the castle she had just escaped from. She did not think she could make herself move.

After what felt like an eternity of silence, Breydon coughed.

"Well," he said. "If the guards went around to the back of the grounds, we should be free to—"

"There!" a voice shouted, and VerGann groaned in frustration. Several blurry figures were approaching through the thinning mist, picking their way along the banks of the moat. Tiaponine saw their blue Draven uniforms and closed her eyes in dismay. She wanted to keep them closed forever.

I can't run right now. I can't.

Next to her, VerGann pushed himself to his elbows, but his exhaustion was pronounced on his face. "If I take them down..."

"Then we get... Get to go through a battle like this," Tiaponine managed to say. Now her teeth were chattering, too—she felt like she would never be warm again. "One way or another... We're finished right now."

VerGann made eye contact with her, his gaze worried. And defeated, she realized—perhaps he could still fight his way out of this if he tried, but she and Breydon were all but useless, and he must view that as a failure on his part.

She at least forced herself to sit up, though her head spun at the exertion. VerGann steadied her as she started listing to the side.

It was warmer there, with his arm around her and her head on his shoulder. Tiaponine closed her eyes again, wishing she could stay there like that. *Maybe, just maybe...*

A strong pair of hands grabbed her by the upper arms, wrenching her away from him. VerGann lurched for her instinctively, only to be pulled back by another two guards. Two more had Breydon on his knees and were trying to pull him to his feet with little success.

"Quite the escape attempt," one guard in a captain's uniform said with a smirk, as they were hauled to their feet and their wrists were bound behind them. "You almost got away." He turned to one of his men. "Send word to the king. Our friend from EliSann has arrived."

CHAPTER 18

"Have you heard anything?" Natty tapped her foot anxiously against the table as KaiDinn reappeared in the back room of VerGann's home. "Did he say when he'd be back?"

The young delpin gritted his teeth, his blue eyes troubled. He sat down on a nearby chair, legs sprawling, pressing a hand to his head.

"No," he said. "No, no. Nothing. He's shut us out, we can't hear anything."

"And the city…?"

"There's too much chaos out there. I can't properly track him like that. That's why I'm back here." KaiDinn sighed, sounding tired. "The others are still looking, but…"

"Do you think he'll be back soon, though? How long until things calm down?"

KaiDinn simply shook his head, and Natty quieted down immediately. It was not often that she saw him this upset—this was troubling him more than she had thought.

"I don't know. I don't know anything about this." He fell silent for a long moment. "Natty, I don't understand him. What he's doing, why…" His voice trailed off.

Natty clucked her tongue in sympathy, flying over to perch on the bedside table next to him.

"He really cares about her." She thought of VerGann dancing with Tiaponine, just a short while ago, and the happy glint in his eye every time he'd looked her way. "I think he'd do anything for her now."

KaiDinn opened one eye to look at her. "Anything?" he muttered. "He's thrown all caution to the wind—how are we to recover him?"

Something in his voice sounded raw. For half a second Natty thought it might be bitterness—then she realized it was a mix of genuine hurt and apprehension.

"To recover him," she echoed slowly. She cocked her head to the side. "You don't think VerGann will come back after this is all over?"

He stared at her for a moment, then groaned, closing his eyes.

"I… Nat, I don't know what he's going to do. I don't think he's figured that part out yet, either." Another brief silence. "You really think he would do *anything* for her? Even…"

He did not finish his sentence, but Natty did not need to read minds to know what he was thinking. *Even leave behind his home, his friends, his family.*

She tried to imagine never seeing VerGann again—tried to imagine his presence simply being erased from EliSann, crossed out the same way the BarLonn had been. She could not do it, but she also could not deny that his attachment to Tiaponine had become part of him over the past several years.

"I think…" She hesitated. It *was* possible, she'd been about to say. But her friend's eyes were wide and afraid as he watched her. VerGann was like an older brother to him. KaiDinn was too young, too *delpin* to understand why VerGann might be willing to leave EliSann for Tiaponine. And Natty could not bring herself to put voice to his fears.

"I don't know," she said instead, and it was true.

KaiDinn sighed. "I just wish…" His gaze shifted as he trailed off, focusing on a point past Natty, and his face paled.

"KaiDinn? What…" Natty followed his gaze and then stopped, her blood running cold. Standing in the shadows on the opposite side of the room was none other than Marlott.

VerGann's leaving for Draven, the delpins' frantic search for him—had they told Marlott any of this? One more glance at KaiDinn answered that question clearly enough. The answer was no, she had been kept in the dark, and based on the expression on her face, the seratine was not happy about that fact.

BriDonn and Vrenler appeared beside KaiDinn. "I checked the dungeons, but no sign—" BriDonn began, cutting off when Vrenler elbowed him hard in the side. Their eyes widened as they found Marlott frowning at them.

No one spoke. It was obvious that the seratine was not at all pleased to find VerGann gone. How much she had heard of Natty's discussion with KaiDinn, Natty couldn't tell. Enough for her to be upset.

In the next instance, Marlott was gone.

There was a collective sigh from all three delpins.

Natty closed her eyes. "Oh, *no*."

The castle was in an uproar.

Everywhere there were soldiers running to the grounds, laden with weapons. As the noise of the battle reached the grand entrance, terrified servants ran the other way, hoping to escape through the gardens or hide in the upper rooms of the castle.

The guards led VerGann, Tiaponine, and Breydon through the chaos calmly, as though nothing was out of the ordinary. As they pushed through the crowd, approaching the doors to the Great Hall, the largest of the guards turned on the group.

"Wait here," he said. A ghastly smile crossed his face, and he leaned in closer to VerGann, as though sharing a secret. "I'll alert the king that we're here."

VerGann crinkled his nose at the guard's pungent breath as he passed and disappeared through the double doors. He tugged at his restraints—the leather straps binding his wrists were uncomfortably tight, and he could feel them rubbing his skin raw. He *could*, of course, just disappear right now. He could disable a few of these guards before they could react. He was tempted to do so.

The issue was that he couldn't manage all of them at once, not when he was standing at the center of a circle of a dozen of them. If he fought, it would be Tiaponine and Breydon that paid the price. It only took a glance to see that neither of them was up to much of a fight at the moment.

Breydon met VerGann's gaze. "He won't have much help inside of the hall. We could take him down."

VerGann wanted to laugh. He had to admire the prince's determination—drenched to the bone and shivering from the cold, shaky and pale from a lack of sleep, struggling to remain standing, but he still wanted to fight back.

"You mean *I* could take him down," he hissed back. "You're exhausted."

Breydon grimaced. "I'm trying to think of a scenario where this doesn't end horribly for us."

"I don't know," Tiaponine muttered, shoulders slumped. "This is all pretty horrible."

"Quiet," one of the guards said gruffly. "No talking."

They fell silent for a few seconds. Then, quietly so that the guards couldn't hear, VerGann said, "If I see an opening, I'll take it. But not if it'll just get you hurt."

Tiaponine met his gaze, opening her mouth to say something. Before she could speak, though, the doors to the Great Hall opened, and the guard returned.

"His majesty will see you now," he said, standing to the side as the guards ushered them inside.

Two days ago, the Great Hall had been full of activity as all the nobles of the city vied for a glimpse of the prince's chosen bride. In the time since, all of the opulent decorations from the banquet—the banners and flowers and elegant table arrangements—had been left as they were, leaving the hall with the eerie feeling of a place abandoned in a hurry.

King Hulbert sat on the throne at the head of the hall, legs crossed, expression fixed in a scowl.

"You returned later than I expected," he said, eyeing VerGann. As he spoke, a deep *boom* echoed through the corridor outside—by the sound of it, something large and heavy ramming into a wall by the grand entrance.

"You're not very wise for a tyrant king," VerGann replied. "There's a battle at your front gates, and you're still here."

"I have more pressing concerns at the moment." The king stood and strode toward them. VerGann felt Tiaponine shrink into herself next to him.

Hulbert stopped several yards away.

"Release them," he snapped. "Might as well give them that."

VerGann's leather restraints fell away as the guards swiftly cut through them. He massaged the raw skin at his wrists, taking in his surroundings quickly. Hulbert knew that they were outnumbered and weak—which was true—but with their hands free, they might have some options here. At least Tiaponine and Breydon would not be hopeless if VerGann managed to make a move against the guards and the king.

"Now." Hulbert pulled something small from his left pocket—the Stone of GraVinn, its aquamarine surface webbed with dark cracks. He tossed it to the ground, letting it skid to a stop at VerGann's feet.

VerGann stared at the stone for a moment. Just like the other day—he felt nothing from it, no energy, no pull. He frowned up at Hulbert.

The king drew himself up to his full height. "You will put back into this the power which you took from it."

Breydon and Tiaponine exchanged a surprised—and concerned—glance. VerGann blinked, taken aback by the demand.

"I... beg your pardon?" he said.

"You heard me," Hulbert growled. "You took the power. Give it back."

Some part of VerGann wanted to laugh. The king gave away his ignorance every time he spoke. For VerGann, a single being with limited power, to be capable of disabling a nearly-eternal thing like the GraVinn, let alone return it to its former power...

But the rest of VerGann, the part that remembered that he was in a precarious situation, was horrified. The fact that Hulbert could actually expect him to be capable of carrying out this request... The man truly *was* deranged.

"I cannot do as you ask," he said slowly. Another *boom* echoed in the corridor outside.

Hulbert snarled, and in that moment, he truly did resemble a cornered animal. His eyes glinted with a feral desperation.

"Don't play games with me, delpin."

"*Your majesty.*" VerGann could not keep the mockery from his voice. He nodded at the stone on the ground. "This is a rock. Nothing more, nothing less. It's worthless."

"It was the key to unimaginable power," Hulbert growled, his face reddening. "Power which you are responsible for removing."

VerGann fixed his stare on Hulbert. "You're the one who removed the necklace by force. Your greed rendered it powerless, not me."

"My…" Hulbert's face went from red to a worrying shade of purple. "*Me?* I have dedicated my life to finding the GraVinn. You will restore it or pay with your life!" He was yelling now, his voice rebounding off the walls.

"Then I'll pay with my life," VerGann bit back. "I cannot—"

"Or perhaps," Hulbert interrupted, nodding at his guards. "*Their* lives."

Tiaponine yelped as a guard grabbed her by the shoulder, yanking her backwards and pressing a knife to her throat. Next to her, Breydon's eyes widened as he found a blade to his neck as well.

VerGann forced himself not to react, tried to keep his eyes off of the blade at Tiaponine's throat. He could protect her, could save her. He could not guarantee safety for both her and Breydon, though, not while dealing with Hulbert at the same time. Someone was going to get hurt here.

"The GraVinn's power far surpassed mine," he said, carefully keeping the quaver out of his voice. "I was never capable of controlling it. No one was. I cannot return what I could not take."

"Stop *lying!*" Hulbert snapped. "Do it now or the girl dies!"

The guard pressed the blade into Tiaponine's throat, and a thin line of red beaded up where it dug into her skin. Her eyes remained fixed on VerGann, her lips pressed tightly together.

"As you wish," VerGann relented, his tone icy. "Release them first."

Hulbert scoffed. "What do you take me for? No!"

"That was not a request," VerGann warned. "Release them."

The corridor thundered with noise again, and this time the distant rumble did not fade out.

"The stone," the king demanded.

Well, he was nothing if not persistent. VerGann held his hand out in front of him. The GraVinn rose from the ground, lifted by an invisible force, and came to rest in his palm.

"Release them both," he said slowly, as though speaking to a child. "Then, and only then, will I give you what you want."

There was a long moment of tense silence. But then the animal desperation in Hulbert won out.

"Release them," he snarled to his guards.

"VerGann?" Tiaponine whispered as the sharp blade was lifted from her throat and she and Breydon were released.

VerGann strode toward the king, his hand still stretched out in front of him. A halo of orange light began to form around the GraVinn, and the hall echoed with the sound of high pitched wails, drowning out the noise from the corridor. Every candle flame along the wall flickered in time with his steps, and he relished the way the guards glanced fearfully around them.

Abruptly, the commotion and brilliant light display came to an end.

VerGann held his hand out to the king. Hulbert stepped forward eagerly, then froze.

The GraVinn was gone; in its place was a small pile of gray dust.

Hulbert's upper lip twisted into a snarl.

"Oh, dear," VerGann said, blowing the dust into Hulbert's face. "Well, that's unfortunate."

The king coughed, recoiling from the cloud of dust. "You—how *dare* you—"

All at once, the noise outside surged to its greatest volume. This was not another resounding *boom*—this was a chorus of shouting, screaming, the clanging of metal on metal and pounding feet.

"Oh, yes, and Tatrus has arrived," VerGann mused. "Did you invite them?"

"Guards—" Hulbert began, but before he could finish, the doors were thrown open, and a soldier stumbled into the hall, face pouring with sweat, uniform dark with blood on one sleeve.

"Your Majesty," the soldier—a captain of some sort, based on his uniform—panted. "They've breached the entrance. We have to get you off of the premises."

"They're *inside the castle?*" Hulbert gritted his teeth, glancing from the soldier to VerGann and back again. "This isn't over," he snapped, pointing an accusatory finger at VerGann. "Let's go! Keep them secure," he shouted at the guards as he followed the soldier out of the hall. "We'll meet outside the western wall!"

Although they had received their orders, the guards in front of VerGann, Tiaponine, and Breydon appeared conflicted. Their eyes kept darting from the still-open door to their charges and back again. The sounds of the battle grew louder with every second.

The largest guard cleared his throat. "Hands behind you," he ordered, only the slightest hesitation in his voice.

Tiaponine slipped her hand into VerGann's. Breydon, although he still looked exhausted, actually laughed.

"Please," he said. "I'd focus on getting yourselves out of here."

The guards did not appear to particularly disagree. Before they could gather their wits about them again, Breydon was running for the doors, Tiaponine and VerGann right behind him.

The corridor was full of people rushing in all directions—Draven soldiers running to assist their comrades, the occasional Tatrine troop pushing past the castle's first lines of defense, straggling servants pulling their friends and families along in hopes of finding safety. Breydon led the way to the back wing of the castle, and VerGann found himself surprised by the prince's resilience, even after all of the stress of the past two days. They might actually make it out of this place…

But Breydon slowed to a stop as they reached the corridor leading out to the gardens. It was clogged with people, blue and green uniforms dropping left and right.

"Is there another way out?" Tiaponine's distress was audible in her voice.

"It looks like they've taken the ground floor," VerGann said. If Tatrus had managed to take both the front and back entrances, it was most likely they'd also taken every other ground floor entrance, which meant that they were stuck inside.

"We'll find somewhere to hide." Breydon pulled them back into the depths of the castle, barreling up the nearest staircase into a hallway lined with doors. He picked an unsuspecting room at the back of the hallway—a supply closet, by the looks of it—and ushered them inside before closing the door behind him.

He promptly collapsed, sliding to the ground in exhaustion.

Tiaponine sat down, too, leaning heavily against the wall, her eyes bloodshot from a lack of rest. VerGann, although certainly in better shape than both of them, felt the tug of exhaustion as well. When was the last time he'd slept? It had been a chaotic couple of days.

They sat in silence for a long while, catching their breath.

"I don't understand," Breydon finally said, leaning his head against the door. "Tatrus has been camped outside of EliSann for days, but why would they attack Draven..."

Personally, VerGann could think of many reasons to have a bone to pick with Draven. But pointing them out would not be productive at the moment. The sounds of the battle could still be heard in the distance, and while their little supply closet was fairly isolated for the moment, eventually someone would come looking for those in hiding. How their next several days went might be very different depending on who took control of the castle.

Tiaponine seemed to be realizing the same thing. She shook her head in frustration.

"It's too late to wonder," she said. "But we need to get some rest."

"I'll keep watch," Breydon began, but VerGann shook his head.

"I'll keep watch. You two rest."

The prince appeared almost relieved. "Very well. But if anything happens..."

"I'll let you know," VerGann agreed.

Breydon shifted away from the door, already half asleep. Tiaponine gave VerGann's hand a squeeze before curling up herself, eyes drifting closed.

VerGann settled against the wall, eyes fixed on the door, and listened as the battle drew nearer.

Breydon woke up to a dull throbbing in his head. He winced as he shifted—everything was still sore from the events of the last couple of days. *Had he even managed to sleep at all?* It sure didn't feel like it.

The sound of yelling and cries of pain had gone. The relative silence from the corridor outside seemed almost material. Breydon opened his eyes slowly.

As he adjusted to the dim light of the supply closet, he found VerGann leaning against the wall.

"Tatrus?" Breydon began. VerGann put a finger to his lips, then pointed to Tiaponine. She was still curled up, eyes closed. She looked small and fragile like this, the opposite of when she was awake.

Breydon could see the warmth in VerGann's gaze as he looked at her. Had Breydon ever looked at her like that? He cared about her, he truly did, but... He somehow doubted it.

He forced his thoughts away from the topic.

"The battle?" he asked, keeping his voice down so as not to disturb Tiaponine. "What happened?"

"It's over," VerGann said. "It's been over for hours."

"Who won?"

VerGann shrugged. "I can't tell. They're searching the castle, though. For the people who hid."

Breydon pushed down the apprehension rising inside of him. He was not sure that any outcome of this battle would be good for him. If Draven had won, he'd have his uncle's wrath to face. If Tatrus had won—well, he wasn't sure why King Sandis had felt the need to attack, but as the prince and heir of a fallen king, Breydon was unlikely to receive favorable treatment.

At least, if Tatrus had won, they would have no reason to keep Tiaponine and VerGann here. Breydon might have dragged them into this mess, but Tatrus could give them a way out of it.

"I'm sorry," he found himself saying. "About this entire mess. I acted like an idiot the other day, and now all of this..." He gestured at the room around them, which seemed a bit inadequate in the grand scheme of what had happened since the banquet.

Tiaponine had forgiven him, almost immediately. Breydon could not imagine VerGann doing the same, not when he remembered the unmistakable fury in the delpin's eyes upon seeing Tiaponine on the ground and Breydon just... standing there. Watching.

As expected, VerGann regarded him coolly, raised an eyebrow, and said, "You did act like an idiot. I'm glad you know it."

Breydon sighed. Well, at least he hadn't been met with complete contempt. In a way, the delpin's blunt words were more comforting than forgiveness would have been. Dry jabs and sarcastic remarks, Breydon could expect from him. That meant that something was normal in the world, at least.

"I suppose, to be fair," VerGann continued, surprising Breydon. "I wasn't exactly useful the other day, either." His gaze flitted back to Tiaponine, the regret plainly on his face. "It still happened the way it did."

Breydon shuddered as he pictured that otherworldly woman, floating in the air like a spirit, glaring at VerGann as he'd tried to push toward Tiaponine. "I somehow doubt that was on you. I think what'll matter to Tee is that you came back."

VerGann cast him a sharp look. Breydon couldn't tell if it was more surprise at the mention of the *other* EliSann creatures at the banquet, or irritation at his using Tiaponine's nickname.

"It *might* matter," he said. "If we manage to get out of this."

Something down the corridor crashed—the sound of a door banging open.

Tiaponine jolted awake. "What..." She trailed off as both VerGann and Breydon shot her warning looks. "What was that?"

she whispered. The sound of a commotion reached their ears, a handful of men's boots on the ground and a voice.

"Come on, out with you. Let's go…" The voice faded down the corridor, but the sound of footsteps grew closer.

"They've been searching for escapees," VerGann said quietly. "I guess that door was locked."

"*This* door isn't locked—" Breydon began, but was interrupted by a sharp rapping on the door, followed by the doorknob shaking as someone tried to turn it. The rusty latch did not immediately release.

"Back away from the door!" a man's voice called from the other side, sharp and loud. "Hands up!"

VerGann and Breydon both scrambled away from the door, and Tiaponine grabbed the delpin's hand, now fully awake. They had scarcely cleared the door when it came flying open, broken by a strong kick on the other side.

At first, Breydon could not see the man in the doorway clearly. The torches in the corridor had burned low after a long night of fighting with no one to tend to them, leaving very little light for his eyes to adjust to.

Blue or green? What color was the uniform? Breydon squinted, even as he raised his hands and got to his feet, Tiaponine and VerGann doing the same next to him.

"Two men and a woman in here," the soldier called to someone behind him. "Not Draven soldiers. Come on, let's go."

They staggered out into the hallway—Breydon's legs didn't seem to want to work after going through so much abuse yesterday—and five armed soldiers surrounded them. Now Breydon could see their dark green uniforms more clearly.

One guard took in their clothing and frowned at Breydon. "This one wears the royal crest on his sleeve."

Breydon clenched his fists at his side to hide his nerves. *Great.* They'd taken the palace and now knew they had a member of the royal family...

"You are from Tatrus, correct?" he demanded, steeling his voice as much as he could. He could not appear weak here, had to remain as in-command as he was able. "I wasn't aware that King Sandis of Tatrus had a quarrel with Draven."

A soldier leveled his sword on him and smiled. "He doesn't. This is a favor."

"For whom?"

Another soldier—the one who had kicked in the door—laughed.

"Come," he said. "I'm sure King Lundane would love to find the usurper to his throne hiding in a closet."

King Lundane... Usurper to his throne...

The soldiers made to move forward, but Breydon stood rooted to the spot. His breath had frozen in his lungs.

Tiaponine and VerGann were staring at him with wide eyes, as though waiting to see his reaction.

"What is the meaning of this?" Anger seeped through his every word. "King Lundane is dead, and even if he weren't, *I'm* no usurper. What game is your king playing here?"

The Tatrine soldiers stared at him for a long moment, as though slowly processing his words.

"No usurper, eh?" one mused. "Do you claim Hulbert to be the rightful king? Your dear father, who tried to have your uncle Lundane killed?"

Something about that question seemed to twist Breydon's brain into a knot.

"Hulbert, the *rightful* king?" he echoed incredulously. "That man is not my father."

There was another long moment of confused silence. A soldier glanced from the royal crest on Breydon's sleeve to his face and back again.

"The... prince?" he whispered.

"That's not the prince," another snapped in response. "The prince was killed years ago. He's dead."

Breydon recoiled at the words, as though he'd been slapped in the face. VerGann raised an eyebrow.

"He looks pretty good for a dead man," he said flatly.

"Shut up," the soldier who had kicked in the door snapped. "Shut up. Grab all three and follow me."

A guard roughly grabbed Breydon by the arm—*he was getting tired of being handled*—and pulled him along down the corridor, Tiaponine and VerGann in tow.

King Lundane, Breydon thought the whole way. *This is a favor... for King Lundane...*

CHAPTER 19

"Your staff will need to be watched for a while," Sandis said. "To ensure their loyalty. If you wish, some of my men will remain to assist you in weeding out the traitors."

Lundane nodded without much enthusiasm as he took in the Great Hall—there had been a celebration here not three days ago, and many of the decorations had been destroyed in the battle, leaving broken glass and crushed flowers strewn across the floor and banners torn from the walls.

He had not stood in this spot for nearly eighteen years. Aside from the mess, it had not changed much. It was an unsettling thing to realize, especially when so much else *had* changed.

Sandis was correct, of course. Such a long time had passed since Lundane had been on the throne, some of the staff—especially the younger ones—had probably grown loyal to Hulbert. That was to say nothing of the state the palace guard and military would be in. Despite his being a tyrant, Hulbert's military policies were much more active than Lundane's had been, and he could easily believe that it would take him years to rebuild a loyal army.

A soldier entered the hall with an old servant woman trailing him. Like most of the staff they had found so far, the woman offered no resistance to being ushered around, although she did appear nervous.

Lundane took one look at her weathered face and smiled to himself. "Madame Farault," he said. "I'm pleased to see the years have been kind to you."

Madame Farault looked around for the source of the voice, and stopped short when her gaze rested on Lundane. Recognition and tears flickered in her eyes, and she covered her mouth with her hand.

"You... your majesty," she stammered, going into a deep curtsy. Her voice trembled. "How...?"

"It's a long story," Lundane sighed, although his heart warmed to see the kindly old woman after all this time. She had practically raised his son back then... He should ask her about Breydon's fate...

He opened his mouth to speak again, but Madame Farault was already looking back up at him, tears falling freely.

"Your majesty, we thought you'd died... How..." Before she could finish her question, her eyes rolled back into her head and her legs gave out.

Lundane started and rushed toward her in concern. The soldier at her side scrambled to catch her before she hit the ground. Sandis winced, watching the unconscious woman with pity.

"I suppose that one doesn't need to be watched," he mused. He took a swig of wine from his goblet.

Lundane sighed, looking Madame Farault over to reassure himself that she was not hurt. Pale, and a bit clammy, but otherwise she looked alright.

"Take her to her quarters," he told the soldier. "Have a nurse check on her."

The soldier nodded and left the hall, leaving Lundane and Sandis staring after him.

"Did you hear that?" Sandis said after a few seconds. He waited for Lundane to look at him. "They thought you were dead."

Lundane thought of the tears streaking down Madame Farault's face as she'd spoken. It made sense that Hulbert would have claimed his older brother was dead before taking the throne—no one in Draven could possibly know that the assassination attempt all those years ago had been unsuccessful. The idea that he'd been thought of as nothing more than a ghost for two decades did not sit well with him, though.

"I would have done the same in Hulbert's shoes," Lundane agreed, trying to keep his voice even. He turned toward the throne at the end of the hall and climbed the steps to sit in it, crossing his legs in as relaxed of a posture as he could manage at the moment. "Speaking of Hulbert, any word on him?"

"My captain sent a report not long ago. He's been apprehended and is in holding in the dungeons, to be dealt with at your majesty's discretion."

"Good." Some relief washed through Lundane at that. He leaned back in the throne. "When we're done here, I'll go down to him."

"King Sandis!"

The Tatrine ruler sighed, taking another sip of wine as he turned toward the doors. "Yes, what is it now?"

A cluster of four Tatrine soldiers had entered, pulling three people along with them. A young woman in a tattered dress, a man with blond hair and a sour expression, and another young man with tousled dark hair, pulling against a soldier's grip on his arm.

The soldier who had first spoken bowed to Sandis before continuing. "Your majesty," he said. "This man claims to be Prince Breydon of Draven."

Lundane froze, his blood chilling at the sound of the name. He leaned forward in his seat, narrowing his eyes at the dark-haired young man the soldiers were thrusting in front of them.

Sandis frowned, squinting at the man suspiciously.

"Prince Breydon of Draven," he repeated slowly, swirling his drink around. "We'll see about that."

The young man yanked his left arm from the soldier's grip in obvious irritation. He drew himself up to his full height, held his head up high, and Lundane felt his heart stop.

There were his own features reflected back at him, in the face of the young man staring defiantly at Sandis.

"Draven and Tatrus have not been at war for over three hundred years," he said, enunciating each word clearly. "I find it curious that you choose to pick a fight now, after so many years of peace."

Surely, if Hulbert had had a child, he would share some familial features with Lundane as well, wouldn't he? That must explain this boy's resemblance to him—that must be it…

But Lundane could not convince himself of that. There was nothing of Hulbert in this boy's face.

Impossible.

"I have no interest in war," Sandis answered, smiling a crooked smile. "But a grave injustice has been done. My presence here is merely to right that wrong."

"And what wrong is that?" the young man snapped.

We thought you had died, Madame Farault's voice sounded in Lundane's head.

"I'm here to take back Draven's throne."

Everyone in the room turned to stare at Lundane as he forced himself to stand. He could not tear his gaze away from the young man as he approached the group. No, there was no way this was Hulbert's son—he had to be in his early twenties, not his mid-teens. And there, on his sleeve, was the royal crest…

They told me he was dead. He's dead.

Even as he tried to fight his hopes down, Lundane spoke. "Breydon?" His voice sounded hesitant, to his dismay.

The young man's face filled with confusion as he looked Lundane over. A moment ago, he'd been speaking confidently, as though merely inconvenienced by his being dragged into the Great Hall. Now, Lundane could see the apprehension in his expression, as well as the disbelief that followed. It was extremely subtle, the tell-tale of someone who had had plenty of practice monitoring his responses to his surroundings and wasn't sure what to do about his shock.

Lundane understood—he felt the same way. Terribly conscious of Sandis' eyes on him—the Tatrine ruler had never seen him so surprised, he knew—he swallowed and spoke again.

"Breydon," he started, and broke off. He tried again, shaking his head. "I—I was told that you were dead. Murdered. I..." He trailed off, closing his eyes. The months following the Tatrine report of Breydon's death had been the darkest of Lundane's life, and he had never quite recovered.

And here was the prince, right in front of him, nothing like the young, wide-eyed child Lundane had left behind, but somehow every bit as recognizable.

"This isn't possible..." He didn't quite realize for a few seconds that he'd spoken out loud.

There was a long moment of tense silence as everyone in the room looked from Lundane to Breydon and back again.

"No, it's not possible." Breydon's expression had gone cold again, although he clenched and unclenched his fists at his sides restlessly. "My father is dead. Who are you, to claim his identity?"

The blond man spoke for the first time, hesitantly, as though he was already regretting his words.

"No, Breydon..." He shook his head, locking eyes with the prince. "It's been a long time since I've seen him, but that is King Lundane."

Lundane thought, distantly, that the blond man looked far too young to have known him before Hulbert had taken the throne. But he could not dwell too much on that puzzling fact, not when his son stood before him, expression shifting again to disbelief.

Sandis looked to Lundane, his eyes filled with concern. "Can you confirm that this man is the rightful prince?"

Lundane heard the suspicion in his friend's voice. He appreciated it, he really did—for all of Sandis' foolishness, he genuinely did not want Lundane to face more pain than necessary.

But all doubt had gone from Lundane's mind by now. He could not find his voice to speak again, but he nodded slowly.

"Hmm..." Sandis squinted at Breydon one more time, and evidently saw nothing amiss in the prince's behavior— although, given how much he'd been drinking, Lundane was not certain how well the man could really see to begin with. He threw back another gulp of his wine and straightened, allowing himself a satisfied smile. "Well, then—this day has been a greater success than we could have hoped for!" He handed his goblet off to a nearby servant and gestured vaguely in the direction of Breydon and his companions. "Although, all three of you look terrible. You need a drink. Shall we call for refreshments?" He turned to Lundane, who had still not managed to tear his gaze from Breydon—now frowning in mild confusion at Sandis' behavior.

What should he do in this situation? Lundane had never expected to see Breydon again, had never considered how a reunion might go. What was appropriate? Part of him wanted to embrace his son, and part of him was all too aware of the years between them, the distance that that must have created.

Breydon's gaze shifted from Sandis to Lundane, and something inside of Lundane suddenly felt raw, exposed. It was too much—too much for this moment, at least—and he swallowed, finally finding his voice again.

"You go ahead," he said to Sandis, nodding respectfully. "I'll go and survey the prisoners." He turned to leave, then paused, looking back at Breydon. "My son..." The words sounded foreign after so long. "Breydon. Would you like to join me?"

Breydon glanced back at his companions nervously. He did not say anything, but nodded once and stepped toward his father.

They left the Great Hall together, father and son.

Tiaponine sighed, leaning back against the windowsill. Far below her, she could see the moat surrounding the castle, its waters cloaked by grey mist. She shivered involuntarily at the memory of plunging into its icy depths and closed her eyes.

She had been ushered back to her old quarters to clean herself up. After three days of absolute chaos, she certainly needed it. Her injuries were minimal—just the bruising across her face and some blistering on her feet from running the day before—but she was exhausted. She could fall asleep just like this, on this windowsill...

A knock sounded softly on the door. "Tee?"

VerGann's voice. Tiaponine sighed and opened her eyes again. "Come in," she called.

He pushed the door open carefully, stepping inside silently. He still looked more tired than Tiaponine had ever seen him before, although he was clearly in much better shape than either she or Breydon were. He offered her a small smile.

"Good to actually get a break, isn't it?"

Tiaponine rolled her eyes, returning the smile. "You have no idea. I could sleep for the next three days straight."

VerGann raised an eyebrow. "You could do that under normal circumstances, too."

She made a show of acting offended. "I am *not* that bad."

"Whatever you say."

They settled into silence for a few minutes, VerGann joining her at the windowsill. The grounds still bore traces of the battle against Tatrus—grass torn up in places from dozens of sets of heavy boots trodding it down, plants flattened in the gardens, the occasional dark stain on the cobbled paths. The staff were in the process of cleaning it all up, a job that Tiaponine did not envy. She forced herself to look past the mess below her and focus on the forest in the distance.

"Something's bothering you," VerGann finally said. He'd been watching her carefully, his eyes tracking her every movement.

Tiaponine glanced over at him. "Something isn't bothering you?"

"Lots of things are bothering me. But you're more on edge than usual."

She bit her lip, trying to push down the apprehension that had stayed with her the whole day—even after King Lundane and Sandis' appearances. "I just don't think we're really getting a break yet. Something's still going on here."

VerGann considered her words for a moment. "What do you mean?"

"I mean—the way that everything ended, so suddenly like that... With Tatrus showing up out of nowhere..."

"They *have* been outside the city for weeks," he pointed out.

"Yes, but that and Lundane, too..."

The delpin shook his head. "That *was* a surprise. But I do recognize him…"

"Right, and I take you at your word that that's really the king. But still—it seems too lucky, doesn't it? For everything to come together so perfectly and so quickly?"

She studied his expression. Although he hesitated at her words, he clearly wanted her to be wrong—and she couldn't blame him.

"We'll keep an eye on things," he said finally, meeting her gaze directly. "If we see anything suspicious, we'll take care of it. But I do think that things are going in a better direction, with the king back."

We'll take care of it. The two of them, as a team, as it always had been. Tiaponine's heart warmed, and she pushed her lingering fear down for the time being.

VerGann's expression was still solemn, though. He took a deep breath, as though debating whether or not to say something.

"Alright." Tiaponine crossed her arms pointedly. "Now it's your turn. What's on your mind?"

VerGann sighed, eyes focused on a point on the ceiling. He took a few seconds to answer.

"I owe you a huge apology. I owe you a thousand huge apologies."

First Breydon, now VerGann. Tiaponine narrowed her eyes, frowning slightly.

"What for?"

"What *for?*" VerGann laughed mirthlessly. "As though keeping the GraVinn secret for so long wasn't enough—"

"We already sorted through that!"

"I left you alone to deal with the king at that banquet. Even though I *knew* something wasn't right. And…" He gestured at her agitatedly, his eyes on her cheek, where the bruises from the banquet had darkened in the past couple of days. "And I should've been there. I'm sorry I wasn't."

Tiaponine resisted the urge to touch the bruising on her face. "VerGann, you couldn't have known Hulbert was going to do all of that *right then*."

"Maybe, but I knew *something* was—"

"Both of us knew. Breydon knew, too. None of us expected that spectacle."

VerGann quieted, his expression troubled.

"Besides, you came back. Twice." Tiaponine's heart swelled at the thought. "Even though you weren't supposed to."

VerGann blanched at that. "Ah…" He buried his face in his hands. "I'm in *so* much trouble…"

Tiaponine giggled. "We'll take care of it," she said, echoing his words back to him.

He smiled, although there was a lot more apprehension in his gaze than she had expected. Just how much *had* he risked coming to get her? How much trouble *was* he in? Maybe she owed him more than she'd thought, too.

"VerGann…" She trailed off. She wasn't sure what she'd even been meaning to say, but she needed to say something. She swallowed and started again. "VerGann, I… I need to tell you something…"

His expression changed very suddenly—eyes clouding over with a strange mix of fear and sadness. The tension in the air between them was almost palpable now, and it felt almost like a warning to Tiaponine—*don't speak. Don't speak.*

VerGann swallowed. "What is it?" His voice was full of tension as well.

Tiaponine clenched her jaw, forcing herself to speak again. "I… We… Well, I—"

Another knock sounded at the door, startling them both.

"Dinner!" a voice from the corridor called. "Kings Lundane and Sandis request that the prince's companions join them for dinner."

Tiaponine didn't quite comprehend the servant's words for a few seconds, but VerGann sprang to his feet. As he did so, the tension around them evaporated—like a spell of some sort had been lifted. Tiaponine frowned to herself at the strangeness of it all.

"Fantastic," VerGann said, sounding significantly more lighthearted than he had only moments ago. He turned and offered Tiaponine his hand, pulling her to her feet. "I'm famished."

Tiaponine followed him out into the corridor, fighting back the sense that all was still not quite as it should be.

After dinner, Breydon and his father headed back down to the dungeons.

Sandis' men had only arrested those whom they had found resistant to Lundane's retaking the castle—meaning that most of the prisoners were the more aggressive among Hulbert's guard and the occasional servant. Breydon had felt no small satisfaction at finding Samuel behind bars, glowering out at him miserably among the rest.

Now, all that was left was to deal with Hulbert. Breydon recalled the crazed look on his uncle's face from days and shuddered slightly—this would not be a pretty meeting.

But this time, he would not bear the brunt of Hulbert's rage. This time, he had his father with him… His *father*…

Next to him, Lundane slowed. "Breydon? What's wrong?"

For about the hundredth time that evening, Breydon found himself startled by his father's voice. He wasn't sure why— he had almost no memory of King Lundane from his early childhood. But something about the way Lundane spoke was still so familiar.

"Nothing, sire," he said quickly.

Lundane's brow furrowed. "*sire*," he repeated, clearly not a fan of the title. It reminded Breydon of his own distaste for formalities. "My son, what are you thinking about?"

Breydon swallowed anxiously. No one had called him *son* for as long as he could remember, and it felt strange to hear a near-stranger saying it.

"How can you be sure that I *am* your son?" he found himself asking. "It's been so long... And everything's changed so much..."

Lundane looked at him sharply. "How can I be *sure?* Do you wish to deny it?"

"No, that's not what I mean." If Breydon hadn't been sure Lundane was who he claimed to be, then VerGann's recognizing the king had put an end to any lingering doubt. "I know who I am. But how do *you* know who I am? It's been such a long time..."

Lundane fell silent for a few seconds.

"To tell you the truth," he said finally. "I don't understand how this came about. I was told you were dead years ago."

Breydon shook his head to himself. It did not sit well with him that someone, somewhere, had been spreading rumors about his death for most of his life. If he thought about it, his father probably felt the same way about returning to a city that had thought him nearly twenty years in the grave. "How does someone even *make* that mistake?"

Lundane sighed. "I don't know. But I have no doubt that it *was* a mistake."

His voice had softened considerably, to Breydon's surprise.

"How?" he asked quietly.

"There are some people that you can recognize no matter how much time has passed between you." Lundane smiled—an actual smile, which Breydon had not seen from him all day. "I could see myself and your mother in you immediately."

A lump formed in Breydon's throat at that, and he stopped walking altogether.

"Father…" He trailed off. He couldn't find any words that seemed suitable for the moment.

Lundane wrapped an arm around him, pulling him into an embrace. The lump in Breydon's throat refused to go away, so he returned the embrace in silence.

"You don't need to prove your identity to me," his father said quietly. "I know my own child when I see him."

Hulbert hummed to himself, leaning back against the wall of the cell.

Why was he humming? He'd certainly never been much for it before. And by all rights, he should be absolutely furious. His nephew had lied to him about Lady Christine. Lady Christine had turned out to be a street rat, and her delpin guard dog had deprived him of the GraVinn he'd worked so hard to find. And now this—his nuisance of a brother daring to return to Draven after all these years, casting Hulbert into his own dungeon.

Yes, he should be furious. But he wasn't—in fact, he wanted to laugh like a madman. He must actually be going insane.

He closed his eyes when he heard two sets of footsteps approaching from the corridor. The Tatrine guards outside his cell saluted the newcomers before retreating further down the hall.

Hulbert spoke first, breaking off his humming.

"Ah, family reunions," he said. "It's been an interesting few days, has it not? Who'd have expected the dead to return?"

"Prince Hulbert of Draven." *Ah, that voice*—Hulbert had hoped never to have to hear it again. It had been almost twenty years, and he still could not stand his brother's stiff, self-righteous tone.

"*Prince*," he echoed disdainfully. "How quickly you demote me. Who took care of your kingdom all these years, brother?"

He finally cracked his eyes open. And there stood Lundane, Breydon at his side. Now that they were in the same space, Hulbert realized just how much like his father Breydon looked. That fact irritated him more than he knew how to express.

"You *took care* of Draven?" Breydon scoffed. "I'd love to hear you explain your protection to all the people whose lives you've destroyed."

"As though either of you have done anything better these past years." Hulbert smiled. "I brought us military strength. I gained the most powerful artifact in the world—"

"And promptly deprived it of all of its power," Lundane pointed out. "Time well spent, I see."

Yes, the GraVinn was deprived of its power and turned to dust. But still—there was still hope. He could get it back, get it all back, if only he could get out of this dungeon…

"Prince Hulbert," Lundane began again. "For your crimes against your king, your blood relatives, and your people whose lives were under your care, you will be charged with treason."

"Hm." Hulbert yawned. "Condemning me to death?" The sudden edge to his voice obviously caught Breydon off guard. The prince clenched his jaw.

"You tried to condemn me to death, once." Lundane turned to leave. "We will return to finalize your sentence."

Hulbert leaned forward suddenly as the two of them started walking away.

"I'm not finished yet," he called after their retreating backs. "You'll see."

They did not dignify him with a response. He laughed to himself and went back to humming.

CHAPTER 20

The captain paced the length of the laundry restlessly, listening for sounds from the corridor outside. Glancing down at the unconscious castle servant leaning against the wall, he tugged at his stolen servant's uniform. The servant boy was smaller than the captain, but it was a close enough fit—chances were that no one would recognize him.

He was exhausted. The battle a few days ago had left him a bit worse for wear, and after losing track of Hulbert before managing to escort him from the castle grounds... Well, that was a mistake that the captain could not forgive himself for. He could at least try to remedy it, though. He'd spent the past half week hiding in closets and spare rooms, contacting the remaining servants and guards loyal to Hulbert, and stealing food from the kitchens when he could. Biding his time until today—until King Sandis' foolish party was underway.

Hurried footsteps sounded in the hallway outside. The captain ceased his pacing, pressing himself against the wall next to the door. When the door cracked open, though, a familiar man in an ill-fitting Tatrine uniform slipped inside, glancing surreptitiously behind him.

The soldier closed the door behind him, and the captain eased away from the wall. The newcomer saluted.

"Sir," he said, voice low. "The party in the Great Hall is in progress. We have men stationed inside."

"And King Hulbert? He's been located?"

"Located, Sir. With the Tatrine troops at the party, we've broken our men from the dungeons. The king awaits his time to make an entrance."

"Excellent." The two men fell silent as more footsteps echoed in the corridor. After a few seconds, the sound faded, and the captain turned back to the soldier.

"You were able to locate what I requested?"

The soldier reached inside his jacket and drew out a small crystalline vial. "Of course. Two doses worth."

The captain took the vial and studied the clear bubbling liquid inside it. "It's from a reliable source?"

"Absolutely. Just half of this will have Lundane and his son dead on the floor."

"Good." The captain tucked the vial into his own jacket. "I'll hold this for the time being."

The Great Hall boomed with the sound of the evening's festivities. King Sandis had pulled together quite the party in a very short amount of time. The room bore no trace of the battle that had occurred just days ago, and had been strung with banners and candles all over again. A small orchestra played at one end of the hall, and servants wove their way through the crowd of Tatrine guests carrying trays of refreshments.

VerGann surveyed the commotion with little interest—although he could not help thinking that the stout little ruler of Tatrus was a buffoon. Lundane had returned to Draven only four days prior. A celebration *was* appropriate, but Sandis' quick timing was ill-advised. Very little had actually been resolved yet. Hulbert and his co-conspirators had yet to be sentenced, and the Draven guard and castle staff surely still concealed some traitors in their midst. Lundane needed time to readjust to life as king of Draven, and Breydon certainly needed time to readjust to having a father.

And here Sandis was, throwing a party.

A chorus of high-pitched giggling sounded above the crowd, coming from a gaggle of women talking amongst themselves in one corner of the room. An entire entourage of noblemen and women had arrived from Tatrus in the wee hours of the morning. How they had come so quickly was a mystery to VerGann, unless Sandis had been anticipating a quick success and subsequent party in Draven from the very beginning. Like their king, those from Tatrus had quickly inebriated themselves and showed no indication of planning to put down their drinks anytime soon.

"I'm glad you're enjoying the festivities," a familiar voice said at VerGann's side. He glanced around to find Breydon approaching him, a slightly amused smile on his face.

VerGann didn't dignify the prince's sarcasm by rolling his eyes, even though he wanted to. "It is quite the party."

"A strange time for it," Breydon mused in a tone that told VerGann that he shared his reservations. "But it *does* appear that things are falling into place. Maybe Sandis isn't quite the fool I think he is. Maybe we *should* relax a little bit."

At that, VerGann had to chuckle. Breydon raised an eyebrow.

"What?" he chided. "I can tell just by looking that you think he's an idiot."

VerGann shook his head. "I think the word I chose was *buffoon*." He watched the stout king take another swig from his goblet on the other side of the room. "Yes, relaxing sounds great... When the time is right. Your father hasn't had time to filter out Hulbert's men from your guard yet. Do you not feel exposed here?"

Breydon sighed. "I don't disagree, believe me. But the king—my father thinks we should allow Sandis to celebrate a bit. It'll keep him happier in the long run."

"A *bit*," VerGann echoed. "Have you seen the man sober yet? Because I haven't."

Breydon laughed. After a few seconds of silence, a more serious expression crossed his face.

"Things might not be perfect yet," he said. "But still—I can't believe this is really happening. Over eighteen years... No one's father comes back after that long. So how..." He trailed off, deep in thought.

VerGann remained silent—Breydon's world had turned upside down in the span of a week, and the past few days the prince had seemed lighter at heart than before. Breydon must still be taken aback by everything. VerGann was sure he would be reeling for weeks if he had a dead parent come back home out of nowhere.

"Well, we'll get back to normal eventually," Breydon continued. "I just wish—"

"Breydon!"

King Sandis' voice boomed loudly from nearby, causing both Breydon and VerGann to jump in alarm. The king strode toward them, listing slightly to the side as he made his way across the floor.

"Come, my friend," he sang, looping an arm around Breydon and leading him away. "Partake in the festivities!"

VerGann tried to suppress his smirk as Breydon paled, a slight grimace crossing his features as Sandis leaned heavily on him.

Catching sight of Tiaponine amidst a group of girls coming his way, VerGann breathed a sigh of relief. At least now he would have company for the ill-conceived party.

"Celia, sweetheart!" a man's voice suddenly rang out over the crowd. A short, bearded man picked up the young woman closest to Tiaponine by her waist and carried her off into the sea of people around them. The girl's giggle echoed above the noise long after she'd vanished from view. VerGann rolled his eyes—part of Sandis' entourage, no doubt.

It was then that he got a full view of Tiaponine.

All of the Tatrine women were dressed to impress, beautiful intricate gowns rustling at every turn. Sandis had evidently made sure that Tiaponine would not be left out. Her gown seemed to glow gold in the candlelight. Black trim accented a modest bodice, and a panel of off-white satin adorned the front of her skirts. She walked a little taller than usual, head held high, and VerGann could not take his eyes off of her.

His smile faded slightly—*here was this mess of emotions returning*. He thought of the tension between them from a couple of days ago. What had she wanted to tell him? She hadn't brought it up again since they'd been interrupted, and he wasn't sure he wanted to know.

Yet he still took a step toward her, as though drawn in by an invisible line.

Then he stopped as she unexpectedly came face to face with a robust little man, grinning at her from ear to ear, clearly intoxicated.

The man managed to wink at Tiaponine before holding his hand out to her. She swallowed hard.

"My lady," he cooed, in what he seemed to think was a seductive tone. "Would you care to dance?"

"Um..." Tiaponine broke off with a gasp as the man grabbed her around the waist and pulled her into the crowd. She finally made eye contact with VerGann, looking alarmed as the stranger flung her grandly off to the side and then, with the same determination, pulled her back toward him. She winced, trying to recover from the forced spin.

These people... VerGann approached the man and cleared his throat, trying to keep his eye from twitching. The man looked up at him, bleary-eyed.

"Sir, you seen my dancin' partner?" the man slurred.

VerGann and Tiaponine stared at him with twin expressions of disbelief. This man had to be far beyond his cups at this point, as he still had hold of her hand and did not even realize it.

"Yes," VerGann answered, releasing the man's hold on Tiaponine and facing him in the opposite direction. "Right over there."

Grinning broadly, he stumbled off. "Oh, thanks," he burped.

Tiaponine burst out laughing as they watched him bump into a dancing couple, nearly pitching face-first into the ground. VerGann smiled at the sound of her laugh and held his hand out to her, leading her deeper into the crowd. They easily fell into step with those dancing around them.

"Well," she said. "Now we know why Tatrine celebrations are so notorious. I've heard rumors for years, but I couldn't have imagined something like this."

"I'm surprised that they can even remember them," VerGann offered matter-of-factly. He glanced at King Sandis, his fist still firm around his goblet. "That man hasn't put that drink down since he's arrived."

Tiaponine's voice dropped to a whisper. "I'm still not sure about all this," she said quietly, taking in their surroundings cautiously. "It's still too soon."

VerGann had to agree with her. "Sandis is a bit of a fool," he said. "But that's not our problem. Let's just take this break and enjoy it for what it is, Tee. A little departure from reality could serve us well right now."

"And what about the trouble in EliSann that you spoke of?"

VerGann missed a step, almost tripping into someone behind him.

"I'd hoped you'd forget about that," he muttered, suddenly uncomfortable.

"Marlott knows you're gone, doesn't she?" Tiaponine pressed. "She'll be looking for you?"

"No." VerGann kept his tone flat. "She knows precisely where I am."

Tiaponine bit her lip, clearly uneasy. VerGann hurried on.

"And I'll return to EliSann to face the consequences of my disobedience." He forced a smile. "With all that's happened, I'm sure Marlott will reach a place of forgiveness soon."

Or maybe he was just trying to convince himself of that. If he dwelled too much on how his last conversation with the seratine had gone—the number of rules that he'd come so close to breaking—that forgiveness seemed quite impossible in the near future.

"And you'll come back to Draven after that?" Tiaponine pressed, the hope clear in her expression.

VerGann remembered Marlott's warning look his way during the banquet last week, and realized that he could not give Tiaponine a favorable answer. He glanced down at the ground.

"I have… quite the mess to clean up at home before that's possible."

Tiaponine's long silence betrayed her nerves.

"Well," she finally began. "Whenever you do get things figured out—"

"Men on the right, women on the left!" a voice bellowed from somewhere in the crowd, startling them both.

"What?" Tiaponine managed just before she was pulled away from VerGann and pushed into a group of women behind her, beginning to form a line.

VerGann barely had time to reach for her before he, too, was pulled back into a waiting line of men behind him. It appeared that everyone else not only understood what was going on, but was excited about it. Given their altered states, VerGann was not sure that was a good thing.

The two lines turned to face each other, the men stepping forward to take the hands of the women across from them, as the orchestra struck up a lighthearted tune. VerGann extended his hand to a Tatrine woman, who stumbled slightly as she approached him.

"Well, hello there," she giggled, hiccupping slightly.

VerGann forced a smile.

Great.

❦

Tiaponine tore her gaze away from VerGann and found herself face to face with Breydon.

"Breydon!" she exclaimed. He smiled and bowed to her, offering her his hand.

"Shall we?" he asked as they fell into step with the line of dancing couples around them.

"I haven't seen you much in the last couple of days," she said after a few seconds. "How are things with your father?"

His smile widened at the word *father.* "Well, there's a lot to be done still," he said. "And everything's a bit of a mess, but… I think things are looking up."

"Good." Tiaponine giggled as he spun her around. "You seem a lot happier than before."

He did not respond to that. After a moment, he spoke again.

"I did… I did have a question for you, actually." He sounded hesitant, uncharacteristically so, like he was choosing all his words very carefully. "I was wondering…"

"Yes?"

"You liked it here, right? I mean, before all this." Breydon gestured at the room around them, but Tiaponine knew he was referring to the banquet last week—when the Great Hall had been decorated rather similarly to tonight.

Tiaponine hesitated, very aware of Breydon's slightly nervous expression.

"Yes," she said slowly. "It's nice here, but..."

"I just wondered if... Well, hoped that..." He swallowed. "You might want to stay here? With me?"

Tiaponine's heart clenched. She thought of their walk in the gardens last week—when he'd almost kissed her.

She really hadn't noticed his feelings for her until it was too late. And she did care for Breydon, but...

"That's quite the offer," she mused. "Do you really think I'd fit in here, Breydon? This is still a foreign world to me."

He shrugged. "I don't think that's what's important. Fitting in or not fitting in. But if you wanted to stay here, I..." He trailed off. "I would love to have you by my side."

Tiaponine sighed. "I appreciate it," she said carefully. "Really. You're a good friend to have. But... I have to turn you down. This isn't where I should be, long term."

Breydon studied her for a long moment. Then he nodded, looking down. "Well..." He laughed. "To be honest, I figured you'd say that. Still worth a try, though." He met her gaze again. "Just know that I really do care about you. And I wish you and VerGann all the best."

Tiaponine blinked. "I..."

The prince laughed. "I'm not blind, Tee. I know how he feels about you. And how you feel about him."

She felt her face heating up. She knew, if she was honest with herself, exactly how she felt about VerGann. But... "How he feels about..."

Breydon raised an eyebrow, eyes full of amusement. "Interesting. Maybe *you're* the blind one."

"I don't…" Tiaponine cut herself off when she realized her voice was an octave higher than usual, and tried again. "You know what, I'm going to ignore that. You didn't say that."

"Whatever makes you most comfortable. Live in denial if you want."

Tiaponine sighed, glancing over in VerGann's direction. "*I'm* not in denial," she said quietly.

They were silent for a few moments.

"You'll be alright, won't you?" she asked, turning back to Breydon. "I mean it when I say you're a good friend…"

He waved off her explanations. "Like I said, I think I've been mentally preparing myself to be turned down for a while now. My father and I are going to have a lot on our plates for quite some time, so… I'll get past this, Tee." He paused. "If either of you ever need anything, though, I'll be more than happy to help if I can."

"I'll keep that in mind," she said, smiling as Breydon spun her again. "Thank you for everything."

VerGann glanced over in Tiaponine and Breydon's direction again, trying not to draw attention as he peered over the heads of the people around him. She seemed to be having fun— she was smiling at something the prince said as he spun her around.

VerGann forced himself to turn his attention back to his own dancing partner. The young Tatrine woman was clearly quite accustomed to this particular dance, whirling around in front of him, very content to be the center of attention. Based on the way she stumbled every few steps, she was also quite drunk. He hoped the end of the line was close.

"I haven't seen you before," the girl shouted over the music, her eyes seeming to devour him. "Are you part of Sandis' court?"

VerGann forced a smile. "No, I'm from out of town."

"Ah." She giggled. "Your first Tatrine party! How exciting."

"I've been to one before," VerGann answered absentmindedly, catching sight of Tiaponine and Breydon again. "I stopped in for Cretisdan's seventieth birthday celebration."

The young woman fell silent, frowning with the effort it took to concentrate. "Cretisdan, the ruler of Tatrus? Didn't he rule some... two hundred years ago?"

"More like a hundred and twenty or so."

VerGann received no immediate response. He winced. This wasn't Tiaponine—he couldn't just say things like that. *Oh, yes, I stopped by Tatrus once over a century ago. Nothing special.* At least this woman looked far too dazed to properly remember this conversation.

After a moment, she giggled. "The ale went straight to your head, I'm afraid." She wrapped her arms around his neck, an unnecessary move that had VerGann once more looking around for the end of the line. At this point, he was practically carrying the girl.

"What can I say," he said, sounding strained to his own ears. "The people of Tatrus really know how to have fun."

Mercifully, the couples around them separated, switching partners to their right. VerGann breathed a sigh of relief as he came to face Tiaponine. Following the lead of everyone around them, they locked hands and began to spin.

"I don't get the point," she shouted over the noise. "I'm getting sick."

VerGann smiled mischievously. "Faster!" She giggled as they kept turning, the music swelling to a climax before the song finally ended. Tiaponine stumbled back as the final chord dissipated into the air around them, catching her breath.

Almost immediately, a new song began. In stark contrast to the lively music from earlier, this one was slow and haunting, beautiful in an eerie way. VerGann was somehow reminded of home—this sounded similar to the music of EliSann. The Tatrine guests around them clearly understood the dance to this song as well, moving together in choreographed steps.

"There you are, my little rum cake!" came a vaguely familiar voice from the crowd—shouting, at odds with the beautiful music. "I've been looking all over for you."

Tiaponine grimaced as the inebriated little man from earlier approached, evidently ready for another try. He stumbled to a stop in front of her.

"Um…" she stammered. "I…"

VerGann managed his reaction, tapping the man on the shoulder. "She's with me. You'll have to find another tasty treat out there."

Tiaponine's nauseated expression faded to relief. The man stared at VerGann, open-mouthed and perplexed, before grinning broadly.

"My apologies," he slurred. "Thank you." His eyes wandered to the crowd around him, disoriented.

VerGann physically faced the drunk in the opposite direction and, with a light shove, sent him on his way. He turned back to Tiaponine and offered her his hand.

"My little rum cake?"

She smirked. "Funny."

"I found it funny."

They circled each other with their right palms together, looking to those around them for guidance. The dance was simple compared to the previous ones, and VerGann soon found himself staring at Tiaponine rather than at the other couples. He'd never associated her with poise or grace, really—those traits were at odds with her feisty nature—but here, somehow... As she swept around him, eyes glittering with reflected candlelight, a soft smile on her face, he felt at peace. *Truly* at peace. Breydon, the Stone of GraVinn, King Hulbert, EliSann—none of that mattered here, with her smiling at his side.

Tiaponine looked up, locking eyes with him, and VerGann realized that he was holding his breath. The music slowed down, ending with one last high whisper of the flute, but he could not let go of her, could not tear his gaze away.

She bit her lip. VerGann felt, more than he saw, the distance between them closing, their hands still pressed together.

Tiaponine reached for him, lightly touching the side of his face. The pressure of her hand was soft and slight, but his skin still burned where her fingers touched. He went perfectly still, maintaining eye contact with her.

"Tiaponine? VerGann?"

Just like that, the spell was broken. Tiaponine jumped, recoiling, and they both whirled around to find Breydon rushing up to them, Lundane at his side.

The prince glanced between the two of them, face flushing in embarrassment. "Um... Sorry. We're just looking for—"

"Have either of you seen King Sandis?" Lundane asked, clearly not sharing in his son's discomfort. "We need to speak with him."

"King Sandis?" Tiaponine echoed, frowning deeply. "Not recently..."

"What's wrong?" VerGann asked, catching onto Breydon's nervous expression.

"Nothing we know for sure," he said. "But something seems a little off—guards not where they're supposed to be, and whatnot. So—"

He cut off abruptly as a servant appeared to his left. "Prince Breydon, King Lundane, a drink?" He offered them one of the glasses of green liquid on his tray.

Lundane waved the servant away. "No, no, not now."

Breydon smiled, but also shook his head. "Perhaps later."

A strange expression crossed the servant's face, but before VerGann could decide what it was, the man bowed deeply.

"Of course, sires. Ah, and I was told to inform you that King Sandis wishes to speak with you in the hall."

Lundane's eyes narrowed. "Sandis? Very well…" He turned to walk off.

Breydon bowed to Tiaponine before turning to follow his father. "We'll get this sorted out," he said with a smile.

Something about the whole exchange didn't sit well with VerGann. The servant watched Lundane and Breydon's retreat with a curious look in his eye, as though he'd forgotten that VerGann and Tiaponine were standing there, too.

"I'll take one," VerGann said, snatching a drink off the tray. "Thanks for the offer."

The servant cast a wary look his way before bowing and turning away, vanishing into the crowd.

"I've seen that man before," Tiaponine mused, watching the spot where the servant had vanished. "Haven't you?"

VerGann shrugged. "We've seen a lot of the staff around." He took a sip of his drink and raised an eyebrow. "You know, this is *really* good, actually."

Tiaponine laughed. "As long as you know when to put it down." She gestured at the Tatrine guests around them.

He smiled to himself and took another sip. "What were you talking to Breydon about earlier?"

She raised an eyebrow. "Were you watching us?"

"I…" VerGann trailed off, suddenly feeling guilty. "Well, I could see you, of course."

She smirked, but her smile faded. "He… asked me to stay here. At the palace. With him."

VerGann forced himself to manage his response. This wasn't a surprise, not really—he'd suspected something along those lines. That didn't mean it didn't hurt a bit. He swallowed, his throat dry.

"And?" he pressed. "You *would* be provided for here. It would be reasonable to want to stay."

She shifted uncomfortably. "Maybe. But you know as well as I do that this isn't actually a place for me." She shook her head. "This was never meant to be something serious. A game, a charade—nothing more."

"I don't think the prince sees it as a game anymore, Tee."

Tiaponine crossed her arms. "He's a good man. And I cannot control his feelings. I only know that this isn't where I should be."

A small part of VerGann felt bad for Breydon. Most of him, though, filled with relief.

"And besides," Tiaponine continued. "Where would you go after returning from EliSann? I mean, if I were to stay?"

"Me?" VerGann laughed. "Oh, our prince cannot get rid of me that easily. I'd pop in every once in a while just to keep him on his toes. I'm sure he'd look forward to that." He nudged her with his elbow, taking another big drink from his glass. His throat was still dry, for some reason—he felt lightheaded. He tried to push away his discomfort; it was probably just his nerves over Tiaponine and Breydon.

Tiaponine frowned up at him. "VerGann? Are you alright?"

He tried to focus on her, but her face blurred in front of him.

"Of course," he said. It took more effort than he had expected to form the words. "I'm…"

Her brow furrowed, and she took his arm, pulling him off to the side of the room to lean against the wall. "You look pale," she said. "Are you sure you're—"

She broke off as the main doors to the hall slammed open. The music stopped abruptly, and the Tatrine guests closest to the door fell back in surprise, some of the women screaming.

There, striding down the center of the hall, was King Hulbert, weary but every bit as determined as ever.

Breydon kept pace with his father as they walked away from Tiaponine and VerGann. He tried not to think too much about Tiaponine's rejection—he truly *had* anticipated it, if he was honest with himself. And regardless, they had more pressing matters to deal with at the moment.

The guards they had sent to keep an eye on Hulbert in the dungeons were long overdue for a report. The messenger they had sent downstairs to check in on them had not returned, either.

"Do you think Sandis has noticed anything wrong?" Breydon asked as they wove their way through the crowd. He couldn't keep the doubt from his voice, which he felt bad about—Sandis was certainly a kind man, but… Well, *buffoon* actually was an accurate description.

Lundane laughed. "Sandis is nowhere near sober enough to notice anything amiss, let alone request an audience with us over it. Something's going on."

"Then why did that servant…" Breydon trailed off, recalling the way the man had inserted himself directly in the middle of his conversation with VerGann and Tiaponine. *King Sandis wishes to speak with you in the hall.*

They reached the edge of the room, where an open door led out into the corridor beyond. Rather than going outside, Lundane and Breydon passed the door altogether, falling silent as they took in the corridor from the safety of the crowd.

The torch sconces along the walls had been blown out, pitching much of the corridor into near darkness. Out of the corner of his eye, Breydon saw a brief movement and caught sight of a shadowy figure near a corner—a curtain? Or a person? Either way, he shuddered. Something told him it would have been a mistake to step out into that hall by himself.

"Sandis is definitely not out there." He swallowed. "What should we do?"

Lundane's expression remained resolute, although Breydon could see the tension in his jaw.

"We need to find him first," he said. "He's got to be in here somewhere."

Breydon sighed, surveying the room once more in search of the Tatrine king. In doing so, he caught sight of Tiaponine pulling an unusually wan-looking VerGann to the side of the hall. As he watched, VerGann tripped over his own feet and leaned against the wall, blinking rapidly.

In his hand was a near-empty wine glass. Breydon thought again of the servant that had approached him and his father, carrying his tray of drinks.

"Poison," he said suddenly.

Lundane looked down at him in surprise. "What?"

"He tried to poison us—"

The doors at the far end of the Great Hall flew open before Breydon could finish his sentence.

The crowd parted as Hulbert, surrounded by Draven soldiers, strode down the center of the room.

Sandis, appearing—finally—at the edge of the crowd of guests, shoved his drink into the hands of the person nearest him, narrowing his eyes at Hulbert.

"What is..." he began. His words slurred together—clearly, he was in no shape for a conflict.

Hulbert passed him without a backward glance.

"I must admit, I'm surprised," he said gleefully. "From Sandis, I might expect such foolishness as this. But you, brother..." He laughed as he approached Lundane and Breydon. "I would have thought you'd be much more cautious. You should take care of your problems before throwing a *party*."

Before he could come any closer, Breydon found himself at the center of a circle of guards—some in Draven uniforms, some in Tatrus uniforms, all armed and facing Hulbert.

Hulbert smirked. "Bless your souls—so loyal. But I do think many of you have been enjoying the celebration a bit too much."

Although he hated to admit it to himself, Breydon agreed. Several of the soldiers around him looked dazed, like it took a great deal of effort to stand here and concentrate. He was glad that he was armed himself—he may not be able to rely on the guards to protect him.

"Prince Hulbert," Lundane began. Hulbert's eye twitched at the title of *prince*. "Another coup like this will ruin you if you aren't careful."

Hulbert sneered. "You were going to kill me anyway. I either win my throne back now or meet my end the way I would have if I'd sat around waiting for your *sentencing*." He turned to the soldiers behind him. "Now—bring me the king."

Lundane squared his jaw, hand going to the sword at his belt as the rebellious Draven soldiers surged forward to meet the Tatrine and Draven guards for the second time that week.

Tiaponine had barely managed to comprehend Hulbert's presence in the Great Hall before the fight broke out. It wasn't just the soldiers that were at risk—Hulbert's men were going after party guests, too, and everyone around her was either trying to fight back or rushing for an exit. She and VerGann, next to the wall, could hardly step further into the room without being pushed on all sides.

Speaking of VerGann—he'd turned a ghostly color of white, his eyes glazed. He dropped his drinking glass, and it shattered against the ground. Tiaponine grabbed his hands. His skin had turned clammy, too, and he was shaking.

"VerGann?" She squeezed his hands. He stirred at the sound of his name, but did not seem to be able to focus on her. "VerGann, what's wrong? Tell me what's wrong."

He opened his mouth, but before he could say anything, his legs buckled. His knees collided with the ground.

Tiaponine glanced at the shards of the wine glass, her blood chilling. *Something was in that drink. Something was in that drink.* She took a deep breath, trying to push away her panic—she had to be thinking clearly right now.

"Stay with me," she said, trying to prop him against the wall. "I need you to stay awake right now."

"I..." His voice was weaker than she'd ever heard it before. His gaze, still unfocused, turned to something behind her.

"Well, look at this," a familiar voice sounded. Tiaponine gritted her teeth, straightening as she turned around.

There, smirking down at VerGann, stood Samuel.

"Seems like someone had a bit much to drink," the servant laughed, confirming Tiaponine's suspicions. "I believe this was *intended* for the king or the prince, but..." He shrugged, kicking at one of the fragments of the broken glass. "I still call this a success." His gaze levelled on Tiaponine. "Whatever will you do without your little friend?"

Her vision flared red. "He's not gone yet."

"He will be," Samuel laughed.

"Shut *up!*" Tiaponine lunged forward, tackling him to the ground. He fell with an alarmed yell that cut off as she punched him square in the nose. The servant stared up at her in shock, suddenly at a loss for words. Perhaps he was just struggling to draw air into his lungs after that impact with the tile floor. Although Tiaponine was sure she would be satisfied at any other point in time, right now all she could focus on was her panic over VerGann's worsening condition.

She punched Samuel one more time and then scrambled to VerGann, pulling him to his feet and draping one of his arms around her shoulder with some difficulty. She pulled him toward a nearby door—she was pretty sure this one led to a corridor facing the grounds. If she was lucky, maybe she could get them to the forest...

VerGann slumped into her, and she almost fell. *How was she going to do this?* He was too heavy for her to drag all the way outside.

"VerGann," she pleaded. "Please—I need you to help me get out of here..."

His eyes were half closed, but he nodded feebly. Tiaponine pulled him closer, and together they stumbled through the door into the corridor beyond.

CHAPTER 21

Leranavi watched the approaching troops from Draven cautiously. The sun had risen by now, casting a shadow over the castle grounds and throwing the combatants into darkness.

By now, everyone in the EliSann Forest knew about Lundane's return to Draven and Hulbert's desperate last fight for the throne. No one was all that surprised. This fight had been long in the making, and at the moment, it was headed straight for the forest.

Leranavi could not remember a time before now that the humans' battles had reached the forest. To her, EliSann had always seemed untouchable by human conflicts. But now, watching the troops rapidly drawing nearer, her home felt far too exposed, far too vulnerable.

Something in the air around her shifted, and Leranavi realized that she was not alone. Looking around, she could see five delpins perched in the trees around her, also focused on the human soldiers with those unnerving stares. *Good.* They were all plenty strong, and she was no slouch in a fight, either—they would be able to run the humans out with little difficulty, together. Prevent them from getting into the forest in the first place, even. They could be a formidable team...

"Marlott is aware of what's going on."

Everyone turned toward the source of the voice. Leranavi glanced back to find Vrenler standing behind her, arms crossed.

"She wants us to refrain from interfering," he continued with a voice void of inflection.

Leranavi frowned. They were supposed to stand here and allow intruders into their forest?

The delpins around her appeared uneasy. GaeLenn spoke up.

"She wants us to stay out of it?" The incredulity in his tone was clear. "Look at how many are down there. They'll tear this place apart."

Vrenler maintained his neutral expression. "At least for now, we're forbidden to interfere." His gaze shifted to Leranavi.

The other delpins followed suit, one by one turning their attention to her. Leranavi swallowed, her determination from only moments ago dissolving. She still was not quite part of this group—they didn't trust her.

Yet, she reminded herself. *They don't trust me yet.* She understood why—she had spent more time away from EliSann than in it for most of her life. And with her heritage...

It was only natural for her people to distrust her. But she would do everything she could to prove her loyalty to them—starting with obeying the Seratine. She nodded once at Vrenler, letting her aggressive stance fade.

Evidently satisfied, Vrenler disappeared, followed by the other five delpins, until Leranavi was left alone.

It had been almost an hour since Tiaponine had half-carried, half-dragged a nearly-unconscious VerGann into the EliSann Forest. She had not gotten far before he'd blacked out altogether.

The delpins, of course, had noticed the moment they had entered the forest. Even though KaiDinn felt terrible watching his friend suffer from whatever ailment had come over him, VerGann was still in huge trouble. As part of the conflict from

Draven, the delpins had been told to leave him and Tiaponine alone for the time being.

They had left them undisturbed, but KaiDinn was not at all keen to leave them unattended. He'd gotten bits and pieces of VerGann's rambling thoughts before he'd gone unconscious—something about his drink at the castle—and although it was clear that he was in the process of fighting off the poison... Right now, both he and Tiaponine were defenseless. She had fallen asleep a short while ago, leaning against the trunk of a nearby tree.

She'd been in tears by then. Panicked. KaiDinn understood to an extent—he was worried about his friend, too. But as a delpin, it would take more than a bit of poison to actually end VerGann's life. Seeing him so ill was surely alarming, but there was no question about his survival.

Tiaponine must know that—she knew how strong VerGann was. So why so incredibly distraught?

Next to him, Natty sighed. "You're thinking about it again."

"Hm?" KaiDinn jolted out of his thoughts, looking down at the sprite. "Thinking about—"

"Your argument with VerGann the other day. You have the same expression on your face now." Natty frowned up at him. "What's so confusing about this?"

"I understand being upset about his condition," KaiDinn said. "But it's also clear that he's strong enough to recover. She didn't need to stress herself out so much..." He trailed off. "Well, with the troops approaching. That might be why she was so upset. That makes sense..." He found Natty shaking her head. "What is it?"

"You delpins are *so* strange," she sighed.

KaiDinn shrugged. "I don't know what I'm supposed to think. They're both acting irrational."

"KaiDinn, you might have full faith that he'll recover," Natty said. "But to Tiaponine, a poisoning like that is deadly. It doesn't matter that she knows he's strong. She sees someone important to her undergoing something that would kill everyone else she knows." She smiled, like she was letting him in on a secret. "Not everyone is as powerful as you, and not everyone can actually comprehend a delpin's power."

KaiDinn considered her words. The delpins were undeniably the second most powerful creatures in EliSann. He had never thought about what that looked like from anyone else's perspective. Maybe it *wasn't* clear to Tiaponine that VerGann would be alright. Take away KaiDinn's understanding of VerGann's power, and maybe he would be panicking, too.

"And anyway," Natty continued, looking up at the clouds and kicking her feet happily. "People are more sensitive to the things that hurt people they love. Logic has nothing to do with it."

He blinked. "You think she's upset because she…" He could not make himself finish the sentence. It was far too similar to the argument he'd had with VerGann days ago. *This isn't about what makes sense.* If Natty was right—if *KaiDinn* was right— VerGann and Tiaponine…

They really might not get him back after all this. That cold fear crept through KaiDinn again.

Natty smiled to herself. "After all that's happened, you're just now admitting it to yourself? You're really good at the denial game."

KaiDinn opened his mouth to argue—although he wasn't sure what he wanted to say—but before he could, Vrenler appeared on his other side.

"The troops have breached the forest. Marlott wants us coordinating ourselves so we can end the whole thing at once." He leaned forward on his elbows. "No stragglers."

KaiDinn's nerves mounted some more. Marlott hadn't been in the best mood recently, and the statement *no stragglers* sounded quite threatening coming from her.

"Alright..." he began, but trailed off as his gaze was drawn once again to VerGann and Tiaponine far below, unconscious.

Vrenler followed his line of sight. Something in his expression softened.

I know, he said silently. *I don't understand, either. We just have to hope he can figure things out.*

KaiDinn nodded, repeating the words to himself. *VerGann can figure things out.* Stressing over it like this would not help anything.

"Natty can stay and keep an eye on them," Vrenler said out loud. "Just to let us know if they need help."

Natty perked up at having been given a job to do. "Definitely!" she exclaimed. "You guys can go and take care of things, I'll be fine."

Despite himself, KaiDinn smiled at her excitement.

"Great," he said. "Just remember—you're here to guard them. Not to eavesdrop."

She only smirked, practically announcing that *she* thought differently. Sighing, KaiDinn followed Vrenler's lead and disappeared.

VerGann groaned as he came around—his whole body felt heavy. Opening his eyes, he forced his vision into focus. The sky was turning the orange of sunset overhead—an entire day had gone by since the Tatrine party. Dense foliage surrounded him. *Home.*

He sat up and leaned forward over his knees, wincing. What had happened? He struggled to remember the party. King Sandis and his ever-present goblet, a dance with Tiaponine...

Tiaponine. VerGann suddenly felt wide awake as he looked around for her. There she was, leaning against a nearby tree, eyes closed. His heart clenched as he saw a few streaks on her cheek where tears must have fallen.

What to do now? He braced himself to stand. Sharp pain shot across his midsection as he did so, and he groaned again. It hurt to stand upright. Why? VerGann searched his memory. The party, the dance, Breydon and a drink...

Ah, the drink. He'd inadvertently managed to be the recipient of an assassination attempt. Lucky him. Or, rather, lucky Breydon.

That didn't account for all of this pain, though—delpins fought off most human ailments and poisons quickly. This was still excruciating. He took a deep breath and managed to straighten up—his legs felt shaky, but he remained standing.

Tiaponine stirred behind him. Her eyes opened as he turned toward her, and relief flooded through him.

"Tee," he sighed, leaning forward to help pull her to her feet. He winced at the effort it took. "Thank goodness."

She looked slightly dizzy, pressing a hand to her forehead, but she immediately checked him over with a concerned expression. "How are you feeling?"

VerGann laughed uncomfortably. "I guess this is a bit more of my human side than the *something extra*," he joked. "I can't say I remember much."

She smiled weakly. "I wish. Hulbert escaped, and you... You were ill." She wrapped her arms around herself tightly. "I didn't know what to do, so I brought you here, but it sounds like a fight followed us."

"Great," VerGann muttered, closing his eyes against the throbbing in his head. Every image from the night before was blurry in his memory, almost indistinguishable. He did remember, though… "Samuel."

Tiaponine stared. "Samuel?"

"I seem to recall you tackling that little…" Clearing his throat, VerGann smiled. "Samuel."

"He deserved it," she countered immediately.

VerGann laughed outright, although he quickly cut off as the lingering pain through his middle increased. "No argument here."

Tiaponine chuckled. Something in her expression looked exhausted. "That, back there… That wasn't our fight. I'm tired of being in the middle of a battle that doesn't concern us, aren't you? Tatrus versus Draven, Hulbert versus Lundane, Breydon versus Hulbert…" She sighed. "It's enough to make your head hurt."

VerGann had to agree—he'd tried very hard to avoid thinking about Draven's political situation for that very reason.

"We don't need to be involved anymore," he said. "They've lost track of us, haven't they? We don't need to be part of their fight."

He thought he heard a whisper through the trees at that—the rustle of disquieted voices—and he shivered slightly. He was much closer to leaving everything behind than he'd thought—as a delpin whose home had been invaded by strange humans, this technically *was* his fight.

But it was not Tiaponine's. And he could not imagine himself leaving her on her own, even with his home in danger.

She watched him with that weary look in her eyes. "Where do we go from here? Back to the city? Stay in EliSann?"

Where do we go. We. VerGann's throat went dry. He couldn't think logically about the question at the moment—all he could focus on was the idea that whatever happened next, it would be with Tiaponine. They'd been a team for a long time, but this felt different, and…

And he did not want to pretend otherwise anymore.

He swallowed, every limb on his body going numb. "Tee…" He cleared his throat, trying to manage his nerves. He had to tell her now—had to, in order to move forward—but the words were difficult to form. Admitting his love for her would make him more vulnerable than he had ever been before.

He tried again, without success. "Tee, I…"

"Yes?" she pressed when he trailed off.

He sighed, studying her. And then, as though drawn in by some invisible force, he took her hand, closing the distance between them. He leaned in, ready to kiss her, and—somehow—she made no effort to back away—

And his head and chest exploded with pain. The jabs in his side from earlier were nothing compared to this—he doubled over, hitting the ground hard. Tiaponine shrieked and stumbled back.

"VerGann?" The alarm in her voice was unmistakable. VerGann could not draw in the breath to respond. All of his concentration was on trying to manage this impossible, unnatural pain.

Unnatural.

Tiaponine reached for him, and he found himself pushed back, out of her reach, by an unseen force. That confirmed his suspicions—someone was intentionally causing this, someone much more powerful than himself.

Tiaponine tried to reach him again. "VerGann—" She broke off as her forward momentum stopped unexpectedly. Her eyes widened, and she struggled to move—it was as though the air around her had solidified, keeping her from going anywhere.

VerGann forced himself shakily to his feet, trembling in pain, and looked around for the source of this disturbance. Hidden in the shadows of the forest around him, he glimpsed the other delpins, all seven of them watching him with a hint of helplessness in their expressions.

"VerGann."

He turned slowly, gritting his teeth to keep his vision clear. There she was, hovering a few feet off the ground—Marlott. She must have known that he was in EliSann long before now. Her displeasure was clear in her expression. He *had*, after all, run off against her will.

"You've done your job admirably," she said, and her even tone had a sharp edge to it that made VerGann's nerves rise considerably. "With the GraVinn destroyed, you are able to return home."

Return home. There she went again—and now that VerGann had formed his resolve, he had to disobey her once more. He glanced sideways at Tiaponine, whose eyes had widened, although she still could not move.

Marlott followed his gaze. "Tiaponine will be fine in the city," she said flatly. "She knows perfectly well how to take care of herself."

"I know that," he relented, trying to keep himself composed even though the seratine's coldness toward Tiaponine did not sit well with him. It was not a personal issue with Tiaponine, he knew—Marlott was scared for him, scared of what he would do next.

But still…

"We can set her up in Draven with a home to rely on," Marlott continued. "And you no longer need to distance yourself from your friends and family. We've all missed you these past years—"

"I know that, too, my lady."

VerGann swallowed as Marlott's eyes flared at the interruption.

"I understand your concerns, but I cannot go back to my old life if Tiaponine isn't a part of it."

"My son, your behavior puzzles me." The seratine's head tilted to the side as she frowned down at him. "This relationship is not permitted. You're aware of our laws, of your position—"

"I have broken the laws of EliSann."

The temperature in the air dropped noticeably. Marlott took a deep breath—and when she spoke, something in her voice sounded almost raw.

"It's forbidden for a delpin to fall in love. Not with a nymph, definitely not with a human. This isn't allowed for a reason, VerGann."

"It's already done," he said.

"You don't understand." Marlott swallowed. "If you go through with this—we don't know precisely what will happen to you. We don't know whether the damage will be permanent. And *I can't help you* with whatever you put yourself through. I can't undo it." For the first time VerGann could remember, the fear was actually audible in her voice. "I never wish to see my children suffer like that."

Even as she spoke, the pain shooting through his chest and head was almost overwhelming. "I fully expect the consequences to be permanent," he said through gritted teeth. "And I will have to accept them."

She closed her eyes, as though trying to compose herself. "And you," she said, turning to Tiaponine. "Do you feel the same?"

Tiaponine swallowed. When she spoke, her words were barely audible. "I have for a long time."

Marlott's gaze steeled. "I need to know that you mean it, child."

Tiaponine flinched, her face pale. "I do. I love you, VerGann."

VerGann's shoulders fell as some of the pain racking his body alleviated—like a weight lifted from him. His disobedience was almost complete. Tiaponine's admission moved him that much closer to leaving his previous life behind.

Marlott studied Tiaponine before turning back to VerGann, her expression softening—she still could not hide her concern, but there was sympathy there, too.

"You're willing to give up the only life you've ever known and have your power stripped from you—all for this human girl?" she asked softly.

VerGann did not respond.

She sighed. "I don't believe you would hurt yourself—or me—in this way unless your relationship with this girl was genuine." In the blink of an eye, she stood directly in front of him, setting her hands lightly on his shoulders. "Very well, my son. This decision is yours to make."

Without another word, the seratine disappeared. One by one, the delpins followed.

The moment Marlott and the delpins disappeared, whatever invisible barrier had formed between Tiaponine and VerGann dissipated.

They were silent for a long moment as Tiaponine tried to process everything that had just happened. VerGann's features were still taut with pain, but he somehow seemed more at ease than before.

Had she hurt him by saying what she'd said? It was true, but she could not bear the thought of putting him through so much pain.

"VerGann," she began quietly. "Are you…"

He swallowed hard, turning to her. "An admission of love from both of us would ensure that my power would be gone. If I am to stay with you, it'll have to be as a human."

"But what about EliSann?" Tiaponine pressed. "Your home…"

"I…" He cleared his throat. "I can ask Marlott for permission to stay."

He sounded almost resigned, and that worried her. "I understand if you don't…" She hesitated. "I mean, this is a big decision."

VerGann shook his head, reaching for her hand and pulling her closer. "There is no decision, Tee." He maintained eye contact as he set his hands on her waist. "It's already done."

He kissed her lightly, and her breath caught.

"I love you," he whispered.

And then his face contorted in pain again, his eyes squeezing shut. He let go of her, but she held onto him by the shoulders. Whatever this was, it was entirely in his head.

"VerGann?" she asked weakly. He winced in response, and she hugged him close. "It's alright, it'll be fine…"

She was not sure how long she held him, but she did not let go until his trembling faded away.

Natty leaned further over the edge of the branch she was perched on, unable to contain her grin as she watched VerGann and Tiaponine below.

"Nat?"

Surprised by KaiDinn's sudden appearance next to her, the sprite squeaked and nearly toppled out of the tree. "I wish I could put a bell on you or something," she scolded as she righted herself.

There was something sad in KaiDinn's smile. "I can't believe you're still up here after all that."

"What, Marlott?" Natty shook her head. "I couldn't have left even if I'd wanted to. I've never seen her like that."

"Yes, well…" KaiDinn's gaze fell to VerGann and Tiaponine. VerGann's shaking had slowed somewhat by now—it seemed that whatever was happening to him was almost complete. KaiDinn, evidently reaching the same conclusion Natty had, looked uncomfortable. "This isn't for us to watch, at this point," he said. "We should go, Nat."

Natty rolled her eyes. "*You* can go, if you want." She froze as VerGann reached out and pulled Tiaponine closer to him, kissing her again. "Whoa…"

KaiDinn looked positively scandalized, and blinked rapidly, redirecting his gaze at the sky. "I'm serious. This isn't our business."

"Oh, very well." Natty took a step back as if to leave, and KaiDinn vanished. As soon as he was gone, she promptly sat right back down, leaning forward eagerly on her elbows. She knew VerGann would be mortified if he knew he had an audience, but that did not matter to her at the moment.

Her view went dark as KaiDinn reappeared and blocked her line of sight with his hand.

"Hey!" she protested.

He laughed, shaking his head. "Natimae, *really…*"

Natty stomped her feet in mock anger. "Fine, fine, I'm going…" With that, she took off into the darkness of the forest.

Breydon gripped the reins tightly as his horse bucked under him, and ducked away from a low-hanging tree branch. At this speed—with the thick foliage and fallen trees in the forest—it would be impossible to outrun his uncle's soldiers here.

They were all idiots. Hulbert's men, Sandis' men, him—they were all idiots for carrying their fight straight to the EliSann Forest. It was only a matter of time before the forest's inhabitants retaliated, one way or another.

The foliage grew thicker as he pressed onward. His horse whinnied in protest—the uneven terrain was not easy on the creature's feet. Breydon could see three of Hulert's soldiers in the near distance, coming his way. He had to keep moving.

His horse halted, its breath coming in short spurts.

"Great," Breydon growled, studying the impenetrable wall of trees ahead. He couldn't back out now; Hulbert's men were right behind him.

One of the soldiers charged forward. Before Breydon could adjust his grip on the reins, his horse bucked sharply, tossing him from its back before fleeing off into the forest. He hit the ground hard, stars exploding behind his eyelids.

He forced himself up onto his elbows, gritting his teeth against the pain. He did not have time to lament over that right now; the soldiers were in the process of dismounting.

Pushing himself to his feet, Breydon drew the sword from his belt. He was outnumbered, but he could at least cause some damage before going down.

In the same moment that he locked blades with the closest of the three men, five soldiers in Tatrine uniforms rushed into the clearing from behind. Breydon lurched backward as one of Sandis' soldiers attacked the man he was fighting with—the man, not expecting a blow from behind, screamed a deafening scream and fell to the ground, eyes open and staring. His two comrades, realizing how close to being cornered they were, pushed past the Tatrine troops and ran, closely pursued.

Breydon winced as he took a step forward and gingerly touched his backside. He would be feeling that fall for quite a while. For now, he needed to keep moving—if he was found here again, he might not be as lucky as he just was.

With the sun setting again, and clouds obscuring the stars, he was completely disoriented. Where should he go now? He picked a direction at random and pushed forward.

He did not get very far before a pair of strong hands gripped his shoulders from behind, yanking him backward. Breydon landed in the brush with a thud just as eight of his uncle's men charged past.

"VerGann!" He scrambled to right himself from his tangled position. "That was close."

The delpin was studying him with an amused smirk. "Everything alright?" he asked.

Breydon realized that he was still, obviously, favoring his backside. He offered a lopsided grin.

"I'm glad I can still amuse you so much," he muttered. "It's nothing that a few days won't take care of." He caught sight of Tiaponine behind VerGann. "Tee, thank goodness." He clasped her hand. "I saw you two leaving the castle. I'm sorry I couldn't get to you." He looked back at VerGann. "I see you're feeling better."

VerGann's attention remained ahead. "Yes, Draven's hospitality set me back a bit," he said dryly.

"You were smart to get out of there while you could."

Hearing the clear sound of approaching horses, Breydon joined Tiaponine and VerGann as they ducked behind a large tree.

"Why, though, would you bring all of this mess to EliSann?" Tiaponine muttered as another soldier surged past. There were dark circles under her eyes—no doubt the past day had been exhausting.

"Not my idea," Breydon replied. "I'd really rather be anywhere else."

Tiaponine sighed. "Well, it's probably best to find cover before—"

"Breydon!" a guttural male voice bellowed from nearby.

Too late. Breydon swallowed as he turned around, already knowing what he would see. Not only had they been spotted, but it was none other than his uncle who had found them.

Hulbert's horse charged, and Breydon just managed to dive out of the way. It was a near enough miss that he could hear the sound of metal cutting through the air right next to his head as Hulbert brought his sword down. Behind him, Tiaponine screamed. When Breydon looked back, she and VerGann were scrambling backward themselves, stumbling into the tree they had been using for cover only moments ago. Tiaponine was holding her right shoulder, wincing—it appeared that one of the horse's hooves had grazed her.

"You two," Hulbert seethed, turning his back on Breydon—still struggling to push himself back upright after one too many falls today. "You cost me the GraVinn."

VerGann pushed Tiaponine behind him. "You cost yourself the GraVinn."

Hulbert sneered. "Isn't it about time you disappeared or something, delpin? Leave the girl to take the fall again?"

Breydon had to admit that by now VerGann *should* be able to do something. The delpin was certainly powerful enough to fight Hulbert with no trouble—so why was he not doing anything?

But he wasn't doing anything, and Hulbert's horse reared for another attack. Breydon stumbled to his feet, recovering his weapon from where he'd dropped it, and started toward Hulbert.

He staggered to a stop as soon as he looked back up.

A thick swarm of bright yellow lights had surrounded his uncle between one moment and the next—they had not been there a few seconds ago. Hulbert recoiled, his horse whinnying frantically as it tried to avoid the little light orbs—which seemed to be targeting the creature specifically, darting around its ears and snout.

And then, all at once, all of the commotion stopped, the little lights freezing in mid-air.

Breydon's breath caught—they weren't orbs. They were tiny people with wings.

Hulbert's horse continued to buck, rearing violently. He cursed as he was thrown clear from the beast. The riderless horse tore away through the forest as the cloud of tiny humans flew upward and disappeared into the treetops.

Hulbert tumbled over and over until he hit a thick hedge. He staggered to his feet, one eye swollen shut, bleeding from small cuts all over his body.

He looked from VerGann and Tiaponine, still backed up against the tree, to Breydon, his eyes dazed.

"I... I will..." he began, but seemed to struggle to piece together his words.

"You've lost, uncle," Breydon said. "You're outnumbered and here, you have no power whatsoever."

Hulbert snarled, an expression that made him resemble a feral animal very strongly. "I may not win this battle, boy, but I'll be—"

He cut off abruptly as the ground beneath him shifted suddenly. Something green wrapped around his ankles, and in the next moment, he was on the ground, being pulled backward into the shadows of the hedge.

He screamed in anguish as he was finally swallowed by the darkness. The yell cut off abruptly only seconds later.

Breydon's mouth dropped open. He turned to find matching expressions of shock on both Tiaponine's and VerGann's faces. VerGann searched the forest around him suspiciously.

"What just…" Tiaponine began.

Breydon ran to the hedge and peered past it. The blood drained from his face all at once.

What had greeted Hulbert on the other side was a cliff. He squinted down into the darkness—he could make out a form all the way down there, but nothing in detail. That was probably a good thing.

VerGann, holding Tiaponine's hand tightly, looked over Breydon's shoulder and grimaced.

"It looks like we have a new ravine now," he said. That statement sent a shudder through Breydon's body.

"You mean this wasn't here bef—"

VerGann shook his head. "I wouldn't think too much about it if I were you."

Tiaponine wrapped her arms around VerGann, very intentionally looking away from the cliff. "Wherever that came from, it saved our lives."

Breydon suddenly felt like an unwanted intruder as VerGann settled a comforting hand on her injured shoulder. Something had changed between the two of them since the party.

He had expected it, but he still had to look away.

"Breydon!" Lundane emerged from the trees nearby. "My son, are you alright? We've lost track of Hulbert."

Not even looking his father's way, Breydon sighed. "Down there," he sighed, gesturing behind him.

Lundane looked over the side of the cliff, and his face went a bit pale as he found the outline of what lay on the ground far below. Everyone was silent for a long moment.

"I see." Lundane swallowed, straightening up. "So this is where it ends…"

"What about the others?" Breydon asked, searching the immediate area. It was dark by now, and even the moon could not penetrate every shadowy recess in the forest. He could still hear the battle around them, but could not see anything specific.

"Hulbert's men captured Sandis," Lundane said. "That's the only group of soldiers that continues to elude us, aside from a few loners, but… Nobody knows their way around this forest. At this rate, it could be days before we account for everyone."

"No," a voice sounded. "This battle ends this very night."

Breydon jumped as a woman—the same lady from the banquet hall—materialized before them, staring at him and his father coldly. Almost at the same time, the seven teenaged boys from before appeared, surrounding the small group.

As Lundane began to raise his sword, Breydon put a hand on his shoulder. "No—it's alright," he whispered. He swallowed and forced himself to speak to the woman. "I am—"

"I know who both of you are," she interrupted. "I am Marlott, Seratine of EliSann. And my patience dwindles with your intrusion. EliSann is not a fighting ground for humans to work out their differences. We will not allow you to invade our home in this way."

"We?" Lundane's entire body was tense.

"The EliSann Forest is home to many, King Lundane of Draven."

Lundane met Marlott's gaze determinedly. "Breydon, did you know this?"

There would be time to explain later. Breydon stared at Marlott with cautious reservation. The seratine—whatever that was—still hadn't made clear what she planned to do about the humans' intrusion.

"VerGann will show you where your King Sandis is," Marlott continued. "And then you'll take your men and leave this place. Any delays will not be excused."

"And Hulbert's men?" Lundane asked.

Marlott's eyes narrowed as she studied the king. "We shall help you with them this once," she said finally.

Lundane nodded. "Very well. Let's go," he commanded.

Marlott vanished, but not before Breydon thought he detected some amount of amusement at Lundane's terseness. The teen-aged boys disappeared as quietly as they came.

VerGann started walking away, his expression neutral. "Follow me, your majesty." Breydon was silently grateful for Lundane's silence as he followed the delpin, although his eye did twitch at VerGann's sarcastic tone.

Breydon and Tiaponine, now alone, did not speak at first.

Finally, the sound of a yell somewhere in the forest startled them both. Tiaponine wrapped her arms around herself protectively. "Goodness…" she muttered.

"Come on." Breydon offered her his hand. "It's probably safer to keep moving."

She followed his lead, but lapsed once again into a troubled silence.

"Your shoulder," he said. "How bad is it?"

"Hm? Oh…" She touched her shoulder gingerly. There was a gash there—she was bleeding—but Breydon could not tell how deep it was. "I think it'll be fine."

He could hear the heaviness in her words. The injury was not on her mind, not really.

"What's bothering you?" He forced a smile. "You know your delpin can take care of himself."

She stopped walking altogether, staring at the ground.

"Breydon, VerGann no longer has his power. He gave up his old life for…" She shook her head. "He gave it all up…"

Breydon thought of VerGann's inability to fight Hulbert earlier.

"He gave it up for you," he guessed. "Didn't he?"

Tiaponine smiled despite herself, although her worry was still clear. "He's human. He can be hurt the same as any human." She swallowed. "Well, he always *could* be hurt, it would just be a lot easier to accomplish now."

"You aren't even coming back to Draven, are you?" Breydon's words were more of a statement of fact than a question.

"No," Tiaponine said. "Hopefully, we'll be permitted to stay in EliSann."

His heart panged slightly, but Breydon smiled at the glow in Tiaponine's eyes.

"Just… promise me that this isn't the last I'll see of you," he said.

She returned the smile. "I promise."

Another anguished cry sounded from somewhere nearby. The color drained from Tiaponine's face. It was not VerGann, but he was out there somewhere in that chaos. Breydon could sympathize with Tiaponine's concern.

"Come on," he said, as they resumed walking. "I still stand by what I said—your delpin can take care of himself."

CHAPTER 22

VerGann backed into the shadows of a tree, keeping a close eye on his surroundings. All around him were the sounds of metal weapons colliding, anguished screams of wounded or dying men, pounding feet on the rough ground. Human men fighting each other to the death—human men who had much more experience defending themselves than he did.

With his power gone, suddenly this battle seemed a lot more dangerous, a lot more deadly. He had never quite realized just how significant having that power had been. Upon finding Sandis a while ago, KaiDinn and Vrenler had made short work of the soldiers guarding him, leaving even King Lundane—a perfectly capable man—standing there uselessly, not unlike VerGann himself. It was disorienting to have to face his own ineffectuality so suddenly, and the middle of a battle was not the ideal place to do so.

And not only was he a powerless, inexperienced human, he was also an *unarmed* human, which left him in even worse shape. He needed to get out of the heat of this fight if possible— if he could get to the stream, he could use its steep banks as cover. Maybe he could even find Tiaponine.

VerGann took a deep breath to brace himself, trying to calm his nerves. Then he broke from the cover of the tree and made a break for the brush.

Not fast enough—he was only halfway there when he found himself being thrown to the ground. His vision went dark for half a second, and when he opened his eyes next, he found a Draven soldier—one of Hulbert's—hovering over him, sword coming down toward his throat.

VerGann kicked at the man before he had time to think, catching him in the chest and sending him stumbling backward. He clambered to his feet, despite the pain in his chest from being knocked into the ground. He hardly had time to regain his balance before the soldier charged toward him.

VerGann braced himself and dodged the next blow from the sword, grabbing the man by the arms—getting himself out of range of the weapon. They grappled with each other for what felt like a long time, although it could not have been more than a few seconds. While VerGann fared better than he'd originally thought he would, he still lacked experience. With a final flip, he was on the ground again, the soldier kneeling over him. He raised his sword above his head. VerGann's eyes widened.

And then, without warning, the blood-stained sword flew from the soldier's grip, leaving him blinking in confusion at his empty hand. VerGann took the opportunity to punch the man from under the jaw. The soldier grunted in pain and toppled over backward, unconscious.

VerGann pushed the man off of him and stood. As he did so, he caught sight of a nymph standing just behind the fallen soldier, grasping the bloody sword. She stared at him with a mild curiosity in her expression.

"Leranavi," he greeted, trying to catch his breath.

She did not respond, but continued studying him with that strange look on her face—obviously, she could tell something was different about him. Whether or not she realized what it was, VerGann did not know, and she did not seem to see fit to ask about it. After a few moments, she held out her hand and offered the sword to him before turning and vanishing into the shadows.

He stared at the sword, lifting it up to study it. It was heavier than he had expected. And he had no idea how to use it. Still, he supposed he appreciated Leranavi's help.

An eerie, high-pitched sound cut its way through the forest. Several of the soldiers fighting in the area paused to look up as a glowing gold cloud of sprites descended through the trees, lighting the night until it was almost as bright as day. VerGann caught sight of Marlott as she materialized a few feet in the air at the center of the clearing, surrounded by the delpins.

He felt a little pang in his chest as he realized that he could no longer hear their thoughts. The feeling dissipated as Tiaponine's voice reached his ears.

"VerGann!"

He turned in time to find her climbing through the brush. Breydon, next to her, pulled her to the ground as a stray arrow flew over both of their heads.

VerGann ran to her, pulling her and Breydon behind an old, twisted tree for cover. He squeezed her hand, thankful to see her, even though the battle was still going on around them.

Not for very long, though. Marlott and the delpins, at the center of the battle, had attracted quite a bit of attention. While few soldiers made to approach them—and those that did found themselves thrown backward without warning—some men ran from the area as the temperature dropped. Those remaining ceased their fighting, realizing that the real danger was the small group of eight strangers in front of them.

"Your quarrels do not belong here," Marlott said finally. Somehow, although she was not speaking loudly, her voice carried through the whole area. "You will leave this place, and you won't return."

Almost as soon as she finished speaking, chaos erupted in the clearing.

Men found themselves hoisted into the air by dozens of sprites and dumped unceremoniously some distance away. Others desperately grasped at their weapons as they were torn from their grips by something invisible before being tossed into the trees.

Whole groups of soldiers were physically thrown together, as though being collected by a giant hand. Their groans and frightened screams echoed louder and louder, the volume rising unnaturally fast.

And then, all at once, the commotion stopped. The remaining Tatrine and loyal Draven troops—many of whom had sought cover along the edges of the clearing—remained where they were for several seconds, expressions still stricken with shock and fear.

Marlott, her expression as neutral as ever, spoke. "King Lundane of Draven, I have fulfilled my promise to you, yes?"

Lundane stepped out from the shadows across the clearing, taking in the fallen men around him with a look of amazement on his face. He stared up at the seratine, clearly at a loss for words.

"You will leave this forest now," she said firmly.

Lundane swallowed. "As promised." He turned to his men nearby—most of whom were still in the process of composing themselves after the display they had just seen. "Gather the fallen and secure the prisoners," he called.

Most of the soldiers simply continued staring at the delpins and the sprites.

Marlott sighed. "My children, you may go."

In the blink of an eye, the delpins disappeared and the sprites flew off into the forest. The soldiers, finally shaking themselves out of their shock, scattered to carry out Lundane's orders.

"I'd better go and help with that," Breydon muttered. He turned to VerGann and Tiaponine. "I don't know when I'll see either of you again, but... Thank you for everything." He took Tiaponine's hand in his. "And remember your promise."

"I will," she promised, as he lightly kissed the back of her hand. He nodded to VerGann before going to help his father with the preparations, bowing to Marlott as he passed her.

"Ready to go, sire," a guard announced from the edge of the clearing.

With an exaggerated breath, Lundane waved the last of his men back in the direction of Draven, turning back to Marlott.

"Very well," he said. "We owe you and your..." He hesitated uncomfortably. "Your *people* a debt of gratitude. I hope to be able to repay it one day." He bowed stiffly. "I give you my word that we will not invade your home again like this."

Marlott offered the king the slightest nod of acknowledgement as he joined the band of retreating troops.

Feeling Tiaponine's hand tighten in his, VerGann smiled.

It was over.

Breydon's horse fell into step with those ahead. He took in the hundred or so men in front of him forming the long line exiting the EliSann Forest.

There were many other men that had entered the forest, but would not reemerge. Peace had been restored, but at a great cost. Over the next several months, those loyal to his uncle had to be identified and dealt with accordingly. Only after most of Hulbert's corruption had been purged could Draven truly heal.

Lingering at the edge of the forest, Breydon let those behind him pass. Taking a deep breath, he turned back to gaze at the trees. The EliSann Forest was as eerie as it ever was. It was difficult to think that Tiaponine was in there somewhere. He already missed her. But she must be happy there—and he should be happy for her.

Catching a movement to his left, Breydon jumped. When he looked around for the source of the movement, though, he found nothing. Even so, he felt the weight of someone's gaze—or many people's gazes—upon him.

What was it with this place and watching him? Breydon shuddered involuntarily. Lingering but a few moments more, he gave a swift kick to his horse and joined the soldiers ahead.

"I'm so sorry," Stradelia apologized as Tiaponine hissed in pain again.

"No, no," Tiaponine said hurriedly, her eyes screwed shut. "You're fine…"

Natty winced as she watched the uncomfortable scene in front of her. Stradelia's continual dabbing and prodding at Tiaponine's wound could not feel good by any stretch of the imagination. At least the injury did not require much more than a good cleaning and bandaging.

They sat in the main room of VerGann's underground home. As soon as all of the outsiders from Draven had cleared EliSann, VerGann had sent Natty to fetch Stradelia to tend to Tiaponine's shoulder. Despite her young age of twelve, Stradelia—the only human to live in EliSann until now—had an unusual knack for medicine, making her invaluable to the EliSann community.

VerGann had promptly been ushered outside by the elder nymphs assisting Stradelia before they began working on Tiaponine. He had not looked pleased—he had remained at her side since the battle ended, and was very reluctant to leave.

"Well, it looks worse than it is," Stradelia said, picking up a bowl with a greenish liquid and rags in it. "You'll be sore for a while, but nothing too bad."

"Thank you," Tiaponine said, her attention moving to the door.

"It's hard to say where the nymphs made VerGann go while we were in here," Stradelia joked. "I'll fetch him."

Natty ducked behind a tree root protruding from the ceiling as Stradelia passed before peeking around the edge of the door again. Technically, the sprite was not even supposed to be here. But she wanted to see what happened—Tiaponine's presence here was a big deal, as the only human to live in EliSann under these circumstances.

"How is she?"

As KaiDinn appeared next to her, Natty sighed. "Oh, she'll be fine. I think she just needs some time alone to get used to things." She paused, smirking. "Well, maybe not *alone*. I'm sure VerGann would be welcome. They *do* have a lot of new things they could get used to—"

"Nat, please," KaiDinn admonished as two nymphs passed close by the door. He—and the rest of the delpins—had been unusually upbeat since returning to EliSann the previous night, probably because it suddenly seemed much more likely that VerGann would get to continue to live in the forest. Still, his new life as a human, not to mention his relationship with Tiaponine, would take them some getting used to, as well. They had managed to keep him in the family, but now he was removed from them in a way none of them were sure how to handle.

Natty was certainly going to try to speed them up in the adjustment process.

"KaiDinn, you saw them in the forest," she protested. "Time alone together would go a long way—"

The young delpin sighed, picking her up by the tips of her wings and setting her on his shoulder. "Let's just leave that to them, alright? Come on…" They turned to leave, but stopped as the door opened and VerGann stepped inside.

"Is Tee—" he began.

"She'll be fine," Natty said.

"We can wait for you outside," KaiDinn offered. "If you want to see her?"

VerGann waved him off. "Don't worry about it, I won't be long." With that, he stepped past them into the main room.

Before KaiDinn could carry her outside, Natty leapt from his shoulder to perch on a shelf.

"You know what?" she said, feigning surprise. "I think I forgot something. You go ahead, I'll be right behind you."

KaiDinn frowned suspiciously at her. "Nat, don't…"

"No worries!" she insisted. "I'm leaving right now. Just have to grab something before I go home."

She was not sure how convinced KaiDinn was, but he left without further inquiry. Natty rushed back to the door, peering around the corner at Tiaponine and VerGann.

"—Not that bad," Tiaponine was saying, touching the bandaging on her shoulder lightly. "Some soreness for the next few weeks, perhaps, but that's all."

"Good." VerGann cleared his throat, running his hand nervously through his hair. "I just hope you can be comfortable here. I…" He laughed. "Well, I wasn't anticipating visitors before tonight."

"It's fine," Tiaponine insisted. "I just feel bad for invading your home like this."

"No, I'll be staying with KaiDinn for a while. Just until everything gets figured out." VerGann took a step back toward the open door. "I talked to Marlott, and she's given us permission to stay." Something in his tone sounded raw, and Natty could see the trace of a smile on his face.

Tiaponine smiled, too. "Thank goodness for that," she said quietly.

"Yes, well…" VerGann took a deep breath. "I should really go. You need to rest, and I told KaiDinn I'd be along soon."

"Wait," Tiaponine said as he turned to go. He paused, turning back to her—she was already out of her seat and reaching for his hand, pulling him closer. He relented with little protest.

She stood on the tips of her toes, leaned forward, and kissed him lightly.

He blinked, evidently not expecting that. She blushed.

"I… don't really know how all this works," she said sheepishly. "But I'm glad I get to be here with you."

VerGann took her other hand gently. "Honestly, I don't have any experience with this sort of thing, either. But…" He placed his index finger under chin and raised her head until they were maintaining steady eye contact. "As long as we know where we stand, we'll figure it out."

Natty's smile widened as they leaned closer to each other. And then, finally, VerGann kissed Tiaponine. She wrapped her arms around his neck, and a moment later, they were lost in a deep kiss.

The kiss intensified, and Natty almost squealed in delight. "*Yes*," she hissed, pumping her fist into the air triumphantly and jumping up and down. Her celebration was short-lived, though, as she was picked up by a gentle hand and dropped into KaiDinn's shirt pocket, effectively cutting off her view.

"Hey!" she protested, glaring up at him.

"I knew you were spying again," he sighed, laughing to himself as he turned toward the exit. "Leave them alone, Nat."

"But—but maybe we should wait for VerGann," Natty argued, trying to pull herself out of his shirt pocket. "Since he'll be staying with us, you know?"

KaiDinn shook his head, still clearly amused. "He'll be along later." He opened the door to leave.

Just before he closed it behind him, Natty climbed onto his shoulder, stealing one more glance at Tiaponine and VerGann, still embracing.

The sprite smiled.

THE END